## Also by Jeanne Cooney

*Hot Dish Heaven: A Murder Mystery with Recipes*

*A Second Helping of Murder and Recipes*

*A Potluck of Murder and Recipes*

*It's Murder, Dontcha Know?*

# It's **Murder,**

## You Betcha!

Book Two in the *It's  Murder* series.

A quirky murder mystery with recipes.

# By Jeanne Cooney

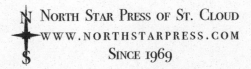

NORTH STAR PRESS OF ST. CLOUD
WWW.NORTHSTARPRESS.COM
SINCE 1969

ISBN: 978-1-68201-148-5
E-Book ISBN: 978-1-68201-149-2

North Star Press of St. Cloud Inc.
www.northstarpress.com


First Edition

Cover and interior design by Liz Dwyer of North Star Press.

# Dedication

I love to write, but it doesn't always come easlly. That's why I'm so appreciative of my writing sisters. These dozen or so female writers are there to encourage, mentor, and celebrate me and everyone else in our writing family. Thank you all. I'm blessed to call you my friends.

# Disclaimer

This is a work of fiction. Characters and incidents are the products of the author's imagination or are used fictitiously. Any resemblance to actual people, living or dead, is entirely coincidental. Many of the towns, roads, establishments, and landmarks, however, are real, and the author encourages you to visit them. They help make the Red River Valley the unique place that it is.

# Acknowledgements

Once again I have to thank my sisters—the biological ones—for serving as my sounding board and my first readers. Especially Mary, who is always there for me. Thanks also to my writing sisters—those female writiers I have come to depend on for encouragement, support, and friendship. This book wouldn't have happened without you. I also want to thank my publicist, Blue Cottage Agency; my web designer, MidState Design; and my publisher, North Star Press. Because of you all, I have achieved a creative goal of mine.

# Chapter 1

"Now don't slip," I warned ninety-year-old Rose O'Brian, as she shuffled across the ice from my SUV toward my son's fish house, one of two dozen scattered across the ice in the middle of Lake Bronson.

The scene called to mind a winter village. Not the kind in a snow globe or a heart-warming tale about the Alps. Rather, the desolate kind you see in *National Geographic*. The land surrounding Lake Bronson lay flat and lifeless, marked by scraggly evergreens and bare oaks, their limbs twisted as if embarrassed by their nakedness.

"Jiminy Christmas, Doris!" Rose's words were accompanied by puffs of frigid air. "It's not as if I had a hankerin' to fall until you warned me against it."

Rose had insisted that we go ice fishing. We usually went a couple times every winter. Yet it was nearly the end of February, and this was our first trip.

After attending mass that morning, Rose and I, along with my sister, Grace, who preferred to sleep in on Sundays, ate a late breakfast in the house we shared, packed our refreshments, and took off for the lake. It was a seventeen-mile drive from where we lived in Hallock, a Scandinavian (meaning conservative) farming community of fewer than 1,000 people in the Red River Valley of northwest Minnesota, twenty miles south of the Canadian border.

Born there sixty-one years ago to a Scandinavian immigrant with a penchant for stars of the big screen, I was christened Doris Day Anderson. I had farmed outside of Hallock my entire adult life, retiring eighteen months ago, following the death of my husband. More recently, I had moved my century-old Sears, Roebuck Victorian farmhouse to the edge of town. My sister, Grace Kelly Anderson, two years my junior and the owner of More Hot Dish, Please, the local café, became my housemate. It was an invitation I had since regretted on several occasions.

"It's colder than a banker's heart out here," Rose grumbled, as I fell into step behind her, ready to catch her if she took a tumble. Truth be told, I had no idea how I'd accomplish that. A nylon bag of snacks hung from one of my arms, while I clutched the key to the fish house in the opposite hand.

"Speaking of bankers..." I paused to watch Rose trundle along, the cuffs of her raspberry-colored polyester sweatpants partially sagging over the fur-trimmed tops of her rubber-soled boots.

Rose O'Brian, an elderly family friend, had resided in the assisted-living wing of the local medical center until, after being the sole witness to a robbery of the adjacent pharmacy a few months back, she came to stay with me "temporarily." Once she had settled in, however, she rediscovered the freedom of residing on the "outside," as she referred to life beyond the brick walls of the sprawling care facility.

Satisfied that she was steady on her feet, I repeated, "Speaking of bankers, what on earth is Gustaf doing with Ed Monson?" I nodded at the fish house owned by local banker Gustaf Gustafson. The most expensive Ice Castle model on the lake, it loomed over the decrepit fish houses on both sides of it, one of them our destination.

Rose halted, and I almost plowed into her. She slowly rotated her head. "How do you know it's Ed who's in there?"

The sun reflected off the snow and her wire-rimmed glasses. With her impish expression and whisps of white hair sticking out every which way from beneath her pink knit hat, Rose, who was short and getting shorter all the time, reminded me of a pixie. Or perhaps a leprechaun, considering she had immigrated from Ireland as a child. How she and her family ever ended up settling in the land of Swede and Norwegian Lutherans, I had no clue. Then, she became my mother's best friend and, later, a second mother to Grace and me.

"That's his pickup." My sister inclined her head, the pile of pink-streaked, bottle-blonde hair on top bobbing in the direction of the red Ford F-150 parked kittywampus on the ice next to Gustaf's SUV. "You can tell because Ed's the only guy around who dares display a Green Bay Packers' decal in his back window. Since he's a deputy, he assumes no one will give him grief about it."

I wiped my nose with my gloved knuckle in an effort to defrost my nostril hair. "A few days ago I saw them together in the café—Gustaf and Ed, that is. And not for the first time either." The bitter breeze whistled past us, prompting me to use that same knuckle to urge strands of my blonde-gone-gray hair from my mouth. "I don't get the connection. Gustaf is almost forty years older than Ed. And he's... Gustaf. Why on earth would Ed want to be his buddy?"

My sister adjusted the oversized bag of beverages cradled in her arm. She had insisted on selecting our drinks for the afternoon: a six-pack of my favorite beer from Revelation Ale, the local brewery, and two bottles of red wine from Hallock's wine bar. "So you've seen them together in the café. So what?"

"It's odd. That's all." I scooted around Rose to key the paddle lock on the fish-house door, as Grace bounced from one foot to the other to stave off the cold. She was the embodiment of a blinking stop light in her tight red ski jacket and leggings.

Grace, like Rose, was short. But unlike Rose, Grace's figure had not lost the war against gravity. While Rose had surrendered to jowls, slap-happy arms, and saggy breasts, Grace continued to do battle. Her primary weapons? Push-up bras and Spanx.

As for me, at five eight, I towered over them both, although shapewear couldn't enhance my figure. Think sturdy, not shapely. Duluth Trading Company, not Victoria Secret.

After starting the generator, located a ways from the fish house, I followed Grace and Rose inside and slid my bag of goodies onto the wood table to my right. At the same time, my eyes adjusted to the dim light from the battery-operated lanterns that Grace had switched on.

The place smelled of fish, stale beer, and cigar smoke. Constructed from a jumble of plywood and knotty pine boards, it measured eight feet wide, seven feet high, and ten feet long. Opposite the door stood a laminate counter with a window above and a heater below. Bending over, I started it up, and it ticked as if previewing it's efforts.

An empty wash basin sat on the counter alongside a roll of paper towels and a three-gallon jug of water. Next to the counter a camouflage curtain hung from a narrow U-shaped track mounted to the ceiling. Behind the curtain a toilet seat perched on a five-gallon bucket lined with a heavy plastic garbage bag.

The setup reinforced a life-long rule: Always use the bathroom before leaving home. Even so, with my penchant for libations while fishing, not to mention my aging bladder, I'd eventually take a turn back there.

Rose plopped down on the single-person bench at the table to the left of the door, and Grace claimed the opposite bench. She emptied the contents of her bag into a mini fridge before offering me a can of beer. After that, she poured wine into two red plastic Solo cups, passed one to Rose, and said, "Drink responsibly, ladies. In other words, don't spill."

◎ ◎ ◎

My son, Will, had phoned earlier to say he had readied the 28-inch fishing poles propped against the fish-house wall. He had also cleared the ice from the fishing holes beneath the four round covers in the wooden floor.

Lifting the cover nearest me, I stared into the black water below, the odor of fish overtaking the smell of stale beer and cigars. "I guess we don't need that one." I gestured toward the lid over the fourth hole. "Too bad Erin had training this week. She would have enjoyed this."

Erin, my 28-year-old daughter and a local deputy sheriff, had driven down to Minneapolis that morning for five days of classes on how to combat international terrorism, a complete waste of time as far as I was concerned. The only "internationals" we encountered in Hallock were Canadians who frequented our campgrounds. And they posed no threat as long as we didn't increase the camping fees or shut down the liquor store.

"God willin', we can get out here once more before the houses hafta be pulled off the lake." Rose selected two rods, colorful lures already attached to the lines. My son had thought of everything.

"Rose, I can't imagine you having another opening on your calendar. You spend almost every waking minute with Lars." In spite of my teasing lilt, a bite accompanied my words.

"What can I say? We're havin' a good time."

"And you deserve it," my sister said.

I set my beer on the table. "Even if you did rob the cradle."

"Oh, don't pay any attention to her," Grace told Rose, who, notwithstanding substantial hearing loss, had heard my slight just fine, as evidenced by her woeful look. "Eight years isn't much of a difference."

"Accordin' to the ladies at the senior center," Rose said, passing rods to Grace and me, "if a man's single, drives his own car, can cut his own meat, and remembers to zip his fly most of the time, he's an eligible manfriend no matter his age."

I plunked my lure into the ten-inch hole in the ice in front of me, the line sliding through my loose grip like silk thread. "Yet

I suspect that most of those men only want to date younger women."

"Lars doesn't." Rose raised her Solo cup to her mouth but didn't drink. "He used to date Etta Wilhelm. She's only seventy-five and can still wear high heels and a belt. She's also hot to trot. But he dropped her for me."

Rose sounded defensive, leading me to apologize. "I didn't mean to imply—"

"In fact, the other day at bingo someone said there comes a time in a man's life when he's more interested in mature women, dontcha know. Women who, for instance, can recognize the signs of a stroke. Lars is obviously at that stage, but Etta wouldn't know a stroke if it came with I.D."

Grace snapped her fingers, and I tossed her the bag of chocolate-covered peanuts. She opened it with her teeth, the scent of chocolate cutting through the fish smell. "Like I said, Rose, don't listen to Doris." Placing the bag on the table, she grabbed a mittful, still maintaining a steady grip on her pole. "She's a misandrist."

"A what?" Rose clicked her dentures.

"A misandrist. Someone who hates men. It was one of the answers in this morning's crossword."

"I am not a misandrist." My voice vibrated with indignation.

"How come you refuse to go out with Karl then?" Grace tilted her head, the shadow on the wood wall mimicking her move. "He's asked you out a bunch of times, but you always have an excuse not to go."

It was my turn to get defensive. "Wait a gall-darn minute. I just went to the fish fry at the Eagles with him."

"That was almost three months ago."

"Well, I've been busy ever since. First, with Christmas." Wiggling around, I attempted to shed my unease, but it clung to me like my holiday weight gain. "And, after that, our trip to Hawaii."

"We've been back from Hawaii for weeks." Grace was like a dog with a bone. She wouldn't let it go. "How many times has he invited you out since then?"

Not wishing to prove her point, I silently contemplated the hole in the ice between my Sorel boots. But because of my genetics, I couldn't allow my sister to get the last word in and said, "Unlike some people, maybe I don't need to date all the time."

"Or maybe you're scared." Of course, Grace had that same predisposition. "Why you're scared of Karl Ingebretsen is beyond me, though. He's the sheriff for God's sake."

"I am not scared. I just don't need a man to complete me."

"Are you suggesting that I do? Remember, Doris, I'm the one who went away to college and culinary school. And I'm the one who became a professional chef and lived on my own in both Chicago and Minneapolis. You, on the other hand, stayed right here and married the first guy who asked."

"Girls, girls," Rose scolded. "Don't start a brouhaha. We're supposed to be enjoyin' ourselves."

To me she then added as she adjusted her John Lennon glasses, "Your sister's only sayin' that datin' might be good for you. And she's right. You spend too much time alone."

"I like being alone. Besides, I have plenty of friends."

"And I counted Karl as one of them," Rose said. "Although you do seem to push him away, which is kinda strange since you used to date the guy."

"Good grief. That was more than forty-five years ago. We were in high school for heaven's sake." I checked my line, hoping against hope that I'd caught a fish. It'd be the only way to divert my companions' focus from my love life—or lack thereof.

With nothing dangling from my hook except a neon-green minnow-shaped lure, I raised my head to find both Rose and Grace staring at me. "Okay! Okay! Karl's nice enough, but he tends to push my buttons."

"Isn't that a good thing?" Grace waggled her brows.

And I rolled my eyes. "I mean, we tend to bicker."

"It's called foreplay."

Another eye roll. When I spent time with my sister, my eyes got a workout. "I have no desire to get involved with another man."

Rose jerked her head as well as her pole. "You mean you're thinkin' about battin' for the other team?" She hurried to add, "Not that there's anything wrong with that."

"No!" I downed my beer, the burn in my throat accentuating my growing frustration. "I don't wanna bat for any team. Or let anybody push my buttons. I was married for forty years, and it wasn't a particularly pleasant experience apart from the birth of Will and Erin."

"It wasn't a pleasant experience," Rose said, "because you married a horse's patoot. Thankfully, not all men are like Bill, may he rest in peace." She switched her rod to her left hand and, with her right, performed a half-hearted sign of the cross.

"Well, I'm not willing to risk going through that kind of anguish again. I'm fine on my own. I'm more confident and happier than ever." I had waged that argument so many times lately that the words practically rolled off my tongue. "I have my old house to work on, my needlework, my books, and my gardening. I also have my friends, two healthy grown children, both of you, and I'll soon have a grandchild. I don't need anything or anyone else."

"Uff-da." Rose sounded far more Scandinavian than Irish. In fact, after eighty-some years here, she rarely spoke with a brogue unless she was terribly upset. "Bein' self-reliant doesn't mean you hafta go it alone all the time."

Grace handed me another can of beer. "Yeah, have some fun. You already proved you can take care of yourself."

She was alluding to a few months back, when I'd nosed around in a murder investigation after my kids had been implicated in the crime. Despite my misgivings, I had forged ahead and apprehended the real culprit. In the process, I'd also discovered that I was a lot tougher than I realized.

"Even self-assured women enjoy companionship and intimacy on occasion." Grace effected the haughty tone she reserved for instances when she wanted to impress upon me her supposed worldliness. "And if that happens to come in the form

of a handsome man, like the aforementioned Sheriff Karl Ingebretsen, all the better. You should—"

A knock at the door brought an end to what would have
been one of my younger sister's lengthy sermons. That's right.
For someone who didn't care for church, Grace loved to preach.

# Chapter 2

Laying my pole aside, I opened the door to frosty air and a pair of Girl Scouts, their chestnut-colored sashes bedazzled with pins and badges and draped over their puffy winter jackets. Each girl sported rosy cheeks and long blonde hair half hidden under her stocking cap.

I didn't recognize the girl in the blue jacket, but the other one, decked out in a rainbow of colors, from an orange scarf to purple boots, was Hannah. She clutched an order form and pen, while Miss Blue Jacket held the handle to a wooden crate affixed to a pair of old skis. Boxes of Girl Scout Cookies filled the crate. My spirits soared.

Hannah's grandma, Dot, hunched over the back of the make-shift sled. Dot was also the daughter of Rose's gentleman friend, Lars. She had graduated from high school with Grace, although they weren't pals. Dot didn't have many of them.

A life-long know-it-all, she found fault with most everybody and everything. Her face had been pinched in disapproval since kindergarten. And though I was positive people had warned her it would stay that way if she wasn't careful, she apparently had failed to heed their advice. Let that be a lesson.

Dot considered me over black-rimmed glasses that rode low on her nose. "I didn't realize this fish house belonged to you." She patted her hair. Short, spiked, and bleached in the past, it now smacked of old-lady sausage curls.

Given Dot's reputation as a busybody, I declined to answer her in favor of addressing her granddaughter. "What in the heck are you doing all the way out here, Hannah?"

"Selling cookies." She motioned to her sidekick. "This is my friend Lisa. Grandma Dot said we'd make a killing on the lake being most people only go ice fishing to get drunk. And once they are, they'll spend—"

"Anyways... " Dot jumped on Hannah's words while circling around me to catch a glimpse of my companions. "Are any of you interested in cookies?" She offered Rose and Grace a smile that never reached her eyes and disappeared altogether when she spotted the wine bottle on their table.

"You betcha," Rose replied, dismissing Dot's disapproval of our alcoholic beverages. "I'll take a box of each."

The girls shrieked. And when Grace and I echoed Rose's order, their ear-splitting cries were answered by the howls of coyotes. Well, maybe not, although it could have happened.

"For cripes' sake." I scrounged through the pockets of my North Face parka. "I forgot my wallet." I retrieved a slip of paper. "But I brought my shopping list—the one I couldn't find when I went for groceries yesterday."

"That's all right." Rose plucked her coin purse from the pocket of her car coat. "I've got plenty of cash. I'll pay the bill."

"You're just like Lars—I mean, Dad." Dot couldn't hide her accusatory tone in spite of ending her remark with a giggle where a period should have gone. "You like to spend money, and you push him to do the same."

"What do you mean?" I didn't care for her criticizing Rose. Not that Rose was perfect. But no one other than Grace and me got to criticize her.

"Well, since Dad has been... umm... spending time with

Rose here, he's gone through money like water down a drain spout after a spring rain. The truth is, I may have to start eating cereal with a fork just to save on milk."

Perhaps Dot could shame some people with her folksy, passive-aggressive repartee, but not me. "Why is that?" I barely managed to keep my cool. "He doesn't financially support you, does he?"

"What?" With an abrupt intake of air, Dot stretched the limits of the zipper on her quilted jacket. She wasn't fat, per se. Just built like an apartment-size fridge. "I earn plenty of money running my bed and breakfast, thank you very much. Still, I expect to inherit a substantial sum when the time comes." No doubt realizing how ghoulish she sounded, she added, "Of course, that won't be for years to come."

Reaching past Dot, Rose paid Hannah for the cookies, and Hannah squealed at the cash before stuffing it in the fanny pack clipped to her waist. She and Lisa then sorted through the cookie boxes.

At the same time, Rose shouldered Dot and said in a voice meant for her ears alone, "Listen here. I enjoy seein' your father, and I plan to keep right on doin' that, dontcha know." Due to her poor hearing, Rose often spoke louder than necessary, so we all heard her, though the girls appeared too busy passing out cookies to pay much attention. "We like goin' places together in spite of the cost. After all, if not now, when?"

"But he's buying stuff like crazy," Dot said. "I happened by his apartment after he got home from your shopping trip to Grand Forks last week, and I could hardly believe my eyes. Bags of clothes, shoes, and whatnot scattered all over the floor. Plus, last night he was supposed to—"

Rose interrupted. "Well, if you're so worried about money, it's a good thing you're out here schleppin' cookies then, isn't it?"

Visibly peeved, Dot wheeled around to leave, as Hannah and her friend shouted, "Thanks, guys! Thanks a lot! This is our biggest sale yet."

❂ ❂ ❂

Once Rose, Grace, and I were alone again, I cranked up the heater, and we all munched on cookies.

"It's hard to believe that Dot is Lars's daughter," Grace said between bites of a Thin Mint. "He seldom comes into the café, yet he seems friendly enough when he does. Dot, on the other hand, is… well… Dot."

Rose dipped her lure back into the water. "Accordin' to him, Dot's always been difficult. Though a couple years back, when he confided in her about his profit from sellin' his sugar-beet stock," she said, referring to the crop grown in the Red River Valley as an alternative to cane sugar, "she got way worse. She became greedier than a graveyard."

Rose clicked her dentures. "Lars doesn't like to criticize her even when it's justified. He's afraid she'll raise a ruckus. Odds are that's been the problem from the get-go. She's spoiled. And it probably got way worse after her sister left town." Rose scrunched her forehead until it resembled a wilted leaf of lettuce. "What was her name again?"

"Janice," I answered. "She was my age. She moved away just before our senior year. From what I understand, she died a while back."

"Well, bein' I didn't get married or have kids, Lars isn't gonna listen to me about child rearin'." Rose played with her fishing line like she had a nibble, but nothing came of it. "He was supposed to have dinner at Dot's place last night and wasn't particularly excited about goin'. When I get home, I'll call him to find out how it went."

"Why didn't you ask her about it when she was here?" Grace wanted to know.

"I don't like talkin' to her if I don't hafta. And she probably would of lied anyways."

I jiggled my line, not because I had a bite but because I was eager for something to happen. I enjoyed Grace and Rose's company. Most of the time at any rate. But, if we were to sit in a stinky fish house rather than in front of the fireplace in my living room or around the prep table in the kitchen of Grace's cafe, I wanted to catch fish.

My sister, conversely, considered these excursions more like social outings and didn't care if she went home empty handed. She often said, "It's called fishin', not catchin'."

"Dot really sounded afraid that you two might spend all of 'her' money." Grace sniffed.

"Yah," Rose said. "She doesn't realize that I pay my own way no matter where we go or what we do. Lots of times, I even treat Lars."

I washed down a Thin Mint with beer. Not a great medley of tastes. "I'm amazed he has any money for her to fret about. I assumed he went broke years ago after paying the fine and restitution levied against him for selling the grain he had used as collateral for his federal agriculture loans."

Grace extended a bandaged finger. As a cook, she always had to nurse a cut or a burn. "Didn't he go to prison for that?"

"Yah." Rose clicked her ill-fitting dentures. "He calls it the federal trifecta: a fine, restitution, and prison time. But that was decades ago. And he insists it was nothin' but a giant misunderstandin'. That's why he only had to spend a year over there in the Duluth prison camp."

"He's just trying to put a good spin on it, Rose," I said. "The fine and restitution were huge if I remember right."

"Well, him and his wife scrimped and saved and paid them off. They planned to liquidate everythin' else too and travel. But she got sick and died before they got the chance." Rose again shifted her jaw. Why she refused to get her dentures adjusted, I had no idea. "Still, he went ahead and sold the whole kit and caboodle. Said he intended to enjoy his 'golden years' since no one knows how many they've got comin'."

With that sentiment hanging in the air, silence settled over the fish house, each of us contemplating her own golden years. Or so I assumed.

Grace proved me wrong when she piped up. "Hey, did either of you happen to read about the guy who sued the Smart Water people because their bottled water failed to make him smarter?"

"Huh?" I did my best to shift my mental gears. During the last several years, they'd become prone to sticking.

"Yeah," she said, not waiting for me to catch up, "leads me to wonder if we might have a case against the Girl Scouts over these Thin Mints."

Finishing off my beer, I realized a couple things: First, I had to duck behind the camouflage curtain. And, second, my sister was on the verge of leading us in another senseless discussion. Neither surprised me. My bladder was the size of a pea. And Grace preferred meaningless topics of conversation whenever we were ice fishing.

To her way of thinking, we couldn't discuss weighty matters while sitting on a frozen lake, drinking booze, and eating junk food. Sure, we occasionally happened upon something thought-provoking, such as Lars's pearls of wisdom regarding old age. But whenever that occurred, my dear sister wasted no time in steering us in another direction.

"What do you propose?" I asked her. "That the Girl Scouts change the name to something like… umm… Weighty Wafers?"

"It'd make more sense."

Getting to my feet, I shook a cookie in front of her nose. "Don't you dare mess with the Girl Scouts or their cookies. I dream about cookie season all year long."

"See?" Grace dipped her head toward Rose. "Doris has no life."

Without further comment, I stuffed the cookie into my mouth and ducked into the makeshift "bathroom." There, I peed in the bucket while singing "Raindrops Keep Falling on my Head."

With no fan to muffle our bathroom sounds, we provided our own noise. The person behind the curtain chose the tune, and everyone else joined in whether or not they knew the lyrics.

After a couple tortuous verses, I wiped my hands and shoved the curtain aside.

"B.J. Thomas has no competition here," Grace muttered, referring to the song's original recording artist.

I corrected her. "I think B.J.'s dead."

"Well, in that case, he's probably rolling over in his grave."

Tucking her fishing pole between her knees, Grace shucked off her jacket. "It's getting warm in here." The front of her long-sleeve t-shirt read, *Fishing's tough, but I can tackle it.* Grace had an ever-growing collection of t-shirts, each with a saying printed across the front. Some were funny. Others, crude. And a few, both.

I sniffed my hands. "I brought disinfectant wipes with me. But the alcohol in them combined with the fish odor in here made my palms smell like lutefisk."

"What's wrong with that?" Grace had insisted she could prepare lutefisk in such a way that I'd "gobble it right down." I had no intention of ever learning if she was right.

Moving to the counter without further comment, I reached for the spigot on the water jug.

At the same time, Rose hollered, "Heavens to Murgatroyd!" I wheeled around, as she added, "I've got somethin'." She yanked on her pole. "Quick, Doris, get the whatchamacallit."

"The net?"

"Yah, whatever." She took to her feet, while I collected the net from where it was racked on the wall.

"He's a heavy son of a gun." She wrenched her line. "But not much fight in 'im."

"Maybe there's nothing there." Grace set her own rod aside and edged closer. "Maybe you're just tangled up."

"No, my line's comin' in." Rose cranked her reel, and it squawked with tension. "It's just slow. He's probably a fat old geezer."

Grace and I lowered our heads over Rose's fishing hole, appearing as if praying to the patron saint of fishing—St. Evinrude if I'm not mistaken.

The taut line flitted about until something flashed below the surface of the water. I readied the net, and Grace warned Rose, "Now, don't reel him in too fast."

The underwater image grew sharper. Nevertheless, I couldn't make it out.

"Take your time," Grace added. "Don't be impatient."

Rose set her jaw but managed to growl, "I know how to land a fish, Grace. I've been doin' it for eighty-odd years." As if to put an exclamation mark on her point, she tugged her pole, causing a shoe to pop out of the hole in the ice. A multi-colored men's sneaker—red, orange, black, and blue—the brand name imprinted on the side.

"Well, I'll be. I guess you showed me." Grace extended an easy elbow to Rose's ribs. "But, in the future, if you plan to fish for footwear, go for something a little less hideous, preferably in a woman's casual, size six."

Without taking my eyes off Rose's catch, I said to Grace, "It's not just a shoe. Look. A foot and a leg are attached."

"What?"

Rose's eyes widened in stunned disbelief, and she stumbled and sat down. "I recognize that shoe," her words barely audible as she sank onto the bench seat. "Lars bought a pair when we went to Grand Forks. Said he just had to have them."

"Are you sure?" Grace commandeered Rose's pole. "No disrespect, but Lars is… ah… kind of old, and that shoe strikes me as something only a teenager would wear."

"Well, he wanted to become a snappier dresser."

I chucked Rose's chin with my knuckle. "Don't jump to any conclusions. Lars can't be the only man with those shoes."

Grace inclined her head and whispered to me, "I wouldn't bet on it, Doris. How many people would hand over good money for a pair of those? They're butt-ugly."

## Chapter 3

It was supper time when we got home. Rose had insisted on staying at the lake until Sheriff Ingebretsen and Deputy Ed Monson chopped through enough ice to retrieve the body. Yes, it was Rose's beau, Lars Carlson.

The trip home felt way longer than seventeen miles. Even though the sun had set, no stars shined in the sky, leading me to drive with my brights on to avoid hitting any deer. I also flipped on the radio, presuming music would fill the void left by the hush in the car, although I kept the volume low to see better. Granted, that made no sense, but that's what I did.

Grace huddled in the back seat with Rose, while I stole peeks at them in the rearview mirror. I willed Grace to look my way. I wanted to signal to her that she should offer Rose words of consolation. But she never met my eyes. As a result, the car crept along the winding two-lane highway with no one speaking until I couldn't take it anymore and provided a few pathetic platitudes of my own. In response, Rose only sniffled.

Once home, I settled Rose at the kitchen table with a cup of coffee and a bowl of chicken-noodle soup. For her part, Grace hurried off to the café, purportedly to prep for the following day. I suspected that was only an excuse to get out of the house. Grace wasn't good at dealing with grief. When our mother died, almost seventeen years ago, my sister left town right after the funeral and didn't return for ten years, when she came home for good.

"How's your soup?" I asked, sitting opposite Rose at the small black drop-leaf table in the center of the room. I'd made it my-self. The soup, not the table. I had opened the can, mixed in the water, and heated it on the stove. In doing so, I also pretty much exhausted my cooking abilities.

"It's fine. Thank you." Drooping her head and hunching her back, Rose folded in on herself.

To ward off my own grief, I looked away, assessing the mun-dane: the empty soup kettle on a hot pad on the butcherblock countertop and the cereal bowls upside down in the dish drain-er next to the cast-iron sink. I even examined the walls and cup-boards I'd recently painted "cheery yellow."

That's when I decided that Grace might have been on to something. Perhaps I could sue the paint manufacturer for false advertising. After all, I didn't feel the least bit cheery.

"I don't get it," Rose said, breaking through my musings. "Lars wasn't scheduled to go fishin'. When we had supper at the bowlin' alley on Friday, he said that before goin' to Dot's on Sat-urday, he planned to take the senior shuttle to Thief River to meet some guys at the casino."

She retrieved a handkerchief from beneath the cuff of her sweater. "He wanted to go really bad since he missed the last couple of get-togethers because, like you said, we've been spen-din' a lot of time with each other."

"Why the shuttle? Why didn't he drive?"

"He planned to have a few drinks. And you know he won't drink and drive. Not after… " Her voice trailed off, but I under-stood what she was getting at.

"Did anyone else from around here go?" I asked.

"Not that I know of."

"Well, he must have changed his mind."

Rose's eyes filled with tears. "He would of phoned me." A tear trickled down her cheek. "At least I think he would of."

"Maybe he didn't get a chance. You said he was supposed to have supper with Dot when he got back. I can't imagine her allowing him to hang on the phone with you."

She dabbed her cheeks with her hanky before wedging it beneath her wire-rimmed glasses and wiping her eyes. "He had all afternoon to get hold of me."

"It probably didn't occur to him. Whether at the casino or ice fishing, he wasn't scheduled to spend the day with you, right?"

"I guess… "

Lars's failure to keep in touch clearly upset Rose, but his sneakers gave me pause. Unlike Grace, I didn't care that they were ugly, though I did have trouble understanding why he had worn them at all. Ice fishing called for boots, even in a fish house. Everyone knew that.

Rose scraped her chair back. "I'm gonna lie down."

"Here, let me help."

She dismissed my offer with a flick of her bony wrist. "I'm perfectly capable of gettin' to my room under my own steam. It's right there."

With a digit crooked from arthritis, she pointed in the general direction of the suite off the kitchen—a suite that overlooked the woods and the river behind the house. Originally, it was destined to be my private area, but I relocated to the second floor when Rose came to stay. I didn't want her climbing stairs.

As for Grace, she occupied the third-floor. I had offered her that entire floor, including a bedroom, bathroom, and sitting area, as incentive to move in. Another debatable decision on my part.

◎ ◎ ◎

Once Rose retreated to her room, I stacked our soup bowls in the sink and answered a knock at the front door. Sheriff Karl Ingebretsen's six-foot-four frame filled the doorway, the overhead porch light supplying nothing more than spotty backlighting.

"Come on in. Coffee's on. It'll take the chill off."

Stuffing his gloves into the pockets of the brown bomber jacket he wore over his khaki uniform, Karl stepped into the entry. Because he lived in a cabin out by Lake Bronson and heated with wood, the space immediately smelled like a campfire.

Whenever close to Karl Ingebretsen, I experienced a wide range of feelings. Sometimes I got butterflies in my stomach. Other times I had the nearly irresistible urge to beat him about the head. But, tonight, I felt sorry for him.

Approaching his sixty-fourth birthday, he had never mentioned retirement. Yet standing there in front of me, he came across as more than ready for it. His jowls sagged. And his eyes, normally reminding me of dollops of dark chocolate floating in heavy cream, now more closely resembled the chocolate-covered cherries I had sat on and squished during his Christmas Day visit.

After stomping snow from his boots, he unzipped his jacket and followed me through the foyer and dining room and into the kitchen. There, he parked himself at the table.

"You're probably hungry after the day you've had." I combed through the cupboards, the "cheery yellow" doors squeaking. "We had canned soup for supper, although I don't seem to have any left. I meant to get more at the store yesterday, but I forgot my shopping list."

"I'm not hungry."

He removed his baseball cap—the one with the county emblem stitched to the front. The glow from the overhead pendant fixture highlighted his prominent cheekbones, his hawk-like nose, and his toffee-colored skin. Physically he took after his mother's side of the family. They were part Ojibwe. In disposition, he was all Norwegian, like his father.

"I probably could have recalled most of what I needed," I said, as if he cared about my shopping challenges, "but everything had been switched around on the shelves again. Why do they do that?"

"Doris, it's fine."

"No, it's not. I hate when they—"

"I mean, you don't have to feed me."

"You've got to eat. You'll—"

"Doris!" Karl was well aware of my propensity to ramble and regularly cut me off. I didn't take offense. It wasn't his fault that my mouth ran amuck whenever I got nervous, and he always rattled my nerves. In other words, his was a losing battle.

"At least have a bar with your coffee." I badgered him about food because it's how we Minnesotans demonstrated that we cared. "Grace brought Scotcheroos home from the café yesterday." In addition to hot dish and Jell-O, bars were a major food group in the region, as demonstrated by every funeral luncheon ever prepared.

"I—don't—want—anything." He carefully enunciated each word. "I only came by to update Rose."

Handing him his cup of coffee, I sat down, somewhat perturbed. The whole enunciation thing was a speck much. "She's lying down. She was all done in. You'll just have to tell me."

He twisted his lips between his thumb and forefinger, most likely debating the soundness of my proposition. Normally, that would have added to my annoyance. But the prospect of hearing the details of Lars's death had left me skittish. Not skittish enough to ask him to forego briefing me. However, I did appreciate a few extra minutes to prepare myself.

"The body's on its way to the coroner in Grand Forks," he said after a while. "We oughtta have a preliminary report as to the cause of death by late tomorrow."

Over the rim of my cup, I repeated, "Cause of death? Lars drowned while fishing, didn't he?" True, due to the man's footwear, I had reservations about the circumstances surrounding his demise. But, to hear Grace tell it, I'd become a "glass half empty" kind of person. She called it my most irritating trait. And because

I longed to avoid irritating Karl, at least until after he brought me up to date, I had resolved to put a less dubious spin on the day's events.

He cocked his head. "You noticed what he had on his feet, didn't you?"

"Of course. But I figured that once he got inside a fish house, his feet got too warm in his boots, so he switched to tennis shoes." That sounded ludicrous.

Karl must have agreed because he looked at me as if my IQ had dipped below the level required for basic deductive reasoning. "And while wearing those shoes," he replied with a smirk that matched his caustic tone, "he slipped through a ten-inch hole in the ice?"

I snarled at his sarcasm. "He could have broken through when returning to his car."

"Lars's car wasn't out there. And no one we interviewed saw him fishing. In fact, Gustaf said he's never seen Lars out on Lake Bronson." Karl tasted his coffee. "On top of that, we couldn't find any of his fishing gear." The right corner of his mouth twitched. "Or the boots he may have slipped off in favor of those tennis shoes."

"Ha. Ha."

"No, Doris," he continued, turning serious again, "it just doesn't add up."

"What? You mean to say that you expect foul play?" Grace was right. I made a poor Pollyanna. I was much more of a Debbie Downer. I expected the worst. Always had. At least ever since marrying my now-deceased, philandering husband.

"Whoa! Whoa! Whoa!" Karl scudded back his chair. "I didn't say anything about foul play. We probably just missed a piece of evidence that'll clear everything up. But it's too dark to do any more searching tonight." He pushed to his feet and pulled his cap over his salt-and-pepper hair. "We'll give it a rest and go out again first thing in the morning."

Maybe Karl's concerns could rest, but mine niggled at me like a colicky baby. Consequently, as I trailed him to the front entry, I couldn't keep from asking, "Are you aware that Lars had arranged to meet up with some men at the casino in Thief River yesterday?" Before he had a chance to reply, I added, "And Dot had him over for supper last night?"

Reaching the door, he pivoted. "Yeah. Ed spoke with Rose out at the lake."

"I was with her. I just didn't know what all he remembered to report back to you. For instance, did he mention that Dot was at the lake too?"

Karl massaged the back of his neck as if something—or some-one—irritated it. "Doris, I realize that you have little regard for Ed's investigative abilities—"

"Oh? He has some?"

The corners of his mouth curved in a barely suppressed grin. "He has a few strengths."

"Could have fooled me."

Karl's hint of a smile morphed into a frown. "How can you say that after the help he provided during that chaos a few months back?"

"He helped?" When Karl's frown remained static, I said, "I... umm... also find him less than transparent."

"How so?" Karl held the door with his shoulder, looking as if prepared to remain like that until I explained myself.

"Well, whenever I speak with him, he comes across as evasive."

"He's shy, Doris. And you can be kind of—"

"What's more," I hurried to say, not wanting him to finish that sentence, "I can't tell what's going on between him and Gustaf?"

"How's that got anything to do with Lars's death?"

"Well, Ed was ice fishing with Gustaf today and—"

"And good thing he was. With Ed already at the lake, we got a jump start on the investigation, which was important since it's still getting dark so blasted early these days."

Having failed to make my point, I raised my voice, as if that might do the trick. "Karl, there's absolutely no reason for Gustaf and Ed to be friends."

The sheriff upped his volume too. "And that's your business because?"

I had to come up with something fast. "Umm… given that my daughter is Ed's partner on the job, I'm naturally interested in what kind of person he is."

Karl's features said, *You've got to be kidding,* but his mouth went with, "Your daughter's pushing thirty, Doris. She doesn't need you—and most likely doesn't want you—checking up on her colleagues."

I hated when he was right. It usually left me nothing to go with except the truth. And the truth often failed to work to my advantage. "Fine. I'm just curious, okay?"

He examined the ceiling as if seeking tolerance. But, unless it came wrapped in cobwebs, he'd have no chance of finding any up there. "Goodnight, Doris."

"Another thing," I said as soon as a more salient notion occurred to me. "I don't want Ed or anyone else dropping the ball on this investigation because they're not one-hundred percent focused. Rose is devastated. And ninety. We have to find out what happened fast."

He spun back around to face me. "We?"

I blew an audible breath. "It's a figure of speech. Nothing more. I have no interest in doing any more police work. I've done enough to last me a lifetime. Believe me."

"I'd like to."

"What?"

"Believe you." His crow's feet crinkled. "Although, if the past is prologue… "

"Yeah. Funny."

Thrusting his hands into his pants' pockets, he jingled his keys and change, his go-to move whenever ill at ease. Had been since high school. "Since you… ah… find me kind of funny," he said, addressing the entry rug, "would you consider going out with me this Saturday? It could be good for a few laughs." His jingling grew more frantic. "I should have all this cleared up by then." He lifted his head, hope brimming in his eyes.

"This Saturday?" My toes curled with desire before something akin to terror overcame me. "You know I was being facetious when I called you funny."

"Even so, you said it. Now, what about Saturday? After all, last time didn't count."

"I… umm… just don't know." While I wanted to accept his invitation—really, I did—a totally different response tumbled from my throat when I opened my mouth. "It's probably a bad idea." It was my turn to talk to the rug. "Rose might need me."

"No one else can take care of her? Not even for a few hours?" His tenor had changed. A sharpness invaded his voice that prompted me to glance up at him. I didn't care for what I saw. Frustration had colored his eyes black. I'd seen it before. On several occasions.

"It's not that." I wrung my hands dishrag style, my own long-time, nervous habit. "It's just—"

"Never mind. I shouldn't have asked. You've made yourself perfectly clear. You're not interested."

"I didn't mean… It's just… " I couldn't finish. I couldn't admit to him that because of my lousy marriage, I was afraid of getting hurt again.

"Don't worry." He pulled the door open. "I'm done asking."

"Karl… "

He lumbered across the porch and down the steps without so much as a "good night."

After easing into his car, a white SUV with "Kittson County Sheriff" emblazoned on the side in black and gold, he turned the engine over, wheeled the vehicle around, and stomped on the accelerator. Exhaust tailed him as he bounded down my snow-coated driveway.

As for me, I lingered in the doorway, the wind howling, the furnace rumbling, and hot air blowing through the heating vent and up my pants' legs.

## Chapter 4

The following morning, I got up around eight, which was early for me. I normally didn't seize the day, preferring instead to poke it with a stick from under my covers. But I couldn't sleep and had spent most of the night tossing and turning when not calculating how much shut-eye I'd get if I drifted off at that precise moment.

As usual, Grace's alarm had gone off at five, the same time my bladder routinely demanded to be emptied. But rather than climbing the stairs to her attic suite after visiting the bathroom, as I usually did, I returned to my room and cuddled my pillow.

Questions crowded my head, yet I had no wish to ask them of Grace or anyone else. If I didn't discuss what had occurred at the lake, maybe the whole ordeal would wind up being nothing but a bad dream.

Of course, that wasn't the case, as I realized when I limped into the kitchen to find Rose sitting at the table in semi-darkness, her posture like a comma. Dressed in her fuzzy bathrobe and slippers, she sipped from a mug, the aroma of fresh coffee wafting through the air, as the coffee maker gurgled and hissed.

White curls matted one side of her head, and behind her glasses, puffy eyes gave the impression that they were holding back tears. But she had cried herself dry. I was certain of that. My old house had thin walls, and I'd heard her off and on all night.

When she set her mug down, her hands trembled, and a lump formed in my throat that rendered me speechless. Still, I patted her arm as I passed by to check the weather through the window. It fit the occasion. The thermometer read twelve degrees, and gloominess had cast a net over the world. Or my corner of it at any rate.

After pouring coffee for myself, I washed down a mega-dose of ibuprofen before switching on the overhead light and occupying the chair across from her. I struggled to get comfortable. My sciatic nerve bothered me, either from sitting too long in the fish house or my restless night. "Want some breakfast, Rose?" My morning voice sounded like the hinges on a rusty gate. "I can scramble you an egg."

"No."

"Are you sure?"

She set her mug down. "Uff-da, Doris, Lars is gone." A bit of a brogue made an appearance in her tone.

Reaching across the table, I caressed the back of her hand. As a Scandinavian, I seldom demonstrated my feelings. We were reserved people. It was part of our heritage, like our round heads, our big-boned physiques, and our fondness for lefse. Nevertheless, I felt obliged to connect with her. "It's only been one night. It'll take time to accept."

"When you're my age, Doris, death isn't all that startlin', unless the circumstances are unusual. Then, all bets are off."

She scratched the rim of her mug with her thumbnail. "Remember when Whitey Wilson got mauled by that black bear out in Caribou a few years back? Everyone had trouble wrappin' their heads around it because black bears aren't supposed to attack people." She arched her eyebrows, and her glasses slid down her nose. "Guess they forgot to tell the bear."

30

She shoved them up again. "Anyways, even though Whitey got drunk and passed out in his deer stand, food scattered everywhere, more or less offerin' the bear a pre-hibernation smorgasbord, we had trouble comin' to terms with his death since the whole thing seemed odd. Same here."

My thigh throbbed, and I kneaded it with the heel of my hand while praying for the pain relievers to kick in. "Karl dropped by after you went to your room last night. He thinks we'll get some answers today."

As if on cue, Karl hollered from the front entry, "Eh? Anybody home?" Before I could coerce my leg into supporting me in a stand, he marched into the kitchen, his boots thumping a military-type cadence.

A quick look my way, then he aimed all his attention at Rose. And, believe it or not, I silently thanked him. You see, I was self-conscious over how things had ended between us the night before. On top of that, I looked a fright.

I hadn't checked myself in a mirror but was positive that the bags under my eyes were the size of my butt cheeks. And when I finger combed my hair, my palm came away greasy.

Plus, I hadn't shaved my legs since October, when I quit wearing shorts for the season. That wouldn't have mattered if not for my knee-length bathrobe. The same one I'd worn every morning for more winters than I could count, the cuffs frayed and the velour all but rubbed off.

If Karl had been disappointed about me declining his invitation for Saturday night, the mere sight of me must have aided in his recovery.

"Rose," he said, "I reckoned you'd want to hear right away what the coroner found." Karl's face typically resembled a relief map with rigid lines and sharp angles. But, in that moment, both his features and his manner conveyed only compassion.

Placing a hand the size of a catcher's mitt on the table, he crouched down until eye to eye with Rose. "Because the coroner suffers from insomnia, he performed the autopsy overnight." He seemingly rooted around in his head for his next words. "His... umm... preliminary finding was that Lars was... umm... struck in the back of the head with a blunt object. That's what killed him. In other words, Lars was murdered. And, afterwards, the killer dumped him in the lake."

Rose gasped. And, in spite of my "expect the worst" outlook, I let out an eek.

"I promise we'll get the person who did this." Karl never shifted his gaze away from Rose, not even to check if I was okay. "I've requested that the State Bureau of Criminal Apprehension give us a hand by sending up a couple agents."

"Okay." A visible shudder rippled through Rose's body. "Now, I better lie down. Will you help me?"

"Of course." Karl practically lifted her off her chair. True, there wasn't much to her anymore. Still, she typically took pride in "doing for herself."

I got to my feet too, mentally ordering my leg to straighten up. Although Karl assured me that he didn't need my assistance.

"How about the doctor then? Should I call Dr. Betcher?"

"No," Rose grunted. "I just hafta rest. That's all."

"What about your high blood pressure?" I said, referring to her recent diagnosis.

"I'll be fine, Doris."

As the two of them left the room, I dropped back onto my chair. My leg pain had subsided, but an onslaught of other feelings pulsed through my body.

◎ ◎ ◎

Lars Carlson was the second murder victim in tiny Hallock in the past few months. Thus, when Karl reclaimed his seat at the table, I said, "At the rate the dead bodies are piling up around here, we might have to update the population sign on the edge of town sooner rather than later."

He failed to respond. He didn't always appreciate my humor. In stressful situations, however, I tended to crack wise. That's how I coped.

"Rose genuinely cared for Lars, didn't she?" He tilted his head.

I stiffened my back. "She'd be in far better shape right now if she hadn't." I didn't mean to say that out loud. I never had anything against Lars. Not really. Sure, he'd spent time in federal prison. And he had done his older daughter wrong. But he and Rose had been companions for only a couple months.

Even so, I had feared that something like this might happen. Not that I could have predicted in a million years that Rose would reel the guy in like a walleye. But, due to his age, I had anticipated tragedy of one kind or another. Yes, Rose was much older than him, yet my brain wouldn't allow me to contemplate her demise.

"I came across the two of them a few times recently," Karl said, "and I can't recall either of them ever looking happier."

I tried to tamp down my bitterness, but I couldn't. Maybe I didn't try very hard. "You also saw her a few minutes ago. She wasn't even able to walk under her own power. So I have to ask you, Karl, was worth it? What she and Lars had?"

Karl rocked onto the back legs of his chair, crossed his arms over his broad chest, and raised a quizzical brow. "How in the hell did you become so bitter?"

Okay, that hurt. "I've had plenty of practice. Years actually."

His eyes opened wide, signaling a lightbulb moment. "Oh, I see. But, Doris, you're not the only person who's been in a bad relationship. It doesn't mean you should give up on people."

He sounded like Rose and Grace. And, for a second, I wondered if the three of them had read the same self-help book. Probably not. I couldn't imagine Karl seeking help from any book. Or any person for that matter.

"Seriously, Karl, she's ninety. What are the odds she'll recover from this? Especially being it happened so soon after she witnessed the pharmacy robbery?"

He lowered his chair as well as his voice. "What if she doesn't? At least her last months will have been enjoyable." His eyes burned into mine. "We all should be that lucky."

I had to look away.

I was on edge, my nerves thrumming, and I presumed Karl was stressed too. That's why I nearly fell off my chair when he reached across the table, chucked my chin, and said with a mischievous grin, "Remember, Doris, 'tis better to have loved and lost than never to have loved at all."

"Huh?" I grunted for lack of a more suitable response.

"It's poetry."

"I know it's poetry. It's also the dumbest thing you've ever said to me."

"I'm offended!" The smile in his eyes undermined his supposed outrage. "I'm more than a handsome native in uniform. I'm a Renaissance man. I can quote all the greats. Shakespeare—"

"Tennyson."

"What?"

"That was Tennyson. You quoted Tennyson."

"Well, Tennyson. Shakespeare. The point remains the same. People need to take a few risks."

"I'm not so sure." Grace was the risk taker in our family. I tended to be risk adverse. I would have loved to claim that my caution was the result of motherhood—and motherhood alone. But, in truth, I had always played it safe. Long before the birth of my kids. And well after they grew up and moved out.

"Anyway... " Karl's countenance shifted. He grew somber, and his jingling stopped. "Doris, did you... ah... ever know that I was married at one time?"

Coffee spewed from my mouth like a fountain gone haywire.

Again, he was oblivious, instead staring at the scratches on my tabletop. "I met her shortly after joining the army. We married before I got deployed overseas the first time."

He spoke without inflection, like he'd get through what he had to say only by pretending it was nothing more than a standard police report. "We were too young. We didn't know each other well. And we weren't in love. In lust, yes. But not in love." He sounded both regretful and resigned. "She divorced me shortly after I returned stateside. Still, since I'd gone into it for keeps, I had a tough time."

I was dumbfounded. I had assumed that I knew Karl, regardless of losing touch with him between high school and seven years ago, when he moved back to town. Sure, we had attended the fish fry at the Eagles a couple months back. But that so-called date didn't amount to much.

You see, nighttime temperatures had plunged to thirty-three below, leading folks to perform all kinds of frigid-weather experiments, something we often did when we found ourselves in the deep freeze. Several inebriated guys in the Eagles even went so far as to soak their blue jeans in water, then hold them up outside until they stood on their own. Suffice to say, Karl had to cut our date short to deal with public intoxication and frostbite.

"You were married? How come I didn't know that?" I posed the question after regaining my composure, which, like my coffee, was spattered all over.

"Well, it usually doesn't come up during the normal course of conversation. But I wanted you to know that despite a bad experience, I didn't give up on people. And you shouldn't either."

While I appreciated his interest in my well-being, my mind overflowed with questions about his marriage. So, as I blotted spilled coffee with paper napkins, I asked, "Any kids?"

"No, which was a good thing. Yet I sometimes think that I might have missed out." He rocked his head from side to side like he was weighing something. "I guess I have a posse of young deputies to watch out for."

"What about her? Your ex-wife? Are you over her?" I had no clue where those questions had come from. Sure, Karl had been my first love. But after discovering him making out with his ex-girlfriend behind the concession stand at the drive-in theater, I quit speaking to him. He had just graduated and soon went off to technical college before joining the army.

I had a couple years left in high school, and I dated but didn't get serious with anyone else until I met Bill Connor, who later became my husband. Nonetheless, I always felt somewhat possessive of Karl. Weird, grant you. But maybe that's how young love worked.

"It's been an awfully long time, Doris. I'd be dumb to still carry a torch."

Because I'd been caught up in my own reflections, my mind was muddled, and I didn't know if he was referring to a torch for his ex-wife or me.

Karl must have picked up on the nature of my confusion because he averted his eyes and surveyed the kitchen. And when done with that, he slapped his thighs. "Yeah, well, I better get going."

I had a dozen more questions, but embarrassment kept me from posing them—or speaking at all—as I accompanied him to the door.

"I almost forgot," he said over his shoulder while grasping the knob, "I dropped by Lars's apartment earlier. His car's in the parking lot, and his apartment is neat, which means there wasn't a fight. Yet we couldn't find his keys, wallet, or phone, so they must have been on him at the time of his death, although they weren't when we recovered his body." He still refrained from looking at me. "A neighbor did see him leave the apartment building on Saturday morning around nine o'clock. He drove away with Etta Wilhelm. In her car."

"Etta Wilhelm?"

"They returned about ninety minutes later, and after dropping him off, she left again. The senior shuttle then arrived at eleven o'clock. But no one saw it take off again. So we don't know if Lars was in it. We'll have to check with Arne and Anders Olafson."

I grimaced. "They're different, aren't they?" No need to elaborate. Practically everyone in town subscribed to the notion that seventy-something Arne and Anders Olafson, identical twins

36

who had semi-retired to Hallock a few months back, were "different," the "Scandinavian nice" term for peculiar. "You never see one without the other. And they always dress alike. It makes it impossible to tell them apart."

Karl ran a finger along his right jaw. "Anders has a jagged scar here."

"I guess I don't get close enough to them—or most men—to check their chins."

"As a rule, Doris, I don't either."

"Yet you're familiar with Anders's minor facial flaw."

"Minor? That scar's five inches long."

I laughed. The awkwardness between us had vanished. Not surprising. Bantering had always come easily for Karl and me, and it left me feeling in sync with him, like the old days.

"Karl?" I clutched the sleeve of his jacket. I wanted a do-over on his invitation from the previous evening. "About this Saturday... " Our eyes locked, physical awareness heightening between us.

After a beat, he blinked. "Doris, I'm sure you were right. We're better off as friends and nothing more."

My grip loosened. "But—"

"Now, I better go." He ambled onto the porch. "I need to get back to work... friend."

As he descended the steps and headed down the sidewalk, every movie I'd ever seen about star-crossed lovers flickered through my mind. But unlike the women in those films, I didn't chase after him or clutch a tear-stained handkerchief to my bosom. Rather, I braced myself against the door jamb and gripped my greasy hair in a stubby ponytail, the hem of my ragged bathrobe riding the bitter breeze and exposing my hairy legs and possibly a whole lot more.

# Chapter 5

With Karl out of sight, I shut the door and banged my head against it. "What is wrong with you? Grace is right. You're an ignoramus when it comes to men." As that truth echoed in my ears, I wallowed in self-pity until I craved ice cream.

With Chunky Monkey and Chocolate Peanut Butter Split on my mind, I trudged toward the kitchen, stopping short when someone reached out and grabbed me. Fear pierced my chest, replaced by anger after I recognized the fist that clutched my arm. "Rose, you scared the crap out of me!"

"Oh, you're fine." She gave me an up-down from behind the archway that separated the foyer from the dining room. "But I'm not. Lars was with Etta."

Releasing me, she stared at the blank wall opposite us. My cuckoo clock had hung there until it went down in a hail of gunfire a few months ago. "I suppose I shouldn't be surprised." She spoke as if in a trance. "Etta couldn't stand the notion of Lars datin' me. Everyone knew that. But I thought better of him." She blinked, breaking the spell. "You were right, Doris. He wanted a younger woman. I'm nothin' but an old fool."

Clutching her upper arms, I backpedaled as fast as I could. "I was wrong to say that. Any man would be lucky to have you for a... lady friend."

"No, like you told the sheriff, I'd be better off if I'd never gone out with him." Her manner contradicted her words. And her words ratted her out.

"Wait. How come you know what I said to Karl? Weren't you napping?"

"I couldn't sleep."

"Well, you shouldn't eavesdrop. Besides, remember what Grace said. I'm bitter."

She snickered. Then teetered. And I caught her as she wobbled.

"Uff-da," she grunted. "I better sit down. I must be more upset than I realized."

"I'll call Dr. Betcher." I led her to the worn couch in the living room, the wood floor creaking as we walked.

"He can't do anythin' about Etta. And I'll be right as rain in a bit."

Realizing there was no point in arguing with her—there hardly ever was—I tucked a lattice-weave afghan, my latest creation, over her lap. "I was about to get some ice cream." I switched on the gas fireplace. The flames offered soft light and subtle heat. "Would you like some? It probably wouldn't hurt."

"No, I'm not hungry."

"A drink then? Hot chocolate? Or something stronger?"

She patted the sofa cushion next to her. "Let's just visit, okay?"

How could I say no? Huddled under that crocheted blanket, her slipper-clad feet not even reaching the floor, she reminded me of a waif in a Dicken's novel. "You betcha, Rose. We'll visit." My ice cream would have to wait.

Grabbing another afghan, I snuggled into the opposite corner of the sofa. Because drafts assailed my old house all winter long, I crocheted a lot of afghans. I enjoyed it, but Grace viewed it as further evidence of my need for more "social interaction."

Yeah, sometimes she went too far. Unfortunately, she always found her way home.

"Doris?" Rose appeared captivated by the reflections in the shiny balls on the Christmas tree I still hadn't taken down. It had been up for so long that I didn't even notice it most of the time. "Would you do me a favor?"

Rose had changed over the years. At one time, she had brought to mind an Amazon woman with her strength, independence, and determination. She had worked at the local court-house, reaching the pinnacle of her career when she became the county's first female clerk of court.

Unlike our mother, who had stayed on the farm, Rose was a "townie" and a "businesswoman." Growing up, my sister and I had admired her cars, her clothes, and her hair. Grace came to emulate her, while I marveled at them both.

Now, Rose didn't drive. Her wardrobe featured polyester sweatsuits appliqued with snowflakes and cartoon wildlife, and her hair resembled the dust bunnies under my bed. Even so, she maintained a formidable will and relative independence with few exceptions, one of them being the last twenty-four hours.

"Whatever you need, Rose. Just name it."

She played with the fringe on her afghan. "Talk to Etta. Find out what happened between her and Lars. See if they hood-winked me."

I would have preferred to jam a pencil up my nose. "I'm sure there's a perfectly reasonable explanation for them being to-gether."

"Well, if that's true, you shouldn't have any problem discussin' it with her."

"But—"

"Doris, it'll eat away at me." She eyed me over her glasses. "Etta worked with me at the birthday celebration at the senior center on Saturday. And while we kept our distance, whenever one of us walked into the kitchen, the other women quit talkin'. Makes me think they all knew what Lars and her were up to."

A pout overtook the bottom half of her face, but I refused to be swayed. "Karl and the BCA are investigating the case. They'll determine what happened."

"They're investigatin' Lars's death. They aren't gonna check what kind of shenanigans Etta and him might of been pullin' behind my back."

"True. But I can't. I almost got killed last time."

"Oh, fiddlesticks." She swished her hand as if wiping away something as insignificant as a fly. "Everything turned out fine. And since what I want to know has didley-squat to do with Lars's murder, it won't be the least bit dangerous."

Her lack of empathy rankled me. I had barely escaped death two months ago. "Why don't you speak to her yourself then?"

"She hates me. I'd be as welcome in her house as a skunk at a Christmas party. And even if she let me in, she'd lie to me, and I'd end up throttlin' her."

I sighed so hard that my lungs practically collapsed. "What am I supposed to say? 'Hi, Etta. I dropped by on Rose's behalf to ask if you and Lars played footsie before he died?'"

"You might hafta be a tad more tactful than that."

"I can't."

"Sure, you can." She slid her dentures from side to side. "True, you're not as tactful as most folks, but—"

"No! I mean I can't confront her. I can't get involved."

Rose resumed toying with the fringe on her afghan. "Listen, Doris. I may not be as young or as shapely as Etta. And I certainly can't cook like her. Or play bridge or whist as good. But I... umm... umm... I forgot where I was goin' with that."

Melancholy shrouded her eyes, and my resolve began to crumble. "Rose, I'd like to help you. Really, I would. It's just—"

"Never mind." That pout again. This time augmented by a trembling bottom lip.

And it was that lip that did me in. "Okay, I'll do it." I should have put up more of a fight, but I loved Rose, and she was hurt ing. "I'll check into what she was doing with Lars. Although, under no circumstances will I ask about the murder."

"Fine."

"I'll also only visit with her one time no matter how much you beg. So, if I don't get the answers you're after, too bad. I won't go back."

"Okee-dokee."

"Well, as long as we understand each other, I'll drop by her place this afternoon."

"Thanks." Rose grinned coat-hanger wide.

And I got the feeling that I'd just been "hoodwinked."

# Chapter 6

The bells on the door jingled as I entered More Hot Dish, Please. My sister, Grace, had owned the place for almost seven years. She did a brisk business partly because of her formal training and extensive experience as a chef. But mostly because it was the only café in town.

Housed in the former jewelry store, the More Hot Dish, Please building featured original tin ceilings and hardwood floors, along with plate-glass windows that framed Main Street. Grace had updated the interior with white paint, black Naugahyde booths, and chrome-trimmed tables and chairs. A Formica-top counter extended the length of the room, stopping just shy of the swinging doors that led into the kitchen.

Open Monday through Saturday, from 6:00 a.m. to 2:00 p.m., the cafe specialized in home cooking—Minnesota style. Grace prepared a variety of hot dishes, Jell-O salads, and bars. Owing to her background in five-star restaurants, she also offered stuffed lobster, beef Wellington, and Coq au vin on occasion, which folks claimed to like "just fine." They even agreed to sample other "fancy dishes," as long as she didn't get "too carried away."

"Hi, Ole." I tipped my head toward the old guy with leather skin who sat alone at the counter. Ole Svengaard, a regular in the café, was crusty from an accumulation of years, but his eyes, almost hidden in an abundance of wrinkles, shined with flecks of gold.

Early every morning, Ole and his cronies occupied stools along the counter and drank coffee and visited, forming a continuous line of John Deere caps. But because it was going on ten o'clock, the place had emptied out. The elderly women who held daily court in the corner booth had left, as had Ole's chums, though I never understood why the old men rushed off. Most of them were retired, their sons and grandsons, as well as a growing number of daughters and granddaughters, now in charge of their respective farms.

Ole had sold his spread "lock, stock, and barrel" several years back. Yet as a life-long "bachelor farmer," he continued to frequent the café for meals and company, claiming the third stool from the end as his own.

"What's up?" I asked like I did whenever we crossed paths.

He always replied with, "Oh, you know, same soup, just reheated."

"Terrible news about Lars Carlson, huh?"

"Yah. Knew him my whole life. Went to school with him. He was a few years behind me." Using only his tongue, he shifted a toothpick from one corner of his mouth to the other. "Never liked him much. Slippery as snot. Chased easy money. That's why he ended up in prison, don't ya know." He plucked the toothpick from his mouth and aimed it at me. "Still, I didn't wish him dead."

"Have you heard anything?"

"Well, I came across Arne Olafson earlier. He said Anders and him drove Lars to Thief River and back again in the senior shuttle on Saturday. But he couldn't say what happened to him once they dropped him off at home."

"Both of them took Lars to Thief River? Why?"

He tapped his toothpick on the counter. "They wanted to do a little gambling of their own."

Not sure where to go from there, I scanned the room. Allie, Grace's premiere waitress, leaned over the booth where Gustaf Gustafson and Ed Monson sat. "On another subject, what do you make of those two?" I pitched my chin toward the men.

Ole cranked his head, the movement achingly slow and seemingly painful. "Oh, they've been together a lot lately. From what I hear, Gustaf's wife is out of town, taking care of her sick mother."

Unzipping my parka, I rested my forearms on the countertop. "Isn't that strange?"

"That his wife is caring for her mother?" Ole waved me off. "Louise may be a shrew, but even a shrew can love her parents."

"No. No. I mean, isn't it strange that Gustaf and Ed spend so much time together?"

Having dropped his toothpick, Ole resorted to sucking his teeth. "Uff-da, I don't know. Although Ed don't appear none too happy about it at present."

He was right. Ed Monson had propped his elbows on the table, cradling his jaw on his fists, like his head was too full of trouble to support itself.

"That's probably how I look whenever I spend time with Gustaf," I said. "But I don't usually do it voluntarily. Ed apparently does. Still, I can't figure out why, which really bugs me."

"Why am I not surprised?"

"Hey!" I swatted Ole's arm, and he pretended to sway from the blow. "How come everyone thinks I'm overly interested in other people's business? I'm only trying to keep track of what's going on around town. You might say I'm civic-minded."

"If that's what you wanna call it." Ole beamed, showing off stained yellow teeth that resembled rotten corn on the cob. "Why don't ya ask the sheriff why they're friends? Being he hired young Ed there, he probably has a pretty good read on him."

"I tried, but he sidestepped my questions."

"Though... Ed wouldn't have gotten hired without Gustaf's approval, since he's the head of the county board and all. So go right to the source and ask Gustaf."

"I have, Ole. I got nowhere."

"Well, you obviously don't know how to get what you want from men." He snickered, and that snicker soon morphed into a wheeze and, from there, a coughing jag. Whipping out a wadded hanky from his pants' pocket, he spit into it and wiped his nose before shoving it back where it belonged.

Like everyone else in town, Ole was well aware that Gustaf Gustafson and I had a contentious relationship. Because we had grown up together, I knew firsthand that Gustaf was full of himself. And after being named president of the local bank right out of college, he became even harder to take. Though I only learned recently that he had never wanted to be a banker. His father, the bank president preceding him, had pressured him into it. In truth, Gustaf hated his job almost as much as his home life.

Grace and I got the lowdown on both one night a few months back, when Gustaf drank more than anyone had a right to and spilled his guts—literally. First, he exposed his deepest secrets. Then, he vomited all over me and my SUV.

Nonetheless, during that evening, the three of us had formed an uneasy alliance. And ever since, my sister and I made a greater effort to tolerate the guy. In return, Gustaf often confided in us.

"Hey," Ole said, bursting my thought bubble, "I have a joke for you." Ole always had jokes, but they were seldom funny. "What do you get from a pampered cow?"

"I don't know, Ole. What?"

"Spoiled milk." The punch line was followed by another snicker and a slap on the counter.

While I groaned as I normally did. "I swear you tell the worst jokes."

"What do you mean? There's no one in here who can match me joke for joke."

"Ole, the place is practically empty."

After bidding Ole goodbye, I pushed through the bat-wing doors that separated the dining room from the kitchen and nearly slammed into 28-year-old Joy Jacobson, better known as Tweety. With a snort that came across as a honk due to her beak-like nose, she barreled past me, a tray of breakfast food held next to her boxy head. The aroma of sausage and maple syrup lingered in her wake, taunting my stomach.

Once in the kitchen, I found Grace bent over the grill, scraping off the remnants of the last order and gabbing on her phone. Two slices of extra crispy bacon lay on a paper towel on the counter next to her. I ate both, deciding that sometimes it was better to seek forgiveness than permission.

"Hey," she groused, slipping her phone into the rear pocket of her tight jeans, "those were for me."

"Oops. Sorry."

"You don't sound sorry."

I wasn't. I sucked the greasy tips of my thumb and forefinger. "I need your advice. But, first, what's Tweety doing here?"

Tweety's mother, Jane, had been best friends with Grace while growing up. So, following Jane's death, Grace had given Tweety a job in the café and a deal on the upstairs' apartment. However, in light of Tweety's recent attempts to implicate my kids in criminal activity, Grace had both fired her and kicked her out of the apartment. Or so I had been led to believe.

"I rehired her this morning." My sister backed against the stainless-steel counter, crossed her feet at her ankles, and reflected on the wood floor. She appeared somewhat chagrinned.

Regardless, if she had glimpsed my way, I would have spit in her eye. "How could you?"

"I didn't have any choice." She maintained her downward gaze. "Lucy Dahlstrom, the waitress from Drayton? You know, the one I hired to take Tweety's place? Well, she turned out to be worthless. This morning she dropped another tub of dishes, breaking half of them."

She sucked air through her burgundy lips. "I didn't yell at her. No, sir-ee. Like all the other times, I simply warned her to be more careful. But she still burst into tears and screamed that she couldn't tolerate any more of my abuse. Then, she walked out. And Allie threatened to do the same if I didn't rehire Tweety."

I felt my forehead wrinkle. "They're friendly now? Allie and Tweety?"

"Not particularly. But Allie's overworked. And though Tweety's a pain in the ass, no one else is pounding down my door, clamoring for a job."

I teased a recollection from the recesses of my mind. "Not that I follow Tweety's comings and goings, but I swear I heard that she was waitressing out at the truck stop."

"She was. She got a job there after I fired her. But she and Destiny Delovely got into a knock-down, drag-out behind the counter on Friday night. And, afterwards, Destiny gave their boss an ultimatum. Naturally, he went with her because she's worked for him since Jesus wore diapers."

"Well, it's no wonder they ended up in a fight. They're like two cats in perpetual heat."

"Yeah, I guess they caused quite a stir." Grace giggled. She enjoyed a good brawl. It's why she watched pro hockey and *Real Housewives.* "Of course, news got around that Tweety got axed, and that's why Allie insisted that I call her this morning."

Grace wrestled her grease-stained chef's smock over her head. Humungous breasts and a baseball cap on top of her hair made it quite a challenge. "To her credit, Tweety came right over." With her dirty smock in hand, she headed to the storage cupboard at the back of the kitchen. "Now, maybe she merely wanted to get out of her grandma's house. God knows, I would. Or maybe she's truly changed her ways."

"You're deceiving yourself, Grace," I called after her. "She'll cause more trouble. Mark my words."

Rather than recognizing the error of her ways and apologizing, my sister got prickly. "Damn it, Doris, I have a business to run.

If you want a full-time job, I'll get rid of Tweety. If not, butt out."

I certainly didn't want to wait on tables on a regular basis. As it was, I grumbled whenever Grace asked me to fill in. "Geez, you're awfully touchy."

"It's been a hectic morning." She tossed her dirty smock into a bin in the closet, grabbed a clean one from the shelf, and pulled it over her head. But not before I read the front of her t-shirt: *Saturday called. She's on her way, and she's bringing wine.* In light of my sister's mood, Saturday couldn't get there soon enough.

Retracing her steps to the counter, Grace poured two cups of coffee and delivered them and a pan of No-Bake Chocolate Oat Bars to the metal prep table in the middle of the room. "As you might expect, there's been a lot of talk in here about Lars's death." She settled on a stool. "And during the telling, you'll never guess what someone shared about Dot?" She didn't wait for me to respond. "A guy named Dirk Dickerson is shacked up with her."

"You mean, he's a guest in her bed and breakfast?"

"Nope. It's supposedly more than that."

"Really?" I said. "Hard to imagine anyone getting close to Dot."

"Be that as it may, people have seen Dot and this Dickerson guy out and about, acting all friendly. But no one has any inkling where he came from. He just showed up out of the blue about ten days ago."

Grace scooped a bar out of the pan. "Can you believe he hasn't been in here?" Crumbs fell on the table as she bit into it. "Dot must be keeping him awfully busy, if you know what I mean?" She gathered the crumbs with the tip of her index finger. "Even so, he managed to make his way out to the truck stop. Tweety said he came on to her out there last week."

"Grace, Tweety thinks every guy comes onto her."

"A lot of them do."

I shuddered.

"Anyway... " After licking the crumbs from her finger, Grace finished the bar, not letting a full mouth prevent her from speaking. "In his attempt to impress her, he mentioned something about soon coming into a large sum of money."

"So?"

"So… " She twirled her hand, motioning me to keep up. "A few days later Dot's father got murdered, leaving Dot to inherit all his money to do with as she pleases."

"Like I already said, you're assuming Lars had money."

"Of course, he had money. All the farmers around here do. Even if he went broke repaying the feds, he had years to recoup." She pitched her thumb into the air as if hitchhiking. "The guys out front say Lars bragged all the time about all his money."

"Whatever." Everyone, my sister included, would just have to wait until the details of Lars's estate were publicly disclosed. It wouldn't be long. Hallock was not much for keeping secrets.

"Anyway," Grace said, "I find the timing suspicious. Dot hasn't had a man in her life since her husband died a decade ago. Then, all of a sudden, this guy shows up, gets involved with her, and—BAM—her dad winds up murdered."

"Grace, you're not seeing anyone right now, are you?"

"What does that have—"

"Your imagination is running wild." I finished my bar, snatched a paper napkin from a stack on the table, and wiped my lips. "If you were dating, you'd have other things on your mind. You wouldn't resort to concocting far-fetched stories about Dot."

"I am not concocting anything." With her knife, she trimmed the row of bars remaining in the pan. Then, she ate those scraps. Like me, she believed that no calories existed in what you ate from a dessert pan as long as you never cut an actual piece. "But I will admit that I'm bored. I don't think I've ever gone this long between boyfriends."

"What happened to that Jim guy from Lancaster?"

"Jim Halvorson ended up being nothing more than a nut in a tinfoil hat. He's certain he's been picked up by a UFO, not once, but twice."

Her disbelief seemed strange. After all, she bought into all sorts of nonsense: ghosts and bad juju, as well as the possibility of permanent weight loss.

"Sure, he may have been beamed up one time," she said. "But twice? No way. He's not that interesting."

Yeah, Grace was nuts. Even so, I told her, "I'm sorry."

"Forget it. He was cheating on me anyway. A month ago, he sent me a text, proposing that we break up. Then, a day later, he followed up with another stating that the first one 'wasn't meant for me.'"

It could only happen to Grace.

"Now, getting back to Dot and her new boyfriend." She didn't appear all that broken up over her breakup. "You know, I have excellent insight into people."

"Huh? You just got done telling me how you were wrong about Jim Halvorson."

"He was an outlier." She tossed the notion of him aside like she was flicking a piece of lint. "But mark my words, this Dirk Dickerson character is up to no good."

"You haven't even met him."

"It doesn't matter. I've got a feeling."

"Grace, you only think poorly of him because he hasn't been in here to eat."

"I'm not petty like that. I just—"

"Grace, please." I could hardly believe what I was about to say: "For everyone's sake, find a new boyfriend."

Chapter 7

With the lunch hour drawing near, the café got busy. Tweety and Allie trotted back and forth with trays of the special, Spanish Chicken Hot Dish, while I loaded and unloaded the conveyer dishwasher. It belched steam every time I opened the hatch, providing me with what Grace liked to call "a working woman's facial."

When there was a lull in activity, I wiped my forehead with the sleeve of my Minnesota Gophers sweatshirt and sidled alongside my sister. She was stooped over the counter, cutting lemon meringue pie.

"I have to take off," I told her while possibly drooling. But who could blame me? Grace's pies were legendary. "Before I go, though, I need your advice."

Grace froze, her knife poised mid-air. "You never ask for my advice."

"Yes, I do."

"Name one time."

I couldn't. The truth was, I avoided seeking my sister's opinion about most everything because it, like her, was usually outrageous. Instead of admitting that, I went with, "I don't have time to play games."

"See?" She finished cutting the pie. "You can't come up with a single instance."

Hoping to avoid an argument, I moved on to say, "According to Karl, Lars spent the first part of Saturday morning with Etta Wilhelm, and Rose wants me to find out why."

Grace dropped her knife on the metal counter with a clang. "Rose suspects that Etta killed Lars?"

"What? No!" Despite her intelligence, Grace's train of thought frequently jumped the tracks. "She's afraid they were seeing each other behind her back."

"Oh, come on. Rose has to suspect her. Especially since Etta was with him right before his death. They were even in here."

"They were? When?"

"Saturday morning." Grace squished her penciled brows together until they formed a "V" over her nose. "I can't believe I didn't put two and two together."

"Grace, no need for math." I slipped my jacket on. "Etta's old. She didn't murder anyone."

"Are you sure? Lars was a little guy. And regardless of her age, Etta's strong. One time, when I picked up Rose at the senior center, I saw Etta move a refrigerator all by herself."

Impressive but irrelevant.

"You said Dick Dirkerson—or whatever his name is—was the most likely culprit." I paused. "Why was that exactly?"

"Why?" My sister slanted her head, apparently bemused by my question. "The murder took place shortly after he—Dirk Dickerson—arrived in Hallock. He's linked to Lars, the victim, through Dot, the victim's daughter. And he's not from around here." She punctuated those three points by raising a finger after each and ended up presenting me with the Boy Scout Salute.

"But even though I'm leaning toward Dirk Dickerson," she said, "I know enough about sleuthing to realize that we have to consider everyone."

"We?" I shook my head so hard I got dizzy. "There is no 'we.' I am not getting drawn into this. Not after last time."

"Who are you kidding? You won't be able to help yourself. You're too nosy."

"I am not nosy." I stared at her for the count of two. "Now, do you have any suggestions for how I might approach Etta regarding her possible dalliance with Lars?" Owing to my desperation—and despite being irritated with her—I appealed to her vanity. "After all, you're so good at dealing with people."

In reality, Grace's people skills were no better than those of most folks and probably far worse than some, as evidenced by the short duration of her own relationships. Though what she lacked in staying power, she made up for in quantity. I couldn't begin to count the number of boyfriends she'd had over the years. And, as she said, she never went long between them. At least until recently.

I, conversely, had opted for a more private life. As an adult, my favorite party trick was not showing up. But that meant my acumen for social interaction had declined dramatically, forcing me to rely on Grace for insight on occasion.

Prior to offering me any, she delivered a tray of pie to Allie, who rested her forearms on the far side of the pass-through window. They exchanged pleasantries, as I read the sticky notes on the pegboard above the counter.

After that, I checked my phone. Then, when they still showed no sign of ending their gabfest, I did what anyone in my position would have done: I grabbed a fork and dug into the lone piece of pie that remained in the tin on the counter.

I was almost done oohing and aahing over the tangy taste when Grace ambled back to me. "You and that pie need to get a room, Doris. You sound darn near orgasmic."

"I don't recall sex ever being this good."

"You must have had the wrong partner." She slapped her palm against her chest and gasped like an actress in a melodrama. "What am I saying? Of course, you had the wrong partner. You were married to Bill."

Unwilling to let her wreck my pie-induced bliss, I raised my hand, demanded silence, and clamped my eyes shut, savoring the final bite of the buttery crust. Afterwards, I tossed my fork into a tub of dirty dishes. "Now, any advice for me or not?"

Grace massaged her chin, either reflecting on my question or checking for wayward whiskers. At our age, whiskers were an ever-present concern. "Be straightforward with her. Suggest that you're piecing things together for Rose."

"Grace, that won't work. Etta and Rose hate each other."

"Oh, I don't know. Under the circumstances, Etta might empathize with her."

I had my doubts. I couldn't recall Etta Wilhelm, my fifth-grade teacher, empathizing with anyone, not even an eleven-year-old girl caught cheating on a spelling test because she'd been too sick the night before to study.

"Order!" Tweety bellowed from the service window, causing both Grace and me to jump.

"If that doesn't work," Grace said, snatching the slip from Tweety's hand, "try–" She broke off her sentence. "I just remembered something, and if I don't tell you right now, I'll forget again." She hustled back to me. "Dot scheduled Lars's funeral for tomorrow afternoon."

"What? The coroner only finished the autopsy this morning. Can the funeral home even prepare the body by tomorrow?" Of course, Grace had no answer for that question, although she did provide an answer for the next. "How'd you find out?"

"Allie phoned Dot a while ago to offer condolences, and Dot mentioned it. She said Dirk Dickerson had advised her against dragging her feet." Grace dropped a hamburger patty onto the grill, where it sizzled. "Just one more reason I'm suspicious of him. I'm not too sure about Dot either. Sure, Lars needs to get buried. But what's the hurry? It's not as if he's going anywhere."

"Wait. Now you suspect Dot too?"

Grace retrieved a recipe card from a tiny box that resembled a treasure chest. "The two of them could be in cahoots." She laid the card on the counter. "Or maybe Dot's been without a man for so long that she's fallen victim to his charm. From what I gather, he's kind of debonaire. At any rate, she hangs all over him."

After retrieving a homemade bun from a plastic bag, Grace sliced it in two and slathered it with butter before plopping it on the grill, next to the beef patty. "Being he came on to Tweety at the truck stop, we know he's not really into Dot. So, what's he up to? And why is he pushing her to hurry with the funeral?" She wielded her spatula in the air. "I'll tell you why. He somehow discovered that Dot's due to inherit lots of money."

"Grace, Lars wasn't even dead when this Dickerson guy came to town."

"Exactly! He died shortly after his arrival. Shortly after Dickerson got involved with Dot. How suspicious is that?"

I rolled my eyes.

"Go ahead, Doris. Make fun of me. But Dirk Dickerson needs to be checked out." Grace grabbed a plate from a nearby shelf. "And you're just the person to do it."

"Me? Why me? You're the one with the marvelous 'people skills.'" I might have employed a smidgen of sarcasm. It happened when dealing with my sister.

It didn't matter. Grace had already moved on to instructing me. "Pop on over to Dot's under the guise of offering to cook something for the funeral luncheon and find out what you can about him—and their relationship."

"My ineptness in the kitchen is the stuff of folklore. Dot will never buy that I'm there to sign up to cook."

She placed the hamburger on the bun and the bun on a plate, complementing it with potato chips and a pickle spear. "Come up with another excuse then. But do it."

A couple years younger than me, Grace had always bossed me around. And while I'd deferred to her more often than I cared to admit, I wasn't about to visit Dot's house or check out her new beau. Even so, I did have to agree that the whole boyfriend thing seemed kind of strange.

"Karl and the BCA agents will interview everyone important

to the investigation," I informed her by way of refusing her demand. "I don't need to get involved."

"Dot will bamboozle them. She's sneaky."

"Karl won't be fooled."

"He may not be the one who interviews her. It may be those BCA agents I heard he requested. Believe me, they won't stand a chance against her."

My head began to throb. "Fine." My sister had the ability to wear me down on a good day. And with everything that had happened during the past twenty-four hours, this was far from a good day. "I'll tell Karl about the new boyfriend. But that's all." Grace went squinty eyed, prompting me to add, "Last night he more or less warned me to stay out of his business."

"Since when do you listen to him?"

"Grace, if I push too hard about this Dirk Dickerson guy, Karl will insist that I reveal my source. And being he has no respect for Tweety, he'll also demand corroboration of some type."

"So get it! Like I said, look into both Dot and Dickerson before you see Karl."

I rubbed my temples. A Grace-induced headache was on its way. I was familiar with the symptoms. I had experienced them ever since my younger sister had learned to speak. "I don't understand. You just got done calling me nosy. Plus, last time there was trouble in town, you were dead set against me going anywhere near the investigation."

"Well, you are nosy, Doris. That's indisputable. As for last time, I ended up supporting you. Hell, I even provided you with assistance."

To my recollection, Grace had hindered me more than assisted me, and she came close to landing us both in jail.

"And, in the end, you took down a killer."

"I had no clue what I was doing, Grace."

Rather than disputing that statement like a supportive sister would, she agreed with me in a round-about way. "Yeah, as Karl said back then, 'Sometimes it's better to be lucky than good.'"

"Huh? He said that?"

"Doris… " She picked up the recipe card from the counter and waved it in my face. "If you don't do everything you can for Rose, you'll never forgive—"

"Why me?"

She dropped the card again. "Well, first of all, you've already caught one killer. Second, Erin's not here to help and neither are most of the other deputies, so someone has to pick up the slack."

"I called Erin. Got her voice mail. Left a message. So—"

Grace spoke over me. "Third, you and Karl have… ah… thing."

"We do not have a thing!"

"Fourth… " Again, it was like I wasn't even participating in the conversation. "We can't count on Ed to assist Karl because he's barely potty trained. And, fifth, the BCA agents won't prioritize Rose, but you can push Karl to do so."

"And pray tell, dear sister, what will you do while I'm 'helping Rose'?"

"I'll be here in the café, of course. Although I will give you a hand—and advice—whenever I can."

"Oh, goodie."

◎ ◎ ◎

After leaving the café, I scootched behind the wheel of my white SUV. It had been idling along the curb for nearly two hours. But that wasn't unusual. During the winter, lots of people around Hallock left their vehicles running. No one wanted to get into a freezing car or deal with an engine that refused to turn over. Sure, some folks had remote starters. But not me, which was fine. My car was good enough the way it was.

Shifting into reverse, I noticed a gym bag on the passenger seat. After considering that I hadn't set foot in the local fitness center since its grand opening two years ago, I knew I'd gotten into the wrong vehicle.

Last winter I'd done the same thing and was almost home when the dog I hadn't noticed in the back seat licked my ear, making me so hot and bothered that I plowed into a snow bank. But it wasn't my fault. Not then. Not now. There were just too darn many white SUVs in the Red River Valley, and they all looked the same.

Anyhow, after concluding that my current gaffe had gone unnoticed—at least no one in the café stared out the window, laughing uncontrollably—I slinked two cars down to my vehicle. I confirmed ownership by the telltale M&M wrappers and take-out coffee cups littering the floor.

As I set my purse on the seat next to me, my cell phone rang.

When I answered it, my son, Will, stated without preamble, "I'm worried about Rose."

My stomach muscles tightened the way they did when I attempted a sit-up, if memory served. "What's going on?"

He had agreed to stay with Rose at the house until I got back. He could do that in the off-season. One of the perks of raising crops over animals. "She refuses to take me on in cribbage."

I let go a breath I hadn't realized I'd been holding. "Is that all?"

"Mom, she's good at cribbage."

"Yeah, I've played her. I think she cheats."

"She loves competing against me. We bet on the outcome, and she cleans me out almost every time."

"Again, she cheats."

"She's… umm… in a bad way." Almost forty, Will still struggled with expressing his emotions. He would pretend that everything was fine. And when he couldn't pretend any longer, he'd pick a fight. Not with a family member, but any other unsuspecting soul was fair game.

Several months back, his wife had insisted that he undergo anger-management counseling. She deemed it necessary because of his pending fatherhood. More recently, he'd also quit drinking. But when I inquired as to what had led to that decision, he changed the subject.

"She wouldn't eat her lunch either," he said. "Sophie sent a Chocolate Peanut Butter Pie with me for dessert, and she refused that too. And you know how good Sophie's pie is."

Yes, I was well aware that Sophie's chocolate peanut butter pie had won first prize in the easy desserts category at the Kittson County Fair this past July. Will never missed an opportunity to retell the story or highlight Sophie's other culinary achievements.

He also repeatedly encouraged me to ask her for tips in spite of knowing that I didn't care enough about baking or cooking to seek advice from anyone, not even my own sister, a trained chef. Yep, after marrying Sophie two years ago, my son had gone all Gordon Ramsay.

"What's she doing now?" I wanted to return to the subject of Rose. Not that I disliked Sophie. It's just that… Well…

"She's back in bed. She's depressed something awful, Mom."

"It might be best to let her rest. She's grieving. She'll probably feel better after the funeral." Which reminded me… "Did anyone call about the service? I guess it's tomorrow afternoon."

"Nope. No one called. And no one's come by. Not even the sheriff, which means no progress has been made in the investigation."

"It's only been a day."

"Well, it's not like law enforcement has lots of suspects to wade through. This is Hallock after all." He paused. "They hafta get moving, Mom. Rose can't handle the stress."

My stoic son had referenced both depression and stress in the span of a minute, causing my own nerves to rattle. "I'm at the café. I had planned to run an errand for Rose, but I can put it off and come home right now if you think I should."

"Ah… no. Go ahead. I only wanted to clue you in on… " Even though his voice trailed off, I sensed he had more to say.

"What is it, Will?"

"Well… umm… while you're out, come up with some way to help Rose." His words hugged my heart. He was a good man and would make a great father.

"I'll call Dr. Betcher and ask him to visit her at the house. He'll probably stop by on his way home from work tonight."

"I don't mean that kind of help." He wavered. "Well, sure,

Betcher should check on her. Mostly, though, I want you to light a fire under Karl."

"He's already called the Bureau of Criminal Apprehension."

"We can't wait for those guys to get here from St. Paul."

"I'm sure they're already on their way, Will. I also left a message for Erin. Given how close she is to Rose, she'll probably come right back from her conference and give Karl a hand."

"She just called me, Mom." That didn't shock me. With her dad dead and more than a dozen years in age between her brother and her, Erin often turned to Will for guidance. "She's positive that even if Karl is fine with her heading home, the members of the county board won't be. In other words, she has to stay put. Although you have an in with Karl, so—"

"Why does everyone say that?" My voice climbed to a screech. "I do not have an 'in' with Karl."

"Well, you could if you wanted."

Pain now pounded both my temples in a steady rhythm. Grace wasn't the only family member who could cause my head to throb. "You really irritate me sometimes. You know that?"

"Oh, come on. You love me."

"Don't be too sure. Remember, you're the reason I pee when I cough."

He snorted a chuckle before reverting to his serious tone. "Mom, Rose is bad off. You hafta do something."

I disconnected and phoned Dr. Betcher. And when done with that, I dropped my phone into my purse, leaned my head against the headrest, and shut my eyes.

While I shared many of the concerns expressed by Grace and Will, I didn't appreciate them badgering me. I wasn't a trained investigator. True, a therapist had explained to me not long ago that I possessed "latent curiosity, the result of doing only what had been expected of me most of my life." Still, an excess of curiosity during middle age didn't automatically make me good at "detecting." Case in point: On more than one occasion, I had failed to identify my own car.

64

Still, the notion of Rose in emotional distress proved too much for me. Notwithstanding my bravado when warning her that I'd speak to Etta Wilhelm about her possible fling with Lars but nothing else, I knew darn well that I'd do everything in my power to restore her peace of mind.

# Chapter 8

I unfolded myself from behind the wheel and shuffled along the cracked pavement surrounding the gas pumps, watching for ice. That's why I didn't notice Dot until she exited her SUV at the pump across from me.

"I'm sorry about your dad," I shouted through the howling wind.

She slammed her car door and plucked her credit card from her wallet. "Yeah, it's extremely unpleasant for me."

I mentally patted myself on the back for not pointing out that it wasn't great for her father either. Instead, I said, "If there's anything I can do, don't hesitate to ask." I couldn't bring myself to offer to cook, and she didn't mention it. More proof that my culinary shortcomings were well known.

"I've scheduled the funeral for tomorrow afternoon at two." She shoved the pump nozzle into her fuel tank. "At Grace Lutheran. Lunch to follow in the basement."

"Why so soon?" I posed the question as if Grace and I hadn't already discussed the peculiar timing. Not that I bought into my sister's theory that Dot's new boyfriend—and perhaps Dot herself—had played a role in Lars's death.

"No good can come of waiting," she answered in a practiced voice, like she was repeating what she had heard from someone else. "Give Rose the particulars if you want, though some folks might object to her being there."

"Why?" The pump thrummed, as the smell of gasoline hung in the heavy winter air. "She didn't reel him in on purpose."

"Doris, she was wrong to convince him to spend Saturday evening with her when he was supposed to be with me."

"What? Rose wasn't with your dad Saturday night. She was at the senior center almost all day, working the monthly birthday celebration."

"A likely story." She tugged her knit cap over her ears.

I wished I had worn a cap. Even though my hair fell past my chin, it failed to insulate my ears, leaving the tips of them, as well as the lobes, burning from the cold. "Ask anyone who was there. I dropped her off at ten-thirty that morning and picked her up at eight-thirty that night. As for Lars, she last saw him on Friday, when they ate an early supper together at the bowling alley."

Dot crossed her arms over her quilted jacket and cupped her elbows. "Well, I went to a lot of trouble to prepare that supper on Saturday, and he was supposed to be at my house at six. I planned to introduce him to Dirk. But he stood me up. Dad, I mean. Not… ah… Dirk."

"Who's Dirk?" While I knew the answer, I wanted to engage Dot in a detailed discussion about the guy. Again, not because I considered him a murder suspect. I just had a tough time envisioning any man dating Dot.

"I'm not telling you a thing about Dirk Dickerson. He's none of your business." So much for satisfying my curiosity. "The fact is, Dad blew me off. And I blame Rose."

"Dot, for all you know, your dad was already dead by six o'clock Saturday." That was tactless. Even for me. "I mean, has anyone from law enforcement briefed you as to when he died exactly?"

"The sheriff just called. He said an exact time of death couldn't be determined because the icy water played havoc with Dad's body temperature." Her voice fluctuated, either from emotion or the weather, I couldn't determine which. "The best the coroner could do was estimate that he died sometime between late afternoon and mid-evening."

"So, as I said, Rose couldn't have done it. She's not to blame."

Instead of acknowledging her mistake, Dot stewed while leaning against her car. It appeared freshly washed. Mine, in contrast, was caked with so much highway salt that I had to remain out in the open, nothing to shield me from the wind whipping me from all sides.

Dot must have spotted the clean-car envy in my eyes. "Dirk washed it for me yesterday morning. He even cleaned the inside." She spoke so sweetly that my teeth ached. "He's such a nice man. Always thinking of me."

I threw up a little in my mouth before returning to the subject at hand. "Did you..." I cleared my throat. "Did you see your dad at all on Saturday?"

"Why do you care?"

"Well... umm... I'm attempting to figure things out for Rose. And... umm... for you too." Yes, that last remark was a bit of a stretch. But after recalling that Grace had suggested I tap into Etta Wilhelm's empathy to get her to open up, I decided to try the same thing on Dot. Not that I was callous or anything.

"Well..." Dot began, her eyes softening behind her glasses, leading me to surmise that Grace may have been right about the whole empathy thing. Although she'd never hear it from me.

"I had to run to the store to pick up a few ingredients for the dish I intended to prepare," Dot said. "I was gone for less than an hour. But that's when Dad called."

Dot attempted to laugh, but the sound died in her throat. And my heart actually ached for her as I recalled what Ole had said: "Even a shrew can love her parents." True, he'd been referring to Gustaf's wife, Louise, a completely different shrew. But tomato, tomahto.

"I had left my phone in the sitting room of the guest suite,"

Dot said, "and when Dirk saw Dad's name pop up on the screen, he answered it. But Dad only wanted to know what kind of wine to buy for our meal."

"Wine?" That threw me. Still, I managed to ask, "What time was that?"

"Around four-thirty. At six, when Dad didn't show, I called him, but he didn't pick up."

"What about your friend, Dickerson?" My breath battled the snowflakes that had begun to fall. "Was he with you then? Or at least in his guest suite?"

Dot arched her back, like an angry cat, and hissed, "Of course, he was."

"How about the rest of the evening?"

"Yes, we were together. Why do you ask?"

A SUV honked as it passed by. And while I didn't recognize the driver—and was in the middle of a tense back and forth—I acknowledged the beep with a flip of my index finger. To do otherwise would have been rude.

I turned back to Dot. "Are you sure you or Dickerson didn't go searching anywhere after your dad failed to show? After all, like you said, you worked hard on that supper."

She contemplated the pavement. "Oh, yeah. I phoned Etta."

"Etta? Etta Wilhelm? Why'd you call her?"

Dot heaved air from her lungs, sending snowflakes tumbling every which way. "Someone saw her with Dad in the café that morning." She spoke as if the words tasted like sour milk. "I thought he might have mentioned a change of plans to her, but she didn't know a thing. Said she never saw him again after dropping him off at his apartment before she went to the senior center for the day."

Dot pursed her lips. "I should have ended our conversation right there, but I couldn't keep from asking why they had been together." She shook her head in obvious disgust. "At first, she acted like she didn't want to tell me, but she eventually said he wanted her to reconcile with him."

"What?" My stomach dropped, and due to my weak core muscles, I had to press my knees together to keep it from falling on the ground. "Are you serious?"

"Doris, I wouldn't joke about such a thing. I don't like Etta. Never have. When she dated Dad, she was almost as bad as Rose at pressuring him into spending money."

I bit my tongue. Now was not the time to argue. I had to stay focused. "Speaking of Rose," I said, holding back the nasty retort on the tip of my tongue, "why didn't you call her? Especially since you assumed she was with him?"

Dot tapped her foot, her patience with me waning. "Frankly, after talking to Etta, I couldn't bring myself to deal with any more of Dad's... lady friends. I decided that if he preferred to be with Rose, fine." She didn't sound fine. "I didn't care one way or the other." Oh, but she did care—a lot.

Yanking the nozzle from her tank, Dot hooked it back on the pump, the pungent smell of gasoline lingering in the air. "When I saw Rose at the lake yesterday, I planned to say something. But before I got the chance, she made me angry enough to chew iron and spit nails. That's why I left in such a hurry. I didn't want to speak inappropriately in front of the girls."

She coughed into her gloves. "Anyways, even if Dad wasn't with Rose on Saturday evening, she's still at fault for all of this." She twirled her arms, indicating that Rose was apparently responsible for everything from her father's death to the falling snow. "If she hadn't been so rude to me, I may have had the wherewithal to find him before—"

"Dot!" With an eye-rattling shake of my head, I did my best to dismiss her crazy talk. "By the time we saw you at the lake, your father was already floating under the ice." Again, not tactful. But I didn't care. As Rose would say, Dot could piss off the pope. And I wasn't nearly as tolerant as the pope. As a result, my heart quit aching for her, although she did prompt significant pain in another part of my anatomy.

# Chapter 9

Due to Hallock's size, I knew almost everybody in town, but I seldom saw Etta Wilhelm, my fifth-grade teacher. At seventy-five years of age, she frequented the senior center, while I only stopped by there to drop off or pick up Rose.

After parking in front of Etta's nondescript 1980's rambler on the west side of the railroad tracks, I previewed our exchange in my mind. Did I really want to know if she and Lars had whispered sweet nothings to each other before he died? No. What purpose could it serve? Nonetheless, Rose had insisted, so I'd make an effort to find out.

Sliding out of the car, I hunched my shoulders against the wind and rushed to the front door. The snow had turned to sleet, and it pricked my nose and cheeks like a thousand needles. Acupuncture by Mother Nature.

Once under Etta's stamp-sized portico, I flicked shards of ice from my hair and jacket before pressing the doorbell. I swore I heard a chimes' version of the refrain from Rod Stewart's "Do Ya Think I'm Sexy?" Presuming I was wrong, I pushed the bell again and listened more closely. Sure enough, the chimes repeated the tune ordinarily accompanied by the lyrics, *If you want my body and you think I'm sexy…*

Through the glass sidelight next to the door, I spotted Etta Wilhelm two-stepping toward me across the baby-blue carpet in her living room. She wore gold lame kitten heels and an emerald-green belted dress with cap sleeves, a scooped neck, and a full skirt that fell just below her knees.

When she saw me, she offered a finger wave, most of her digits sparkling with rings. Not to be outdone, her ears featured large gold baubles that weighed on her lobes, while a multitude of chains competed with the skin drooping from her chin. Given her substantial frame, not to mention her abundant ornamentation, she brought to mind the Christmas tree still standing in my living room.

When she opened the door, the smell of rose-scented air freshener, cheap perfume, and firm-holding hairspray assaulted my nostrils. "I'm not interrupting, am I?" My sinuses seized.

"No, it's fine. Come in." Her eyes bulged behind cat-eye glasses, which she removed and left dangling from a gold chain. "I'm going out for dinner in a while, but I got ready early. I didn't want to keep him waiting." With one blue-veined hand, she patted her henna-red curls, and with the other, she palmed her abundant cleavage. "What can I do for you?"

Shifting my attention away from her fleshy breasts, my gaze settled on a wall stencil that urged everyone to "Live, Love, and Laugh." I cleared my throat. "Well, I'm sure you've heard about Lars."

She uh-huhed. "A tragedy. A real tragedy." Her tenor belied her words. She didn't sound any more broken up than if I had announced the death of the guy who plowed the snow from her driveway.

Then, again, when my husband had died, Rose sent out for lottery tickets, claiming it was her "lucky day." Naturally, I balked at her insensitivity, only to have her remind me, "Everyone grieves in their own way."

"Would you like to sit down?" Etta gestured toward the living room.

"I better not." Melted sleet puddled at my boots. "I can't stay. I… umm… only wanted to ask you a few questions. For instance, what were you doing at the café with Lars on Saturday morning?"

Etta's perfect-hostess smile slipped right off her face, tumbling, I suspected, into the abyss between her breasts. "Why do you want to know?"

"Well… " I couldn't bring myself to come right out and accuse her of aiding Lars in two-timing Rose, so I hedged. "I'm attempting to learn how Lars spent his final days."

"Again, why?"

I wasn't handling myself particularly well. In other words, I was doing pretty much as I had expected, and Rose deserved better.

"Miss Erick—I mean Etta—let me start over." I wrung my hands. She had always put me on edge. "As you're probably aware, Rose O'Brian is living with me for the time being, and she's terribly distraught over Lars's death. That's… ah… why she didn't come here herself." Not exactly the truth but not altogether a lie. "Anyhow, when she heard you were with him on Saturday morning, she wondered if you might be able to shed some light on what happened that day."

Etta puckered her lips, her cranberry-colored lipstick oozing into the fine creases bordering them.

"Please," I pleaded. "Rose is heartbroken. She cared deeply for Lars. Of course, I realize what I'm asking may cause you discomfort, since he broke up with you to go out with Rose, but—"

"Well, I'll be… " Etta appeared gobsmacked. "Who told you that Lars dumped me?"

I couldn't confess that it had been Rose, so I faked amnesia, praying Etta wouldn't catch me in the lie. She'd been good at that fifty years ago. "I… umm… can't recall."

She opened her mouth, but a buzzer went off at the back of the house, cutting off what she was about to say. "That's the oven timer," she informed me instead. "Slip off your boots and come with me into the kitchen. We'll have a snack—Cinnamon Bread—and I'll set you straight about Lars Carlson."

◎ ◎ ◎

Passing through the archway that led into Etta's kitchen, the aroma of cinnamon tickled my nose, thankfully replacing her over-the-top personal scent. An incident a few months back had dimmed my opinion of cinnamon. But my aversion to the spice had apparently passed. It couldn't have happened at a better time.

Etta's kitchen was similar to her living room in that it was painted tan and trimmed in medium-stained oak. Oak cabinets lined two walls, and tan print vinyl covered the floor. I sensed that the house hadn't been updated since it was built in the 1980s, with one exception: Etta's kitchen appliances were stainless steel, commercial grade, and first rate.

Like Sophie and Grace, Etta Wilhelm's baking skills were highly regarded throughout the county, and my salivary glands went into overdrive when she pulled the cinnamon bread from the oven. True, I'd already eaten plenty of sweets, but I couldn't deny her the pleasure of feeding me, could I? Besides, bread didn't really count as a sweet.

"Have a chair." With a bob of her head, she motioned toward the round oak table at the far end of the room. A deck of playing cards lay across it in a half-finished game of solitaire. "Some coffee while the bread cools? Cream or sugar?"

Using my thumb and forefinger, I wiped anticipatory spittle from the corners of my mouth. "Black is fine." I draped my jacket over the back of a chair and inspected the county fair baking ribbons pinned to the corkboard on the wall next to the sliding-glass patio doors. Outside there was nothing to see but a dimming sky and deck furniture swallowed up by snow.

"Now," Etta said, handing me a dainty blue-patterned cup with matching saucer, "about Lars." Holding her own cup in one hand, she swept the cards aside with the other and sat down. "If I'm not mistaken, Rose began seeing him in mid-December. But I had ended things with him several weeks earlier."

"Oh? Why did you break up?" Uneasy about questioning my former teacher, even at this stage of our lives, I added, "If you don't mind telling me."

Clasping her glasses, she chewed on one of the bows, something she'd also done back in the day. "He ate Thanksgiving dinner at Dot's house and was to have dessert here with me. I had baked pumpkin pie, although I always use squash. Pumpkin's just too darn stringy. But I can't very well call it squash pie, now, can I?"

Feeling obliged to say something, I opened my mouth but only stammered.

Apparently realizing that I had nothing coherent to contribute, she went on to say, "Well, Lars didn't show up. He never phoned either. And when he stopped by the next day, he shrugged it off, as if standing me up were no big deal."

Hurt dampened her eyes, but she blinked it away. "After dinner at Dot's, he supposedly ran into a few guys who convinced him to join them for poker." Again, she chomped on the bow. "Had I known about his gambling habit, I never would have gone out with him in the first place."

While surprised and more than a little uncomfortable with Etta's candor, I was downright flabbergasted by the revelation that Lars was a gambler. "I wasn't aware," I stated. "Sure, he went to the casino in Thief River on Saturday. But I presumed that was more of a social outing. An opportunity to spend time with friends."

"Well, I can't speak to Saturday. But I know he got into gambling a couple years ago, after his wife died and he sold everything and moved into that apartment." She held her hand to the side of her mouth and lowered her voice. "Not to speak poorly of the dead, but he totally lost control."

"On Thanksgiving?"

"Oh, my goodness, Thanksgiving was just the last straw."

She aimed her attention at the dated brass light fixture above the table, as if it illuminated the past in its glow. "You see, we began spending time together on Labor Day, at the senior center's end-of-summer fling, doncha know."

Her gold earrings sparkled in the light. "I didn't have a whist partner until Lars wandered in. Everyone was surprised to see him because he seldom went anywhere. At least around here."

As she spoke, I breathed in the yeasty smell of the cinnamon bread. I suspected that it was cool enough to eat. Yet Etta made no attempt to get up or offer me a slice.

"Anyways," she said, as disappointment pooled in my stomach, where cinnamon bread drenched in melted butter should have been, "we teamed up. And wouldn't you know? We beat Stan and Mildred Olstrom in the championship round. We got a trophy and everything."

Wistfulness passed over Etta's features. Despite how things had ended between Lars and her, she had been enamored by him initially. "After the tournament, he insisted that we celebrate, so we went to dinner at Hastings Landing in Drayton the following evening."

"And?"

Nostalgia over those early days gave way to the acrimony that had likely fueled the end of their courtship. "Following about a month of dating, he began cancelling on me. And his excuses were ridiculous. He had an acute case of acid reflux. His gout had flared up. Or his IBS was giving him trouble." She shook her head. "If it wasn't one thing, it was another."

She twisted her glasses to the left, then the right, as if weighing the pros and cons of sharing anything more. "Before long," she said after making her decision, "he also began asking for money. At first, only enough to tide him over until he received a dividend check or whatnot. But later, far more. And he never paid me back." She paused, her coffee cup halfway to her mouth. "Did he do that to Rose?"

"Ah… no. I don't believe so." I then recounted how Rose had mentioned paying Lars's way on occasion. Distress clogged my throat. "What… umm… did you do about it?"

Etta flapped her arms, loose skin fluttering like kimono

sleeves. "I confronted him, of course. I accused him of gambling away my money, and he had the audacity to say I was out of line."

Her voice vibrated with anger. "I demanded that he repay every dollar I had lent him, and he became livid—so livid that I ordered him out of my house for my own safety." She lowered her voice. "I also told him that we were through."

I assumed she had finished her story. Yet, with her next burst of emotion, she said, "He apologized right away. He also promised not to let anything—least of all, gambling—come between us ever again."

Her eyes revealed embarrassment but also sought understanding. "He seemed so sincere that I relented, which was a terrible mistake. Less than a week later he gave me the brush off again. On Thanksgiving no less."

"Why did you go to the café with him this past Saturday morning then?"

Etta opened and closed her mouth like a guppy. "That... umm... had nothing to do with his death."

"Even so, tell me. For Rose's sake."

She plucked a paper napkin from the holder in the middle of the table. "Uff-da, Doris, that's not the best way to coax me. Rose and I aren't exactly on borrowing terms. I find her to be a bully."

I silently agreed. After all, she had bullied me into coming here. "Just the same, Etta, what did you and Lars discuss?" I felt odd pressuring my teacher for answers. Years ago, it had been the other way around.

"If our visit had pertained to Lars's death, the sheriff would have visited me by now, don't you think?"

"You're probably right. But—"

"Doris!" She slapped the table. "Stop badgering me!" She dropped her eyes, her cheeks turning far redder than what her rouge had achieved. "I'm sorry." She shredded her napkin into tiny pieces. "It's just that... "

No need to be a great detective—and believe me, I wasn't— to realize that Etta Wilhelm was holding something back. And because I sensed that it pertained to her relationship with Lars, I steeled my spine and asked, "Were you and Lars seeing each other behind Rose's back? Is that why you were together in the cafe?"

She flinched. "Now see here, Doris, you have no right to speak to me in that manner. It's unacceptable."

I slouched in my chair, once more the insolent fifth grader. As soon as I pictured Rose curled up in the corner of my sofa, however, I sat ramrod straight again. Then, with equal measures of purpose and impatience, I asked, "What did you and Lars talk about?"

Etta eyes skidded from her coffee cup to the pile of napkin bits and, from there, to the playing cards scattered to the side. "I can't say. I just can't."

I sucked in a lungful of air, hoping that the extra oxygen would aid me in pushing her harder. But before I got the chance to say anything more, the doorbell rang. *If you want my body, and you think I'm sexy, come on, sugar, let me know.*

Etta gasped at the plastic owl clock on the wall. "Oh, goodness gracious, look at the time. I have to go." She scrabbled to her feet, unable to conceal her relief. "My gentleman friend has dinner reservations for us out of town. You and I will just have to finish this conversation another time."

"Wait!"

"No, really, you have to go. But we'll get together again real soon." She didn't sound at all sincere.

Consequently, I vacillated. I needed an answer about her and Lars. And, to be perfectly honest, I also wanted a slice of that cinnamon bread. Even so, when she exited the kitchen, I had no choice but to leave too. After a parting glance in the direction of the bread, I followed her back through the living room and into the entry.

There, I bent down and stuffed my feet into my boots, doing my best to avoid the puddles of melted snow around me.

At the same time, Etta opened the door, her greeting chock-full of the kind of excitement usually reserved for schoolgirls on first dates or me whenever I discovered an Amazon package on my porch.

The wheezy voice of the man on the stoop sounded familiar, but I couldn't place it. I raised my head and stretched my neck to catch a peek of the guy on the stoop. And that's when I fell over, my butt finding one of the aforementioned puddles.

The man, you see, was none other than Gustaf Gustafson. And, like Etta, he was all gussied up. But, unlike Etta, he was married—married to Louise—who was in Alexandria, tending to her sick mother.

# Chapter 10

"Well, spank me cross-eyed," I mumbled as I plodded back to my car. "Gustaf and Etta. Who would have thunk?" Easing behind the wheel, I stared into the dark sky, now free of snow and sleet. "Just goes to show, there's a lid for every pot."

While avoiding sitting on my damp butt cheek, I checked my phone: a voice mail from a guy in India, worried about my car warranty, and a text from Will, stating he had to go home. Nothing urgent, he said. Sophie was under the weather, that's all. Eight months pregnant, Will's wife still experienced morning sickness at any time of the day.

He assured me that Dr. Betcher would remain at the house with Rose until I got there. He also asked that I pick up a prescription the doctor had called in to the pharmacy.

According to the dashboard clock, the workday was almost over. But, if I hurried, the trip across town to the medical center and pharmacy would take fewer than five minutes. Such was life—and traffic—in Hallock.

While the wind had settled down, and the precipitation had given up the fight, the roads remained slippery. I clutched the steering wheel with a white-knuckle grip as I cleared the railroad tracks, the glow from my headlights bouncing up and down.

At the stop sign, the driver opposite me motioned me through the intersection, but I didn't go, choosing instead to motion him right back. In this version of a game I called "Minnesota chicken," politeness won out. But because I didn't have a moment to spare, I conceded to my opponent and headed south on Highway 75.

Once I had Rose's prescription in hand, I exited the medical center and slip-slided back toward my car, coming to a halt when I spotted the senior van idling along the curb, under a streetlamp. Both Arne and Anders Olafson appeared to be inside, probably waiting to give someone in the medical center a ride home.

On a whim, I shoved Rose's prescription bag into my coat pocket and strolled toward the van, hoping the twins might share something about their time with Lars on Saturday that I didn't already know. After all, Dot had provided me with little and Etta, even less. That's not to say I had given up on either of them. But, for now, I'd see what I could get out of the Olafson brothers.

Because the twins unnerved me, I gave myself a stern talking to while shuffling down the walk. Then, feigning far more confidence than I felt, I said hello by way of twiddling my fingers.

The van's passenger window lowered with a hum, bringing me face to face with Arne Olafson. I knew it was him because his right jaw, illuminated by the streetlamp, was scar free.

"Hi!" I crossed my arms, propped them on the window ledge, and welcomed the warm air from the dashboard heater. "I'm Doris Connor." Arne provided me with a curt nod but remained silent, prompting me to fill the void. "I'm… I mean… my sort-of relative, Rose O'Brien, lives with me. And she was close to Lars Carlson." Because Arne still refrained from speaking, I went on running at the mouth. "I'm reconstructing the events of Saturday in an effort to provide her with some closure. And when I saw your van, I decided to ask about your trip with Lars to the casino."

Arne and his brother were stereotypical older Scandinavian

men. Both sported thin, slicked-back white hair and black horn-rimmed bifocals that framed milky-blue eyes. They had ruddy round faces absent most of the wrinkles associated with old age, although they did possess deep marionette creases along the sides of their mouths. Given that Arne still said nothing, I concluded that his marionette strings were either tangled or broken.

I eased my attention over to his brother, Anders, who was seated behind the wheel. As Karl had demonstrated, a jagged scar ran the length of the man's jaw, giving him a menacing presence.

I trembled before opening my mouth. And rather than addressing him, I spoke to the silhouetted figure standing outside, his arms folded against Ander's open window. "I'm sorry. I didn't see you at first."

The mystery man stooped until the window framed his head alongside Anders's. "No problem."

Despite crouching, I couldn't get a decent look at the guy. But, as a life-long resident of Hallock, I expected to recognize something about him. I didn't. Even so, I extended my arm past both Arne and Anders.

The man clasped my hand in a firm grip. "I'm Dirk Dickerson. Nice to meet you."

Although I schooled my features, I was downright giddy. I had wanted to meet Dirk Dickerson. Like I may have mentioned, I had difficulty imagining anyone volunteering to date Dot. "Oh, so you're Dot's… ah… friend."

"I'm staying at her place, yes." He rescued his hand from mine.

"We're probably after the same thing then."

He tipped his head. "How so?"

"Well, I want answers for Rose about Lars's death, and you undoubtedly want the same for Dot."

"Arne and Anders don't have much to tell." He patted Anders's coat sleeve. "They picked Lars up at eleven, drove him to the casino, and dropped him at his place again just after five." He slapped the window ledge, as if to put a period on his sentence and an end to our conversation.

I wasn't ready to be done. "Wait a second." I regarded both brothers. "Did either of you gamble with Lars?"

"No," Arne replied, at last speaking and, in doing so, startling me into bumping my head on the window frame above me. "He was into blackjack. We play poker."

With a soft touch, I checked my head for blood. "Did you recognize any of the people he was with?" No blood but I'd certainly end up with an egg. The price for being tall.

"We didn't see him with nobody. But even if we did, we probably wouldn't have recognized 'em. We've only lived here a few months."

"Yah, just a few months," Anders echoed.

"How about when he came back to the van? Did he mention anyone then?"

"Nope," Arne said, his brother again mimicking him.

"Ah… umm," I sputtered, a bit unnerved by the myna-bird routine. "Did he ask you to stop anywhere on your way back to Hallock? Perhaps a liquor store?"

"Nope," Arne repeated, his brother once more following suit.

I released a pent-up breath. I was cold, tired, and hungry. And Anders's shtick was irritating me. All the more so because I hadn't learned a thing. "What did you guys talk about during your trip?"

Anders looked in Arne's direction, his eyes clouded with concern as well as cataracts.

"We didn't talk about nothing." Arne glanced between his brother and me, as if trying to placate us both.

"I find that hard to believe." I stared at Arne, his bifocals appearing to slice his eyes in half, causing me to shudder. "Thief River is more than an hour away. That's a long time to go without talking."

Anders's right eye twitched, which, apparently, led Arne to say, "Oh, well… umm… I remember now. Lars got a phone call."

I bent my head, looking directly at Dirk Dickerson through the open window. "Was that your call with him?"

He stumbled backwards. "Me? Why on earth would you think that?"

"Well, I saw Dot earlier today. And she mentioned that you spoke with her dad around four-thirty on Saturday. Something about the kind of wine he should bring to supper."

"Oh… umm… yeah." He reclaimed both his composure and his place next to Anders's window. "That's right." The wheels in his head began to spin. I couldn't see them, but I heard them in his voice. "I forgot about that."

"Really? You forgot that—"

Arne interrupted. "Ma'am, we hafta go."

"Only a few more questions." While my priority was to find out something of importance for Rose, I also longed to unearth information to prove to Karl that my previous success as a sleuth hadn't been just a case of luck. It had. But I didn't like him believing that.

"No, we hafta go now. We have—"

"What happened after you dropped Lars off?" I hurried to ask.

And Arne grumbled, "How the hell would we know? We took off right away."

"Where did you go?"

Arne cut his eyes toward his brother. "We… ah… went to supper in Karlstad. Right, Anders?"

"Umm… right. Karlstad." Anders's eye twitched like he was sending a warning via Morse code.

And upon receiving that message, Arne insisted, "We need to leave now." He tugged on his brother's coat sleeve. "Remember, we have that rider waiting."

Judging by the expression on Anders's face, I expected him to say, *What rider?* But he must have discerned what his brother was up to because, after just a moment's hesitation, he said, "Oh… umm… yah, that rider." And, after that, he shifted the van into gear and took off, forcing me to jump back or get my feet run over.

◎ ◎ ◎

"What did you make of that?" I asked Dirk Dickerson once the van had gone, and we were alone under the blue glow of the streetlamp.

He raised his head. Seeing him in full light, I found him handsome in a preppy sort of way. His hair was black, thick, and styled off his forehead, a trace of gray at the temples. Slender, clean shaven, and well dressed, he donned khaki pants, and he paired his dark wool dress coat with a plaid scarf. He also sported tasseled loafers, something seldom seen around here. I guessed him to be around sixty. And, of course, he had mental-health issues. Why else would he be interested in Dot?

"Are you sure you didn't get any more out of them before I arrived?" My breath billowed white in the crisp air, and I shivered without the van's heater to keep me warm.

"No, they didn't tell me anything." He stuffed his bare hands into his coat pockets. "I hadn't met them before. I introduced myself and posed a few questions. They told me the same thing they told you." He sounded rational enough. Still…

"You didn't get the impression that they were stonewalling us?" I pulled my gloves on and rocked from side to side to keep from freezing.

"No." He chuckled. "They're kind of odd. That's all."

Not having expected to come across Dirk Dickerson, I hadn't prepared any questions for him. "Well… ah… how do you like Hallock?" Like the answer to that would blow the investigation wide open.

"Oh, it's nice enough."

Due to his abbreviated answers, he struck me as somewhat aloof. Hard to fathom, given he hung around with the likes of Dot and Tweety. Then, again, maybe Dot had warned him about me, although I couldn't imagine why.

In an effort to get a better read on the guy, I increased my charm index, which merely entailed pasting a fake smile on my face. "Tell me, Mr. Dickerson, what brought you to Hallock in the first place, if you don't mind my asking?"

He scoffed. "Call me Dirk. And, from what I understand, you'd ask whether I minded or not."

"I beg your pardon?" No need to wonder any longer. Dot had obviously provided him with a less than flattering appraisal of yours truly.

"I'm sorry." He withdrew one of his perfectly manicured hands from his coat pocket and raised it, palm out. "Bad joke."

"That's okay." It really wasn't. "I didn't take offense." Yes, I did. "I only asked because we don't often get your type around here." I pointed at his professional attire. "We're more of a Carhartt and North Face community."

"Well, I plan to start a business in Hallock."

"Oh? What kind of business? And why here?"

This time he had enough sense to withhold his snide remarks. "Well, as you're undoubtedly aware, Mrs. Connor, the Red River Valley has some of the finest top soil in the world." He hiked his shoulders, his plaid neck scarf brushing his earlobes. "Folks up here also have a reputation for hard work. That's why I plan to merge those two assets and start a company that packages and sells top soil nationwide for landscaping purposes."

I chased the idea around in my head. Not bad. But I wouldn't admit that to him. He was a scoundrel. A first-class scoundrel. Who had terrible taste in women.

Which led me to ask, "So, how exactly did you meet Dot?" Yes, his business concept interested me, but I wasn't about to give him the satisfaction of asking any more about it.

"Well…" Initially caught off guard by my abrupt conversational u-turn, he quickly recovered. "Since there was no room at the inn, so to speak, I got referred to her bed and breakfast."

At that point, we suspended our back-and-forth while a white SUV passed by, the person behind the steering wheel slowing down to get a good look at us. Again, I didn't recognize the driver, nor could I distinguish the car from any other white SUV in the area. But I knew for certain that, come morning, tongues would be wagging in the café.

While I couldn't do anything about the gossip, I could dig deeper into Dirk Dickerson's relationship with Dot, so that's what I did. It would prove far more interesting anyhow. "This thing with Dot is recent then? You haven't been with her long?"

"Excuse me?" Dickerson appeared confused. And that made sense. After all, there was no rhyme or reason to my questions because I had no idea what I was doing.

"Your romance with Dot. You two are an item, right?"

Pulling both hands from his coat pockets, he pushed back on my assertion. "Whoa! I wouldn't say that. I'm staying at her bed and breakfast, and we're having some fun. But, mostly, she's just showing me around town and providing me with names of potential investors."

"Mr. Dickerson," I said, my tone disbelieving, "she prepared a special dinner on Saturday night so you could meet her dad. Believe me, that's not normally included in the price of a room."

He poked at the icy pavement with the toe of his loafer, the tassels swinging. "Well, Mrs. Connor, the purpose of that dinner was to present her father with details of an investment opportunity we had in mind for him. An investment in my company." He made a dismissive sound. "Though none of that matters now. He's dead, and Dot has far more important things on her mind than money."

Positive proof that Dirk Dickerson didn't really know Dot Ingstrom or what she deemed important. But I didn't alert him to that fact.

Instead, I said, "You mentioned that you spoke to Lars about the kind of wine to bring to supper. Although, as you just heard, Lars never asked the Olafsons to stop anywhere on the way home from Thief River."

He narrowed his wolf-like eyes. "I suppose he planned to buy it here in town."

"Isn't that strange?" The wine thing had bothered me ever since Dot had mentioned it at the Cenex station.

"Excuse me?" He stretched his back, giving him a few inches

on me. "You think it's strange that the guy shops locally? Isn't that what all you small-town people want everyone to do?"

His condescension threw me. "No… I mean… yes… but Dot doesn't drink and doesn't approve of it. Not since her husband died in an alcohol-related car accident a decade ago."

I expected him to falter after hearing that, but he didn't. "I'm fully aware of the circumstances surrounding her husband's death." He spoke with confidence. "In fact, after I relayed Lars's message to her, she concluded that Lars must have wanted the wine for toasting. That's all. See, Dot intended for him to become the biggest investor in my company. Aside from me, that is."

He certainly had put me in my place. "Was… umm… Lars truly eager to invest?"

"Of course, he was. He merely wanted to review the particulars."

He then attempted a smile, but it didn't quite fit his lips, as if he hadn't practiced it much. "Say, Mrs. Connor, are you interested in investing? Dot mentioned that you're a retired farmer who might like to be a part of a venture that could grow this area."

His charm offensive was every bit as dismal as mine. Still, I played along. "Well, it's possible, I suppose. How many other folks have bought in?"

"There's substantial interest." He gazed up and down the road, everywhere except at me. "But most people were waiting for Lars to make the first move, considering his standing in the community—financial and otherwise."

Lars's family had farmed in the area for generations, and his father had been held in high regard. Even so, folks found Lars lacking. Among his shortcomings, he had played fast and loose with government regulations, something God-fearing Scandinavians couldn't tolerate. Yet he had managed to capture Rose's fancy, which I couldn't understand.

"When things settle down," he said, "maybe Dot will proceed with the deal herself. As… ah… a memorial of sorts."

"What about you, Mr. Dickerson? How much money have

you personally pumped into this venture?" While my words were friendly enough, my tone was far more barbed. I couldn't help it. My instincts warned me that even if this guy was innocent of murder, he was trouble.

"I'm not inclined to go into details, Mrs. Connor. Not unless you're sure you want to invest."

"Fair enough." I had goaded him all I could for one night. "Let me consider it."

"You do that." He offered me his business card, hanging on to it a moment too long, as I tugged it from his hand.

"Now, I better go. I have to get this medication home to Rose."

# Chapter 11

After dropping Mildred Wilson off at her house because the Olafsons had left the medical center without her, I headed back across town.

During my drive, all thoughts of Dot, Etta, Dirk Dickerson, and the Olafson brothers gave way to those of my bra. Specifically, how it had rubbed me wrong all day. I needed to toss it in the trash. To date, I had refrained from doing so because the prospect of shopping for a replacement pained me almost as much as the chafing.

Steering down my driveway, I spotted Dr. Andrew Betcher's black Humvee. It blocked my side of the garage, forcing me to park in front of Grace's bay. As I killed the engine, I reminded myself to move my car before she got home.

Crossing the driveway, my boots crunched against the ice crystals lying on top of the snow, while under the flush of a three-quarter moon, salt glittered on the sidewalk.

A wind gust chased me up the front steps. As I ran, I rolled my shoulders in an attempt to "adjust" myself. With Betcher in the house, I'd have to postpone ditching my bra for a while longer.

Pushing through the door, I met a burst of hot air. "Betcher must be close by," I uttered under my breath with a smile.

In all fairness, Dr. Betcher was popular with his elderly patients, particularly those with Alzheimer's. Again, not nice and perhaps not even true. But I didn't care. I found the man arrogant, personally and professionally.

Years ago, while on a date with Grace, he'd gotten fresh, stopping only after she put the kibosh on his antics with a right jab to his groin. And, a few months ago, he had set his sights on me and became downright frightening when I failed to demonstrate adequate interest in return.

Nevertheless, he remained Rose's doctor, in spite of me urging her to consider other options. On more than one occasion, she'd actually called him "the cat's meow."

Tracking the aroma of coffee, I padded into the kitchen in my stocking feet, startling the doctor, who was glued to his iPad at the table.

"I'm sorry," I apologized, as he fumbled the device. "I guess you didn't hear me come in."

As he righted himself, he said about Rose, "She ate a little before Will left. And, afterwards, I gave her a sedative that may keep her sleeping until morning. She needs the rest." He pointed to the pharmacy bag in my grip, proceeding in a tone devoid of any warmth. "Administer one of those pills twice a day, starting in the morning. They'll help with her anxiety."

As I may have mentioned, Betcher's current attitude toward me was primarily driven by my declining his offer of a date. Although, in the interest of full disclosure, I must admit that I also accused him of murder a few months ago. Nonetheless, his opinion of me never affected his care of Rose, despite having to endure my presence at her clinic appointments and when seeing her at my house.

"Will she be all right?" I placed the pharmacy bag on the table.

"Her blood pressure is elevated, but she's resilient." He twitched his nose, his horn-rimmed glasses bobbing up and down. With his white hair and pink complexion, I likened him to an overgrown lab rat with a stethoscope. "Odds are, she'll come through this just fine." Another twitch. "Still, you'd be wise to return her to assisted living, where I could keep a closer watch over her."

He had waged that battle numerous times, but I never waffled. "Rose will let me know when she wants to return to assisted living."

He gave up a sigh, my response evidently regrettable but expected. "At least keep her calm then."

Easier said than done. My life had been quiet, if somewhat dull, until Rose moved in. Not that she had caused the ensuing bedlam. But she was at the center of most of it.

I poured myself a cup of coffee and rested my backside against the edge of the butcherblock countertop. While too late in the day for caffeine, cradling the cup gave me something to do. "Can she go to Lars's funeral tomorrow?"

"Unfortunately, Will already mentioned it to her, and she assured us both that she planned to attend."

I didn't like him criticizing my son. "He couldn't very well keep her in the dark about it, could he?"

The doctor responded with a shrug that implied that Will could have—and should have—done just that. "It's a moot point now," he stated. "She's determined to go, and I gather you will take her."

Already annoyed with the man—it never took long—I willed him to leave. When he didn't, I asked him about something that had grated on me ever since my stop at Etta Wilhelm's house. "You serve on the county board with Gustaf Gustafson and—"

"He's also on the board at the medical center that oversees my work there." The doctor sounded pained. Dr. Betcher had no time for Gustaf and vice versa.

"Well, do you know what's going on with him? Or, more accurately, with him and Louise?" I had to speak cautiously. I couldn't reveal who I had seen at Etta's house. Betcher was a rumormonger. Every bit as bad as Gustaf. "I heard that Louise went to Alexandria to help her ailing mother."

"Yes, she left," he said. "But God only knows the real story."

"Pardon me?"

"Doris…" He spoke my name with impatience, as if I were a bothersome child. "Gustaf is thrilled that Louise is gone. He said as much at our last county board meeting. Not directly, mind you. But I knew what he meant. I'm quite perceptive. A good doctor has to be." He waited, likely allowing me an opportunity to contemplate the full measure of his medical acumen.

"Trust me," he then said, "Gustaf is much happier now. More pleasant too. Although, with him, the bar's set awfully low." He chortled. It sounded like a turkey gobble. "Anyway, from what I've gleaned, Louise will remain in Alexandria indefinitely, and he'll go and see her on occasion, like when hell freezes over."

"He said that?"

"No. I did." Another gobble. He considered himself funny.

I didn't. Even so, I agreed with him about Gustaf and Louise. Everyone in town knew that Gustaf loathed his wife, and she reciprocated in kind. They lived together for one reason and one reason only: money.

In a manner of speaking, theirs had been an arranged marriage. Seeing dollar signs through their children's union, Gustaf's father, the primary banker in town back in the day, and Louise's father, the most prosperous farmer in the area at the time, coerced their respective 19-year-olds down the aisle.

At least Gustaf later confessed to my sister and me that he had felt coerced. For her part, Louise initially enjoyed the spotlight, yet the shine eventually dulled for her too.

"With Louise elsewhere," Betcher said, "Gustaf can do as he wishes. He's ice fishing more. In fact, I saw Ed Monson drop him off at the courthouse just last week for a county board meeting." He twitched his nose. "Gustaf said they'd been out at Lake Bronson." Another twitch. "Once Gustaf got out of the truck, Lars Carlson crawled out from the back seat, his own fishing gear in hand,

and sat up front with Ed. You could have knocked me over with a feather."

I almost dropped my coffee cup. "That can't be. Lars and Gustaf haven't spoken in nearly fifty years."

"Doris, I know what I saw."

◎ ◎ ◎

After showing Betcher to the door, I drove my car into my side of the garage and scrambled back into the house. The outside temperature had begun to fall. The forecast for morning was thirty below.

Recounting that I had thrown clothes in the washer and dryer earlier that day, I retraced my steps into the kitchen and stopped at the laundry closet. The sports bra I had wanted to wear until my chafing healed was damp, so I set the timer on the dryer for another thirty minutes.

Heading back toward the staircase, I slipped off my bra. But after choosing not to trek all the way upstairs, I tossed it over the newel post. While I had intended to throw it in the garbage, there really wasn't anything wrong with it other than it was miserable to wear. Consequently, I decided to keep it as a "bra of last resort." A bra for when my others were dirty, but I was too lazy to do laundry.

Standing in the foyer, I pulled my sweatshirt down and weighed my supper options. They were grim. Recalling the cinnamon bread I'd been forced to forego at Etta's house, I almost cried.

Hearing Grace's jeep, I watched between the blinds as her garage door opened and closed with a steady hum before she trundled up the walk, a kettle of something from the café in her hands.

Entering the house, she said, "Leftover Cowboy Stew. I just reheated it."

I stole the hot pads and the kettle and made tracks to the kitchen.

"I'll have some too," she hollered from where I'd left her. "While we eat, I want to hear about your afternoon."

She stepped into the kitchen, lolling her head to the side. The bun on top rocked, as other whisps of hair stuck straight out from static electricity. "First, though, how's Rose?"

I ladled a large portion of stew into two bowls and, after setting them on the table, grabbed silverware and bottled water. Taking my seat, I gave Grace a spoon, a water, and a rundown on Rose, ending with, "Betcher just left."

"Thank, God, I volunteered to close the café myself today. Otherwise, I would have been here a lot sooner, which wouldn't have been good. Whenever I run into that man, I want to punch him again."

"Yeah, if I even mention your name, he crosses his legs." With my first spoonful of stew, hearty flavors erupted in my mouth. "Still, Rose believes he walks on water."

"I wish he'd drown." Grace sliced the air with her spoon. "But enough about him. What happened this afternoon?"

"Well," I said after a thick swallow, "I ran into Dot at the Cenex station. For some reason, she blames Rose for everything."

"Pay her no mind. She's deflecting."

Psychological mumbo-jumbo. Grace loved it and everything associated with it. After my husband died, a normal sister would have sprung for a cruise or something to take my mind off the tragedy. Grace offered to pay for therapy.

"Deflecting?"

"Yeah," she said. "She doesn't want anyone looking too closely at her or her new boyfriend."

With my mouth full again, I held up my spoon like a caution flag until I swallowed. "I think you're wrong," I said when I could. "She seemed genuinely upset about her father's death. As for Dickerson, he isn't her boyfriend. At least not a serious one. I met him just before I came home. And even though he's about as pleasant as throat phlegm, and he and Dot probably deserve each other, he insisted that they were only out to have a good time."

"Really? I heard that he expects people to buy dirt from him. How dumb is that?"

"It's not dumb, Grace. It's innovative. But if you ever mention to him or anyone else that I said so, I'll call you a liar."

For the next several minutes, we concentrated on eating, our voices yielding to the slurping of stew gravy.

After scraping my bowl clean, I set my spoon on the table. "Dot supposedly wanted Lars to be a major investor in Dickerson's company."

"But? Do I hear a but?"

"But he died, Grace. He just got murdered. Jeez, sometimes you're… " I let my words fade. What was the point of needling Grace for being… Grace?

"Anyhow," I tried again, "Dickerson said that Dot's now too grief stricken to think about anything, including money."

My sister laughed so hard that she almost fell off her chair.

◎ ◎ ◎

Grace cleared our dishes from the table. "I finally saw him today."

"Who?" I slouched in my chair and rubbed my bloated belly. I had to start eating more slowly.

"Dirk Dickerson. He came into the café this afternoon."

"How did you know it was him?"

Grace sat down, wiggling in a visible attempt to find a comfortable position. Never a good sign. It usually meant that I was in for a long-winded story. "First of all," she began, "the Olafson brothers came in for pie. They ordered the lemon meringue. But that was gone, thanks to you, and they had to settle for apple."

I rolled my hand, motioning her to hurry and get to the point, if there was one, which I doubted.

"Anyway… " She drew the word out, and I lost all hope of her speeding things along. "Except for them, I was alone in the place. I'd let Allie and Tweety go home early. It was nearly closing time anyway, and Tweety wanted to move her stuff back in the apartment above the cafe."

I rolled my hand some more.

"Well," she said, "no sooner had Allie and Tweety left by way of the back door than I heard shouting out front."

She scanned the kitchen, as if hunting for eavesdroppers—or an audience. "Now, I'll admit that Arne and Anders Olafson give me the heeby-jeebies. That whole identical twin thing brings to mind those spooky girls in *The Shining*. That's why I only watched them from the kitchen."

"Grace, get on with it!"

"Okay, okay. To make a long story short… "

If only she could—or would.

"Dirk Dickerson hovered over their table." She spoke in the ominous tone normally reserved for narrating horror stories.

"Again, how did you know it was him?"

"Well, he yelled at Arne and Anders, and one of them yelled back, 'Listen here, Dickerson, we don't want any part of it."

"Wait. When was this?"

Annoyance shadowed her face. "I already told you. Just before closing at two o'clock." She then paused, ostensibly to re-establish where she'd been in her story. "Anyway, the three of them went back and forth until Dickerson banged his fist on the table and said, 'You will help me. Don't think you won't.' After that, he stormed out, slamming the door so hard that the windows shook."

Dickerson had assured me at the medical center that he'd just met the Olafsons. Yet three hours earlier, he had been at odds with them in the café.

"The Olafson brothers were really wound up," Grace said in what sounded like the conclusion to her story. "I half expected them to leave without paying. But they threw enough money on the table to cover their tab and give me a generous tip to boot. That's how I knew something was wrong. Allie always says that the Olafsons have short arms and deep pockets."

# Chapter 12

After Grace left the kitchen, I checked on Rose by standing outside her bedroom door. The familiar sound of her earth-shaking snoring confirmed her wellbeing. How that little body could raise such a ruckus while sound asleep was one of life's great mysteries.

Entering the living room, I passed the Christmas tree with barely a glance before flipping on the gas fireplace.

Grace had already curled up in the corner of the couch, her legs drawn to her chest and one of my crocheted afghans bunched around her ankles. Even though she regularly complained about me spending too much time crocheting, she never failed to grab an afghan when chilly, a common occurrence in my drafty old house.

"Did you get a chance to visit with Etta Wilhelm?" she asked.

"Yeah." I sat down on the opposite end of the lumpy sofa, the springs loudly protesting. "The way she tells it, she dumped Lars—"

"In the lake?"

"What?" My sister was more squirrelly than usual. Forty years ago, I would have guessed that she was stoned. But those days were well behind her. "What is wrong with you?"

She burrowed farther into the corner. "I may have had too much coffee today."

"You think?"

"Well, I couldn't stop dwelling on this... kerfuffle," she said, borrowing one of Rose's favorite words. "Rose has been through enough."

"I agree. But we've got to be sensible."

I stared at the metallic balls on the Christmas tree, the flames from the fireplace mirrored in their shine. "Etta said she broke up with Lars right after Thanksgiving due to his gambling."

"Lars was a gambler?"

"Not a good one. He asked her for money—money he never repaid. Made me wonder if Rose gave him money too. Remember when she mentioned that she often 'treated' him?"

Grace angled toward me, her tone conspiratorial. "If he took advantage of her, I'll—"

"What? Kill him? Someone beat you to it."

She leaned back and toyed with the afghan's tassels. "I just don't get it. If Etta was fed up with Lars and threw him to the curb, why was she with him Saturday morning?"

"That's the million-dollar question. Of course, Rose is positive that they were scheduling their next hookup. But when I asked Etta about it this afternoon, she evaded answering me until her new boyfriend arrived. Then, it was too late to find out anything."

I held my tongue for all of two seconds before adding, "You'll never guess who it was. The new boyfriend."

Grace dropped the tassels. "Gustaf Gustafson."

I leaned toward her. "How did you know?"

"I spotted them heading out of town a few days ago."

"And you didn't tell me?"

"I forgot."

I wasn't so sure. While I shared everything with Grace, she

had a tendency to keep things to herself. It was the characteristic I disliked most about her.

"Now, as far as what you were saying," she said, overlooking my pique, "why would Etta drop Lars because of his gambling, only to date Gustaf, another gambler?"

I let go of my anger. No sense in holding on to it if she failed to take notice. Better to save it for a day when it would prove useful. "She probably has no inkling that Gustaf gambles," I said. "Most people don't. And being he's good at it, he's unlikely to hit her up for money."

Grace tapped her fingers on the frayed arm of the couch. "How much did Lars borrow? Etta can't be rich. She's a retired school teacher, for Pete's sake."

"Whatever the amount, It was a lot to her. She said Lars got 'scary' angry when she demanded that he return it." The wind whistled at me through the living room windows. These days, it was the only whistling to come my way. "She said he frightened her so much that she ordered him out of her house."

A fragmented notion played at the edges of my mind, and once it became whole, I said, "You don't suppose that's the real reason she took him to the café, do you?"

"Huh?"

"What if Etta wanted to ask for her money again but didn't feel safe doing it in her house or in his apartment?"

My sister donned a confused expression. "I thought they went to the café to discuss reconciling?"

"What if they didn't? What if Etta only said that to hide the truth?"

"Doris, why would she want to hide the truth?"

"To save herself embarrassment. From personal experience, I know how tough it can be to admit that you've been played a fool. Especially where a guy is concerned."

I took to my feet and paced around the room. "Think about it. Why would Etta and Lars go to a public place to talk about something as private as their relationship? It makes no sense. And why on earth would she consider rekindling things with Lars when she has Gustaf? Not that Gustaf is any great prize. But he does seem to care for her. Plus, he has lots of money."

"Still, she doesn't really have him, does she?" It was more of a statement than a question, so I waited for my sister to say more. "He's married. And I can't imagine him ever divorcing Louise. Their lives, including their financial holdings, are too intertwined." She snuggled deeper beneath her afghan.

"What are you suggesting, Grace? That Etta somehow figured that out, and that's why she considered going back to Lars?" I couldn't resist yanking Grace's chain. "Or, while they were in the café, maybe Lars again refused to repay her, so she later killed him."

"You think?"

"Of course, not. Etta didn't kill Lars. She was with Rose at the senior center all day." Realizing what that meant, I shook my head. "It will burn her buns to find out that Rose is her alibi."

◎ ◎ ◎

After rummaging through the house for my phone and finally discovering it in a kitchen cupboard, I placed a call, hoping to resolve another issue that had plagued me for the past several hours. Then, I left a note for Rose on her nightstand, next to her teeth. If she needed either Grace or me, we'd be less than five minutes away, no matter where we went in town.

"What's up?" Grace asked from the passenger seat of my SUV, as I backed it out of the garage a bit later.

"I phoned the motel. They haven't been full in weeks."

"That's not unusual."

"Dirk Dickerson told me that he ended up at Dot's place because there was 'no room at the inn.' But since Hallock only has one inn, we know he lied about that too."

Grace smirked. "Are you saying that you finally agree with me that Dirk Dickerson must have had something to do with Lars's death?"

"Not necessarily. But being my head's spinning with possible suspects and motives, I want to stop guessing and start getting some real answers. And because Dickerson has proven himself a liar, we may as well begin with questioning him."

Taking the corner just shy of the bowling alley, I hit a pothole and smacked my head on the roof, my new bump compounding the one from the Olafsons' van. I rubbed my noggin, while Grace, who was too short to ever smack the top of her head on anything, accused the local road maintenance crew of colluding with area auto mechanics.

Slowing down to pass Dot's place, I spotted light in the front part of the house, where she resided, but saw no vehicles in the driveway. "Her car must be in the garage."

"Where did Dickerson park?" Grace craned her neck. "Her garage only has a single stall."

"He drove a black Tahoe away from the medical center. But I don't see it. And it wouldn't fit in her garage."

"How on earth do you know the make of his car?"

"I read it on the tailgate." With a laugh, I turned the corner. "Let's try downtown."

Downtown was a bust too. No sign of the Tahoe at the brewery, in front of the wine bar, or around the Eagles. During the week, Hallock often resembled a ghost town. Come the weekend, though, folks would be everywhere.

Reaching the south-side gas station, I turned left and drove past the Catholic Church before meandering through the snowy side streets. As I passed the Olafsons' house, situated in the middle of a block of post-war bungalows, I noticed that the senior citizen van was parked out front, but the house was dark.

An alley bisected the block, and I proposed that we check things out from that vantage point before giving up and going home. Grace didn't respond, which I took as acquiescence. Although I may have been wrong, seeing how grumpy she looked.

Counting off the detached garages that lined the alley, I came to the one belonging to the Olafsons. It matched their house in style and color. Diffused light burned inside, while Dirk Dickerson's Tahoe crowded the fence along the property line. Exiting the alley, I parked along the curb.

"This isn't a good plan," Grace warned.

"What do you mean? We don't have a plan."

"Precisely. So let's go home and come up with one."

I stared down the row of garages. "This may be our chance."

"To do what?" My sister's voice rose to dog-whistle range. "You aren't really going to question him or accuse him of lying or murder are you?"

"I don't know." I itched with misgivings but wasn't about to let that hold me back. "Let's just peek in the garage. See if anyone's even in there."

"I don't want—"

"Fine. Stay here. I'll go by myself." I retrieved a black stocking cap from my coat pocket.

"Yeah, right. I'd never hear the end of it." Grace pulled her own black cap over her head. "Just keep in mind that I'm not in favor of this."

"Why are you acting this way? Last time we went snooping, you were all for it. If memory serves, you even suggested it. What's more, all I've heard from you since Lars's death is that I should look into whether or not Dickerson killed him, possibly with Dot's help."

"Doris, there's a big difference between speculating behind someone's back and accusing them to their face." She added in a small voice, "Being I've had lots of free nights lately, I've gotten hooked on *Dateline*. And now I see danger lurking everywhere."

"Oh, brother." I opened my door, and the car's interior light flashed on. I blinked against the glare. "You're all talk, you know that?"

We both unfolded ourselves from our seats and stepped outside.

"Doris," Grace said as she walked around the car to join me, "we've already had two murders in town. I just don't think we should tempt fate." She burped. "Remember, Dickerson's probably a killer." She rubbed her sternum.

"We don't know that for sure. That's why we're here. To learn more about the guy." I started down the snow-encrusted alley, the only light guiding me coming from sconces mounted on the garage to my left.

Grace chased after me. "We know he's a liar and a shady character, and the Olafson brothers are probably no better. Don't forget, they're all acquainted." Another burp, this one more threatening sounding than the last.

"Are you okay?"

"Indigestion." She pounded her chest. "Remember when we could eat whatever we wanted without a problem? I miss those days."

Claiming her cell phone from her pocket, she switched on the flashlight app. "I don't want to twist an ankle in one of these icy ruts." The words had barely escaped her lips before she slipped. "Oops!"

"Shush! They'll hear you."

She switched off the flashlight. "They're far more likely to hear me if I fall, break my ankle, and scream in agony."

Reaching the Olafsons' garage, we skirted the window that faced the alley, our backs to the wall.

Hearing voices inside, I ginned up enough courage to look through the bottom corner of the dirty window. With my hands cupped against the glass, I made out a single lightbulb dangling from the rafters. Dirk Dickerson stood beneath it, facing the Olafson brothers. Thankfully, none of them faced me.

While I had an adequate view, I couldn't determine what they said. We needed to move closer. I motioned to Grace, who, at first, appeared thrilled. She obviously assumed we were headed back to the car. But she was wrong.

When initially driving down the alley, I had noticed that the pedestrian door at the rear of the garage was open a tad. Suspecting that we'd be able to hear without any trouble from there,

I slinked in that direction, towing my reluctant sister along.

Indeed, due to a buildup of snow along the threshold, the door was slightly ajar. So, with a flick of my wrist, I directed Grace to inch her way behind it. She refused, the look on her face and her extended middle finger giving me the distinct impression that she didn't care for my plan—or me—at that moment.

Too bad. We had no choice.

I glared at her, as only an older sister could, before mouthing something about her walking home. Not surprisingly, she got into position. Grace, you see, was a lot like me. She didn't fancy exercise of any kind.

Once each of us had taken position, I aligned my ear with the gap between the door and the frame and heard Dickerson say, "There's no risk."

One of the Olafson brothers countered, "Who do you think you're talking to?"

"Well," Dickerson said, "I took you two for smart guys. Now, I'm not so sure."

"Get the hell out of here."

"Come on. You gotta help me."

"No, we don't. This is your mess, Dickerson. We ain't going down for it."

"No one will ever find out."

"Don't be too sure."

"If you guys won't help, I'll have no choice but to let the guys on the east coast know exactly where you are."

"You wouldn't dare."

"Really?"

Metal clanked against metal, and I peered through the gap to see Anders holding a claw hammer high above his head. Arne stood in front of him, his arms and legs spread wide. "Dickerson, you better go. Anders goes crazy sometimes, and I can't always settle him down."

Dickerson backed toward the door. "Fine. I'll leave. But this isn't over."

It was for Grace and me. With a shake of my head, my sister took off toward the car. And even though my legs were far longer than hers, I struggled to catch up, reaching her only after earning a stitch in my side.

"I can't believe you pressured me into doing this," she hissed.

"I didn't pressure you into anything." I bent over and gulped air. "Besides, we're fine."

I'd spoken too soon.

Competing with the squeak of the garage door, Dickerson hollered, "Hey, you two, stop!"

Of course, I had no intention of doing as he ordered. Yet I froze. When he shouted a second time, however, I miraculously thawed and took off again.

Reaching the car, we both dove inside. I cranked the engine over. Grace screamed, "Get the lead out!" And I stomped on the gas.

# Chapter 13

A block later I flipped on the headlights just in time to see Karl in his squad car at the intersection by the courthouse. I didn't stop. For all I knew, Dickerson was in his Tahoe and gaining on us. I swung a sharp right, and Karl fell in behind me.

With the sheriff riding my bumper, my fear decreased. Yet it cranked right up again when Grace wondered out loud, "What if he knows it was us?"

To calm myself, I replied in a voice brimming with bogus composure, "He only saw us from behind."

"If he recognized your car, he could come after us later. Or at least after you."

I showed her the evil eye. "At the medical center, I parked in the side lot, among a bunch of other white SUVs, so he probably has no idea what my car looks like."

"Doris, not everyone is as dense about cars as you."

Knowing she was right, I swallowed hard as my pulse thumped in my ears. And when I spotted an alley, I jerked the wheel in that direction, the rear end of my SUV fishtailing. Karl, in turn, switched on his colored lights. I muttered. And Grace cursed a blue streak out loud.

"Does he really believe we're trying to evade him?" She asked once she had exhausted her four-letter vocabulary. "Hell, we haven't even hit thirty."

Nevertheless, I slowed down. And approaching the next intersection, I used my blinkers.

That must have convinced him that we posed no risk of flight because he flipped off his flashers.

⊚　⊚　⊚

Once home, I hid my car in the garage before Grace and I slow-walked toward Karl. He leaned against his squad car, his leg cocked, his right arm dangling awfully close to his gun.

"You want to explain what that was all about?" He fixed me—and me alone—with a no-nonsense stare.

"Not particularly."

"Well, do it anyway."

Without responding, I headed up the steps and into the house, knowing full well that my sister was on my heels and Karl, on hers. Grace and I toed off our boots and threw our hats, gloves, and jackets in the general vicinity of the entry closet before padding into the foyer. Karl stayed right with us.

"I'm not leaving until you… umm… tell me what you were… umm… up to." He had gotten distracted by the bra on the newel post.

Pretending not to notice or care, I proceeded through the dining room and into the kitchen, where I flipped on the overhead light. Grace followed, giggling. And Karl brought up the rear. God only knew what he was thinking.

"Want some hot chocolate?" I asked with what I determined was fairly smooth detachment, considering that I couldn't meet the man's eyes for fear of blushing. After all, the bra on the banister was clearly mine. No one could confuse it with one belonging to Grace. Or the cantaloupes she carried around.

Karl dropped himself onto a chair at the table and unzipped his jacket. "Hot chocolate?"

"Sure."

Not that I should have been embarrassed. Women wore bras. It was a fact of life. And despite being uncomfortable, that particular bra was kind of pretty, not a safety pin in sight.

As I rummaged through the cupboards for three large mugs, hot chocolate packets, and a bag of miniature marshmallows, Grace stretched her arms and play-acted a non-convincing yawn. "None for me," she said. "I need to get to bed. Another early day tomorrow. And my stomach's queasy."

Mine was too. But I didn't think that would afford me a pass.

With an ear against Rose's door, Grace went on to say, "She's sleeping like a baby, if that baby's a parade of farm equipment rumbling through town. At any rate, you shouldn't have any problem with her." As she left the room, she winked in my direction.

Meanwhile, Karl stared at me until I couldn't take it anymore.

"Fine," I said. "Grace and I took a drive. We were keyed up about everything that's happened."

"And?"

"And someone started following us." Yes, it was a lie. And I regretted it. Truly, I did. But not enough to be honest and subject myself to the reprimand that would surely follow.

"That's why you took off like a bat out of hell? With no headlights?" Mistrust dimmed his eyes.

"Yeah. That about sums it up."

Placing two mugs of milk in the microwave, my fingertips brushed my chest. I had forgotten all about being "au naturel" beneath my sweatshirt. I immediately hugged myself. "Would you... umm... like something to eat?"

I pivoted toward him, my arms wrapped around my torso. "I have some cowboy stew. And don't worry, I didn't make it. Grace did. Down at the café. She brought home the leftovers. It's really good, though it might sit heavy in your stomach."

He looked at me funny. But why wouldn't he? I was wrapped

up like a burrito. "Are you okay?"

"Just… umm… a little cold." I shivered for effect.

"Well, I don't want any food."

"Are you sure? It's no bother to heat something up. Besides, you—"

"Doris!"

I hollered back, "I don't know what else you want me to say!"

"Try the truth!"

The microwave dinged, as if signaling the end of Round One.

I had to uncross my arms to remove the mugs, but I compensated by hunching forward, my sweatshirt ballooning out in front of me. I set the mugs on the table and tossed him a hot chocolate packet and a spoon while describing how I'd seen Dirk Dickerson late that afternoon at the medical center. "He was visiting with the Olafson brothers. And after they left, he told me that he had just met them."

Sitting down, I slouched to keep my sweatshirt baggy in the front. "Yet Grace heard him arguing with the Olafsons earlier at the café. So, obviously, he was already acquainted with them, which means he lied."

Karl ripped open his packet of chocolate powder, poured it into his cup, and stirred, his spoon clinking against the side and the smell of chocolate curling through the air. "What does that have to do with what happened tonight?"

To make it through the minefield that was to be my answer, I had to concentrate. I placed my own spoon on the table and folded my hands in my lap. "Well… umm… Grace and I saw Dickerson's vehicle at the Olafson house. We debated stopping in and asking why he had lied but decided against it." Not the whole truth, but…

"That still doesn't account for your speedy getaway." A muscle worked in his jaw as he apparently gauged the veracity of my version of events.

"We… umm… got scared that he recognized us."

"Why would it matter if he recognized you as you drove by?" His countenance shifted, his jaw tightening as the truth dawned on him. "You didn't stay in your car, did you?"

"Ah, not exactly."

I dropped a ridiculous number of marshmallows into my cup, my scrutiny never veering from my task. "Marshmallows?" I asked in my most accommodating tone. "They make the hot chocolate good and creamy."

He squinted at me until I had no choice but to offer him a play-by-play of our time outside the Olafson garage as I remembered it. Or, more accurately, as I wished to remember it. "The house was dark, but there was light in the garage. We presumed the three of them were out there. Anyhow, as we walked by, Dickerson hollered at us. That's why we hurried back to the car and drove off like we did."

Karl remained mum, giving nothing away.

Because I couldn't handle his silence, I said, "There's something fishy about that guy."

"Oh? Why do you say that?" It was a rhetorical question—a snide rhetorical question—as I discovered when he added, "Just because he got ticked off that you were lurking—"

"We weren't 'lurking.' He lied to me. He knows the Olafsons, although they don't like him. On top of that, no one around here knows anything about him. He showed up out of nowhere, supposedly to start a business. But why Hallock? He has no ties here."

I sounded like Grace, which was unsettling. Even so, I couldn't stop. "He also claimed the motel was full. That's why he went to Dot's. But I called. The motel hasn't been full in weeks. Another lie."

When I stopped, I recalled what Grace had asked me to share with Karl. "And another thing: According to Grace, Dickerson hit on Tweety last week, bragging to her that he'd soon come into money."

As expected, Karl dismissed mention of Tweety with a huff.

But even that didn't stop me. "It was just a few days before

Lars got murdered. Now he's pushing Dot to hurry up with the funeral. Grace suspects that he's trying to get his hands on Dot's inheritance."

"Do you two think he killed Lars?"

I went back to stirring my chocolate. "I don't know. But, as Rose would say, Grace is chewing on that bone. And I'll admit I'm leaning more in that direction than I was this morning."

Karl sipped his drink, then licked his lips. And, for some reason, my stomach performed a cartwheel that had nothing to do with my indigestion or nervousness or my fondness for gymnastics. Yep, even in tense situations, my stomach could act like a hussy. I wasn't sure why. I was done with men, Karl included. Still, every once in a while...

"Well," he said, interrupting my ruminations, which was a good thing, considering where they were headed, "I'll pass all that on to the BCA guy assigned to checking out Dickerson. I'm assigned to Arne and Anders. And, don't forget, they also showed up here out of nowhere."

"But... umm... they've been—"

"Are you okay, Doris?" Karl eyed me sideways. "Your cheeks are red."

"Yeah, I'm fine." I needed to get a grip on myself and think about something other than x-rated images of the man across from me. "It's... umm... just my hot chocolate." I gulped down what was left in my mug, my mouth burning and my eyes watering. "Now, what were you saying?"

Karl pinched the bridge of his nose. He thought I was crazy.

"The Olafsons were the last people to see Lars alive as far as we know," he then said. "They insist that they dropped him off at his place just after five. We're trying to get confirmation from the tenants."

"You've interviewed the tenants?"

"Most of them. A couple are out of town. We're tracking them down."

"And the Olafsons? Have you questioned them?"

"Yep." As he spoke, the fridge hummed, adding an underlying current to the tension in his tone. "They swear it was a standard trip. They took Lars to Thief River and brought him home again but didn't watch him go inside his apartment building."

"Sounds as if you don't buy their story."

"Oh, they went to the casino all right. All three of them appeared on the surveillance tape."

Rose's comment about the purpose of Lars's trip reoccurred to me, as did Arne's assertion that he never saw Lars with anyone. "Karl, Rose said Lars planned to meet some people there. Did you get a chance to speak with any of them?"

"He didn't meet anyone. He gambled on his own all afternoon."

"But he told Rose… "

"Maybe they couldn't make it." Karl's inflection gave lie to those words. "Or maybe he spun that tale so Rose wouldn't suspect him of having a gambling problem. He obviously does—or did."

He picked up his mug, and I dropped my eyes until certain he was done drinking and licking his lips.

"Speaking of Rose," Karl then said, "how's she doing?"

I raised my head, halfway relieved and halfway disheartened that his tongue was back in his mouth. Pathetic. "Betcher came by earlier. He prescribed some anti-anxiety medicine and sedatives. Said she should be fine."

Mentioning Betcher had me recalling what he had said about seeing Gustaf with Lars. I wasn't convinced that it was true but figured Karl still should be aware. "Say, have you known Gustaf to speak to Lars Carlson at any time since you've been back in town?"

"What in the world led you to ask that?"

I repeated the doctor's contention, emphasizing that it was just last week that he had supposedly seen them in Ed's pickup. "He said Gustaf mentioned that they'd been fishing out at Lake Bronson."

"You've got to be kidding!"

"No. Betcher said they'd—"

"He lied to me!" Karl clambered to his feet. "I have to go."

# Chapter 14

The next morning, I found Rose in the kitchen, soft sunshine stealing through the widow above the sink. After pouring myself a cup of coffee, I joined her at the table, the bump on my head aching and my knees creaking. "Ugh. I used to move without sound effects."

Her lips remained tight. She wasn't in the mood for humor.

So, I got down to business. "I'll take you to the funeral today if you're up to going."

"Oh, I'm goin', all right. I'll get ready in a bit. First, though, what did you find out from Etta? You spoke to her, right?"

"Yeah, but I wish our time together had lasted longer. We got interrupted before I learned what you wanted to know."

Her shoulders sagged, misery weighing on her.

Longing to lift her spirits, if only for a moment, I said, "It was her new boyfriend, Gustaf Gustafson."

I expected shock or dismay or at least an inappropriate comment. But all I got was, "Yah, I heard they were seein' each other."

"What? You knew?"

Rose ignored my disappointment at not being the one to

break the news to her. "He claims they're just friends. But when it comes to men, Etta's not the friend type. She's always on the prowl for someone to wine and dine her. As for Gustaf, he probably only calls her a friend because he's married. Although I'm sure Etta's doin' her best to put an end to that." She clicked her dentures. "The trollop. She thinks she deserves two men."

"Rose, if you ask me, the fact that Etta's dating Gustaf is further proof that she wasn't running around with Lars behind your back. She wasn't at all complimentary of him when I spoke with her. And she said she put the kibosh on their romance right after Thanksgiving, weeks before you began seeing him."

Rose harumphed.

"She ended things once he started asking her for money. Money he never repaid. I guess he had financial problems due to his out-of-control gambling."

I watched for a reaction, and she obliged by silently studying her lap.

"When we went fishing, Rose, you mentioned to Grace and me that you occasionally treated Lars. I assume that meant you paid his way. How often? And did he ever come right out and ask you for cash?"

She picked up her cup and slurped coffee, her eyes hooded.

"Rose?" Without saying a word, she had answered my questions. Yet I wanted specifics and repeated, "How often did you loan him money?"

She righted her glasses. "A few times."

"Did he pay you back?"

"No." Her countenance was one of defiance. "But he intended to."

"How can you be sure?"

"He said so."

"Rose! I can't believe—"

"Doris! It's none of your business."

Anger simmered in me. It was my business. It was my job to ensure Rose's money lasted her lifetime. "He took advantage of you, just like he did Etta. The difference is, she sent him packing."

"Then, why was she with him in the café on Saturday?"

While furious, I refused to repeat what I had heard about Lars allegedly pursuing Etta. It would destroy Rose. And, for some reason, it didn't ring true. "Like I said, Gustaf interrupted us before I learned anything definitive. Although it's now clearer than ever that Lars wasn't a nice man. Of course, he didn't deserve to die but—"

"You hardly knew him!" Rose's pale Irish complexion flushed with blotchy color, and her brogue tainted her words.

"Well, I know he got sent to federal prison. And you don't go there for being an upstanding citizen."

She balled her brittle-looking hands. "That was a long time ago."

"I also know that he accepted money—a payoff of sorts—to guarantee his pregnant daughter, Janice, left town and never returned."

"That money covered expenses when she couldn't work. And it later helped with her baby. Besides, that was years ago too."

Rose wasn't about to back down. But neither was I. "He took money from you recently."

She clicked her dentures with such force that I feared they might crack. "It was mine to give!"

"Rose, as a co-signor on your accounts, I have the right to look at them. So just save me the trouble and tell me how much you gave him."

Rose narrowed her eyes, her glasses riding high on her scrunched-up nose. "You promised that I could spend my money however I saw fit." Apparently, her dentures were fine.

"That's because you always demonstrated sound judgment—until now."

She pounded her fists on the table, and our coffee sloshed over the rims of our cups. "I gladly loaned him money! And I'd do it again!"

"Rose!"

In that moment, we both caught our breath, embarrassed by our outbursts.

I rose from my chair and made my way to the laundry closet. To bide my time while I cooled down, I checked the clothes in the dryer. Because they were a mass of wrinkles, I set the timer for another fifteen minutes and pushed the start button.

"I liked havin' someone special in my life." Her lips trembled, and her voice was barely audible above the rumble of the dryer. "Was that so wrong?"

I had to swallow my emotions before I answered. "It wasn't wrong. But you don't have to pay for companionship."

"Oh, really? No man has offered me the time of day for years. Decades even. I'm invisible to them. Then, Lars came along. He made me feel special. And everyone wants to feel special once in a while. Never mind their age."

"You don't need a man for that, Rose. You're special to me. To Grace. To lots of people."

Her nostrils flared. "Don't patronize me. It's not the same thing, and you know it." She grabbed a couple napkins from the middle of the table. "Art Peterson took Verna Olson home from bingo a couple weeks back and got her heart racing so fast in her driveway that her pacemaker malfunctioned, sending her garage doors up and down."

She wiped up our coffee spill. "Mind ya, I'm not talkin' about sex. Just romance." She glimpsed at me. "I'd still enjoy an occasional glitch in my garage door." Another look in my direction. "But bein' you don't give a hoot about romance, you probably don't–or can't–understand."

"Wait a minute. I give a hoot about–" I stopped myself. Who was I trying to fool? I had flunked romance.

"I don't care if it costs me money." She spoke softly, as if to herself. "Folks pay for happiness all the time. They pay for hobbies, trips, wine. They pay–"

"That's different. Lars lied to you. He used you. He had no intention of repaying you."

"You don't know that."

"He didn't repay Etta."

"I'm not Etta." And, with that, she rose from her chair, tossed the coffee-drenched napkin ball into the garage can under the sink, and left the room.

◎ ◎ ◎

The bells on the front door of the café jingled to announce my arrival.

Wishing for a truce with Rose, I had called in an order for Taco Salad, one of her favorites. We'd eat lunch at the house and, if all went well, smooth out our differences before the funeral.

I had barely shut the door behind me when Gustaf shouted from a nearby booth, "Hey, Doris, I have a bone to pick with you."

An image I could have lived without. Still, I slid in across from him to escape the attention of the other customers. "I don't have much time." My voice was just above a whisper. "I'm only here to grab a take-out order."

"You can spare me a minute. You owe me that much."

"What do you mean?"

He wiped his shiny Mr. Potato Head with a hanky. A rotund man with an uncanny resemblance to the aforementioned child's toy, Gustaf spent a lot of time wiping sweat. "The sheriff just left here after ripping me a new one."

I unzipped my jacket. "What does that have to do with me?"

He leaned over his coffee cup, his stale breath finding my nose. "I might have had a hangover on Sunday."

"Oh, really? I couldn't tell." Okay, contrary to what I stated earlier, I didn't confine my use of sarcasm to my sister.

"Very funny. But you're right. I was messed up. I couldn't have found my ass with both hands in my back pockets." Another image I could have done without.

"Anyways," he continued, "I assured Karl that Lars never fished out at Lake Bronson. But last night you set him straight, telling him that you'd seen Ed, Lars, and me coming back from there last week."

"I never said that. Is that what the sheriff claimed?"

"Well, no. But I saw his car at your place and put two and two together." He tapped his temple to empathize his deductive skills.

"Gustaf, you're lousy at math."

"No, I'm not. I'm the banker."

"And ain't it a shame?"

He snarled as he finger combed the half-dozen greasy hairs that comprised his combover.

"I didn't tell anyone I saw the three of you together," I said, "because I never did." No need to mention that I had, however, relayed what Dr. Betcher had purportedly witnessed.

"How'd he find out then?"

"Hallock's a small town. Anyone could have seen you. And no one around here can keep a secret."

I gave him a moment to consider all of that and, hopefully, dismiss me as a possible stool pigeon before I asked, "Why'd you lie to him in the first place? He's your friend."

"He's also the sheriff, and I didn't want to get tangled up in his investigation."

"How would telling the truth—"

"Louise left me." He made the remark in a hiss-laced whisper accompanied by flying spittle. Thankfully, I had moved out of flying-spittle range. "She's living with her mother in Alexandria. As far as anyone around here is concerned, her mother's sick and needs her assistance."

It was my turn to take a minute to process things. "I heard that Louise had left town. And after seeing you with Etta yesterday, I decided it must be true. After all, even you wouldn't date another woman with your wife around."

"Even me?"

"Gustaf, when it comes to moral fiber, you've got to admit you're sorely lacking."

He squinted until his eyes nearly got lost in his puffy face. "You shouldn't talk. Your husband was—"

"Hold it right there." I splayed both hands in the air to empha-size my seriousness. "If you're bringing up my husband, I'm out of here." When it came to my late husband, I maintained a strict "don't ask, don't tell" policy.

"No! Don't go!" With his ham-hock fist, he grabbed my fore-arm. "I need you!"

Checking the room, I prayed that no one had heard him. The stretched necks indicated otherwise.

"Doris, I have to find out who's blabbing about me and Lars." Gustaf's nasal condition caused everything he said to sound whiny. In that instance, though, he sounded even whinier than normal. "As of yet, Louise hasn't mentioned divorce, and I want to keep it that way."

I brushed his hand off my arm and inched my way back to the middle of the bench seat. "Why do you care if she divorces you? You already have a new girlfriend."

"Etta and I are just friends. Plus, Louise wouldn't give a hoot if I took up with another woman. Although, if she ever discovered that I'd been ice fishing with Lars, I'd be in a heap of trouble. She'd hire detectives to dig until they uncovered all the money I've squirreled away."

He lowered his head to match his voice, the former almost grazing the table and the latter nearly unintelligible. "That in-cludes my gambling winnings, some of which I may have forgot-ten to declare to the IRS. And since she can be as mean as a cat getting baptized, she'd then file for divorce and notify the authorities."

"Gustaf, given that Lars is dead, you have nothing to worry about. No one will ever see you two together again." I expected him to be relieved, although he looked anything but.

"What if it's too late?"

"For what?" When he failed to answer, I pressed him. "I don't understand why you went fishing with Lars in the first place. You must have known it would cause trouble with Louise if she found out. And why on earth did you let Ed tag along?"

Gustaf gaped at me as if willing me to comprehend something he didn't want to say out loud. But when I failed to translate his telepathic message, he massaged his temples with his sausage fingers and said, "I suppose I can tell you. It's gonna get out soon enough anyways. I'm kind of surprised it hasn't already."

"Huh?"

"Someone phoned Louise and squealed on me." He swiped the air, as if backhanding the lowlife who had made the call. "So she up and left. Told me she wouldn't stand by while I traipsed around town with my 'bastard son.'"

"What? Your bastard son? I don't understand."

"Well… umm… see, after Janice left town forty-some years ago, she gave birth to our daughter."

"Everyone knows that. She left a month before our senior year."

"Yeah, but everyone may not know that our daughter died of a drug overdose eighteen years later."

"Actually, Gustaf, a lot of us know that too."

He sighed. "Well, did you also know that I went to see Janice afterwards to help with the burial?"

"No."

"Probably because I lied to Louise and everyone else in town about where I was headed." He patted his sweaty face with a napkin. "It was good to see her again. Janice, that is." He stared beyond me, looking into the past. "Well, one thing led to another, and we spent the night together."

"I guess old habits die hard."

"The next morning," he said, disregarding my smart-aleck comment, "we agreed that nothing could come of it. So I went back to Hallock. Janice moved somewhere else. And being there was no need to provide financial support for our daughter anymore, we lost touch."

"Okay. So…"

He grunted. "Do I have to spell it out for you, Doris?"

"Evidently, because I—"

"Ed's my son."

"Oh, my!" My thoughts scrambled in my head like eggs on Saturday morning. "Your son? And Louise found out?"

"Yep. Someone ratted me out."

"Who? Who else knew?"

"That's what I'd like to know. I didn't have a clue about Ed myself until he came to town, looking for me, last year."

I pressed the sides of my head, like that might keep everything inside from spilling all over the place. "He knew you were his father?"

Gustaf nodded once.

"How did he locate you?"

"Janice had left some information about me in an envelope in her dresser. He discovered it when he went through her things after her death."

"Did he tell Louise?"

"Nope, he's never spoken to her."

"So, back to my original question. Who else knew about him?"

He drank more coffee before filling in the blanks. "Well, Karl found out last year, when I did. But he never said anything to anyone."

The question-mark look on my face prompted him to explain. "You see, Ed was trained in law enforcement. He's only twenty-four and doesn't have much on-the-job experience, but he wanted to stay in Hallock being he had no other family." With another napkin, he wiped his eyes. "As head of the county board, I persuaded Karl to hire him on as a deputy."

"So, Ed's your son." I drew out each word, like that might assist me in making better sense of them. "Which means Lars was—"

"Ed's grandfather. And, not surprisingly, the kid wanted to meet both his grandpa and his Aunt Dot. But I held off. I reckoned he'd be disappointed. Who wouldn't? I remember Janice one time saying that her family tree must have been a cactus because all her relatives were pricks." He chuckled. "Be that as it may, Ed insisted. So I had no choice but to arrange things. I started with Lars."

"Too afraid to deal with Dot?"

"She's kind of scary." He waited a beat. "Anyways, Ed and I met with Lars for the first time in my fish house a while back. Shortly after, Louise confronted me. She didn't say how she'd found out. And she didn't say anything about Lars. But she ordered me to make Ed leave town. I told her I wouldn't."

"And that's why she moved out?"

"Yep. I figured she'd cool off and come back, but she hasn't budged."

"Well, I can't really blame her. You did have a child out of wedlock with Janice—twice."

Tweety emerged from the kitchen, a paper bag in hand. She motioned to me from behind the counter, and I pinched my thumb and forefinger to indicate I'd be with her shortly. I then refocused on the man across from me.

Gustaf leaned over the table, his head within a foot of mine. "Louise had... umm... female troubles when she was young, dontcha know. She couldn't have kids, and she refused to marry me unless Janice left town. See, she didn't want to see Janice and my kid around here."

"And?"

Gustaf gauged the room, apparently to confirm that no one was paying us any attention. They weren't. They were focused on a hockey game on the television mounted high above the counter.

He refocused on me. "My old man and Louise's father weren't about to let my pregnant girlfriend stand in the way of them consolidating their financial fortunes, so they paid Lars to keep Janice away. And they continued to pay him until Janice's daughter—our daughter, that is—died." He again wiped his eyes.

"I'm sorry, Gustaf. I had several miscarriages over the years, and that was devastating. I can't imagine losing a teenage child."

He replied in a hollow voice, "I didn't know her, Doris. She was seventeen when she passed away, and I had never even met her."

An uncomfortable silence settled over us until Gustaf slapped the table. "Anyways, despite going along with the payoff, Louise never got over the idea of her family being beholdin' to the likes of Lars Carlson. She truly hated him."

Tweety once more hollered from behind the counter. "Doris, come and get your order, or I'll chuck it in the trash. I don't have time to stand here while you doodle back there."

"Doodle?" Gustaf repeated.

"I think she means dawdle. While I dawdle back here."

He guffawed, clearly relieved for a break from rehashing the old days. "I didn't know you spoke Tweety."

"I can pick out a word here and there."

He glimpsed at her over his shoulder. "She really has it in for you. Even more than usual."

"Why? I haven't done anything to her lately. I couldn't even convince Grace to fire her again. And, trust me, I tried."

"Well, I guess it has something to do with you being seen with Dirk Dickerson outside the medical center yesterday."

I didn't bother to ask how he had come to learn about that. I had anticipated our brief encounter would become the talk of the town.

"Even though he's Dot's beau," Gustaf said, "Tweety's interested. She thinks he might be her ticket out of here. And you know how much she wants out. So, she doesn't take kindly to competition from anyone, especially you."

"Oh, brother."

# Chapter 15

Because I'd gotten waylaid at the café, Rose and I were late to the funeral. The family had been ushered to their seats in the church, as had most of the other guests.

After stowing our coats on a rack in the vestibule, I pointed down the aisle. "How about that pew, Rose?"

"Huh?"

I raised my voice. "What do you think of that spot?"

"Oh, you betcha. I could use a shot. But we probably shouldn't drink in church. Not even a protestant one."

I shut my eyes to count to ten.

She interrupted me at three. "I need a minute." Without another word, she toddled down the hall, and I hurried after her, wondering if the people staring at us were offended that we were there, as Dot had suggested they might be, or if they merely found us loud and obnoxious.

"Turn up your hearing aid," I halfway whispered before realizing how ridiculous that was. "Rose," I then said in a far more commanding voice, "turn up your hearing aids. You're wearing them, aren't you?"

Rose fumbled with the mechanisms behind her ears, more than likely only then switching them on. "Yah, yah, I hear ya."

I caught up to her as we rounded a corner, where we came upon Dirk Dickerson and Tweety. They were all over each other in the doorway of the church nursery, directly across the hall from the women's bathroom.

My inclination was to duck inside the bathroom because I still wasn't sure if Dickerson had recognized me in the alley behind the Olafson house the night before.

Rose had other ideas. "Well, now," she said to the accompaniment of organ music from the choir loft, "isn't this a fine howdy-do."

Tweety spun out of Dickerson's embrace. Although, when she saw me, she nuzzled him some more. "Why, hello, Doris," she trilled in her Tweety Bird voice. "Dirk and I were just… umm… talking."

"Knock yourself out." I pushed the bathroom door open, thinking Rose and I could disappear inside before Dickerson had a chance to accuse me of "lurking" near the Olafsons' garage.

But, again, Rose had plans of her own.

She shuffled toward the pair, leaving me holding the door both figuratively and literally. "Who on earth is this fine-lookin' man?"

"This is Dirk Dickerson," Tweety cooed while clinging to his arm. "Hasn't Doris mentioned him, Rose?"

"Can't say that she has." Rose perused the man as she would a side of beef. "He's a might old for you, isn't he?" She winked at me. "Not that age matters to me. But some folks have an issue with it."

Dickerson clasped Rose's hand.

"Oh, now I know you," she said in lieu of a formal introduction. "You're the guy who's shacked up with Dot."

She showed no sign of embarrassment, so I blushed for her.

And Dickerson? He only smiled that pitiful smile of his. "Happy to make your acquaintance, Rose." He dropped her hand. "Like Tweety said, she's providing me names of people who might want to invest in a business opportunity I have for the fine people of Hallock." He tilted his head in my direction and held my gaze until I looked away. "I already asked Doris."

"Oh?" Rose pivoted toward Tweety. "And what about you? Have you 'invested' with Mr. Dickerson here? After all, I heard he's interested in dirt."

Tweety gasped in obvious outrage, while Rose laughed until she snorted.

Realizing that no good would come from whatever followed, I urged Rose to leave. "We're missing the service."

She opened her mouth, but any comment she intended to make got stepped on by Tweety. "Wait a minute, Rose. Before you go, let me say how sorry I am Lars planned to break up with you."

"What?" Rose's jaw dropped open.

"Oh, silly me," Tweety squealed, her hand fluttering. "You didn't know." She could hardly contain her glee. "When Lars and Etta were in the café on Saturday morning, he asked her to go back to him."

In three strides, I reached Rose and chucked her mouth closed to keep her dentures from falling on the floor. "Rose, you can't trust anything Tweety says."

"I was there, Doris."

"You're also a liar. Now, Rose, let's go."

Rose flicked my hand from her sleeve. "What exactly did you hear, Tweety?" Her voice quaked.

"Well… " Tweety reveled in her trouble-making. "I heard it straight from the horse."

"You mean the horse's mouth?" That was me.

"What? Horses don't talk." Tweety looked at me like I was a fool. And perhaps I was for attempting to converse with her.

"Yeah," she then proceeded to say, "when I saw Etta go into the bathroom at the café, I marched right in after her and demanded to know what she was doing with your beau. That's when she said he wanted her back. I guess he was tired of you."

"Doris is right. You're a liar." Rose shook a gnarly finger in front of Tweety's crow-like beak.

For her part, Tweety dismissed both Rose's pique and her arthritic digit. "At first, Etta acted like she didn't wanna tell me nothing. I suppose she felt sorry for you, getting dumped and all. But, after a bit, she blabbed everything."

"Etta Wilhelm is dating Gustaf Gustafson." I made that statement more as a reminder to Rose than as an argument aimed at Tweety.

"Whatever," Tweety nonetheless replied. "Lars would have preferred Etta anyways. After all, she's way younger."

Rose appeared on the verge of attack, so with dogged determination, I clutched her elbow and steered her down the hall. We were still within earshot of Tweety, though, when Rose said in a raised voice, "Yah, Tweety's so dumb that she asked Dot when she planned to take the bouquet off Lars's coffin and toss it into the congregation to see who was next."

◎ ◎ ◎

Following the service, everybody tagged along with Lars's immediate family to the fellowship hall in the church basement. The smell of scorched coffee collided with the scent of Pine Sol and musty hymnals to create an odor unique to church basements everywhere.

Against a backdrop of tan walls, white acoustical ceiling tile, and speckled industrial flooring, a buffet waited. Tuna noodle hot dish, green Jell-O salad with shredded carrots, and a variety of bars graced a long table covered in red tissue paper undoubtedly left over from the Valentine's Day pie social.

Because we had eaten lunch at home, Rose and I bypassed the food. Then, after Rose selected a glass of lemonade, she deserted me and my Styrofoam cup of coffee.

I milled about the room, listening to snippets of conversations as they bounced off the walls and ceiling until Karl motioned me over to his table at the back of the room. Next to him sat Deputy Ed Monson.

Unlike Karl, who looked disheveled, the deputy wore a clean and pressed uniform with polished dress shoes. His hair was freshly trimmed and shampooed. Normally, Ed was not a memorable guy, but I took notice.

"You look good, Ed," I dropped onto a metal folding chair.

He only grunted before getting up and walking away.

"What's with him?" I asked Karl.

He shoved his plate toward the center of the table, nothing left on it except two noodles and a wrinkled paper napkin. "He probably didn't hear you. He's preoccupied. And moody. Has been ever since he dragged Lars's body out of the lake."

The memory of that moment sent a chill down my spine, although I may have shivered anyhow. Church basements in Minnesota were cold, especially during the winter. Another non-denominational thing. Yet the basement at Grace Lutheran had to be the coldest. In spite of wearing corduroy pants and a wool blazer over a turtleneck, I longed for a hot flash.

"Speaking of Ed," I said while rubbing my arms to generate heat, "Gustaf confided in me that he's Ed's father."

For a moment, Karl appeared dumbstruck, leading me to second-guess myself for saying anything. "So… ah… you understand why he's having such a difficult time," he finally said after a couple false starts. "Janice was the only family he ever knew until this past year, when he located Gustaf. That's when he also learned he had a living grandfather. But he barely got acquainted with him before the guy was murdered." He shook his head. "To make matters worse, Ed was the one who pulled him from the lake."

"Yeah… well… I'm still grappling with all of that."

Karl regarded me over his tented fingers. "I realize that the news will soon be all over town. But given the circumstances surrounding Lars's death, I'd really like Ed to have some more time to deal with everything before becoming fodder for the gossips."

Did he just imply that I'd blab about Ed's situation? The possibility raised my hackles. True, I had been unrelenting in my quest to determine Ed's connection to Gustaf, but that didn't mean I'd gossip about my discovery.

Even so, a wave of guilt washed over me. But because I'd never been good at dealing with guilt—not even after converting to Catholicism decades ago—I changed the subject. "Who informed Louise about Ed? Gustaf wasn't sure."

"I have my suspicions." Karl dipped his head in the direction of the table at the front of the room. Dirk Dickerson had joined Dot, their chairs and hips pressed together. "Only a few people knew of Ed's circumstances. And I didn't say anything. Neither did Gustaf. That leaves Lars and Dot. And, according to Gustaf, Louise said the caller was a woman."

"How did Dot—"

"Lars confided in her a couple months back. Told her that even though her sister was dead, a part of her lived on through her son. He figured Dot would be thrilled that she had a nephew."

"Let me guess…" I took my cue from his countenance. "She wasn't."

"She warned Lars not to alter his will."

"You're kidding."

"Nope. She's all heart."

"So, what did Lars do?" I hugged myself. My coffee had done nothing to warm me. In fact, by the time I sat down, it had gone cold.

"Gustaf says that as of last week, Lars hadn't changed anything. Although he—Lars, that is—was sick and tired of Dot ordering him around. Two of them had quite a row over the whole thing"

"And?"

"We'll find out this evening. That's when the will's getting read."

"Karl, is Dot a suspect?" I posed the question while watching Dot whisper in Dirk Dickerson's ear. And, when Karl failed to answer me right away, I followed up with, "It's hard to imagine someone killing their own father."

"The BCA guys interviewed her." He sipped from his cup. Apparently, he enjoyed iced coffee.

"I bet she ate them alive."

"Not really. From the sound of it, she was evasive. The fact is, they plan to take another crack at her." He scratched his chin and the whisker stubble covering it. Either he hadn't had time to shave that morning, or he had been up all night. I suspected the latter. "Dot claims that she didn't leave her house again after she returned from the store around five o'clock on Saturday. Even when Lars failed to show up for supper, she insists that she only called around for him."

"That's what she told me when I saw her at Cenex yesterday. She said she phoned Etta Wilhelm."

"Yep. Etta confirmed she received the call around six-fifteen. She's certain of the time because she was at the senior center, washing dishes, and noticed the time on the clock above the sink when her phone rang."

"So, what's the problem?"

"Well, earlier, at about quarter past five, one of the tenants in Lars's building spotted Dot's SUV pull in next to Lars's Caddie in the parking lot. He remembers because Dot's car has those oversized fuzzy dice hanging from the rear-view mirror, and he wanted to know why I hadn't ever ticketed her for them."

"Was he certain of the time?"

"Yeah, he said double-jeopardy had just gotten underway."

I shook my head at the thought of a criminal investigation hinging on network programming.

If Karl noticed my glibness, he didn't comment on it. He merely said, "After *Jeopardy*, the nightly news came on, and that's when the same tenant swears he saw Dot leave the apartment building."

We halted our conversation while Lisa, little Hannah's friend from the lake, approached our table. One of several young ladies delivering bars, she beamed, her braces twinkling in the fluorescent lighting, as she set an assortment plate in front of me.

I thanked Lisa and tried not to salivate over the treats. "Karl, why would Dot drive to Lars's apartment just after five when she expected him at her house at six? And more importantly, why would she lie about it? Did she simply forget?"

"Naw. She definitely was evasive with the agents."

"Well, can't Dickerson confirm her whereabouts? He was with her, wasn't he?"

Karl selected a bar, while I recounted everything I'd eaten for lunch and concluded that I couldn't have one. Per the scale that morning, I'd have to swear off sweets until sometime in May. Yep, of all the things I'd lost over the past decade, I missed my metabolism the most.

"Ed's setting up a meeting with Dickerson for tomorrow morning." Karl's voice pulled me back into our conversation,

"What? Why on earth would Ed—"

"Calm down. He's scheduling the meeting for the BCA agents. They're gone today but should be back late tonight."

During the lull that followed, my eyes wandered to the dessert plate. Then, as if my hand had a mind of its own, it swiped a Mounds Brownie and shoved it in my mouth. Not all at once, mind you. Still, I had no choice but to finish it, rationalizing that by eating it, the bar would be out of sight, allowing me to concentrate more fully on our discussion.

"Oh, you might be interested in this." Karl raised a finger. "I spoke with Gustaf about Lars's finances. And while he wouldn't give me actual bank account data without a court order, he did confirm that Lars was a terrible gambler. Sure, he won on occasion. You know, even a blind squirrel finds a nut every once in a while. But, mostly, he lost big."

I licked chocolate from two fingers and was about to suck a glob off the tip of my thumb when I thought better of it and grabbed a napkin. "Well," I said, wiping my hands, "based on my conversation with Dickerson yesterday, Dot had led him to believe that Lars had plenty of money." I studied the head table. As luck would have it, Dickerson met my gaze, staring at me long and hard.

Chapter 16

Gustaf's booming laugh rang out over the cacophony of other sounds in the church basement, prompting Karl and me to look in his direction.

"By the way," Karl said, his attention remaining steady on the banker, who sat at a table in the middle of the room, Ed now beside him, "thanks for letting me know what you heard about Gustaf fishing with Ed and Lars. It was helpful."

"You're welcome." A curious notion scratched my brain. "Is that why you just shared information about Dot with me? One good turn deserves another?"

"Yeah. Something like that."

"Huh. And here I thought you finally realized that I'd make a good confidant."

He snorted.

Uncertain whether it was a teasing snort or a dismissive one, my insecurities took hold. Still, I kept my eyes and my fingers off the dessert bars. I was determined to fight the urge to soothe my fragile ego with more sugar. "Karl, please don't mention to Gustaf what I told you. When I saw him in the café at lunch time today, I had to do some fast talking to avoid getting blamed for you being irritated with him."

Betraying me once more, my eyes meandered to the dessert plate, where they stalled on a Chocolate and Peanut Butter Dream Bar. Another of my favorites. I probably should have picked it in the first place. But the mounds brownie had spoken to me, and I had felt compelled to listen.

Karl smothered a grin with his hand.

"What's so funny?"

"Nothing. Nothing at all."

Preoccupied with the scrumptiousness in front of me—the bar, not Karl—the question I wanted to pose came in fits and starts. "Why didn't... umm... Ed say anything to you... umm... about Lars spending time out on Lake Bronson?"

Out of the corner of my eye, I noticed that the sheriff was barely able to keep a grin at bay.

"Karl! What on earth is so darn funny?"

A devilish glint danced in his eyes. "If you want another bar, Doris, just take it."

"What?" For the first time since arriving at the church, I felt warm. Embarrassingly warm. "I don't want another bar. Whatever gave you that impression? I'm not a pig."

He flashed stop-sign hands. "All right. All right." Removing any hint of good humor from his expression and his tone, he got back to business. "Naturally, Ed presumed that Gustaf had been truthful. At least that's what he told me. But, at some point, he—Ed—must have discovered that Gustaf had withheld information. He just didn't know what to do about it. Family versus job and all that."

I stared at him, vowing not to allow my eyes to stray. "That... umm... doesn't seem very professional on Ed's part. Though it does explain why he looked so distraught while sitting with Gustaf in the café yesterday morning. He must have been upset that his long-lost father had put him on the spot."

"Could be. Though it's all fine now. Or as fine as it can be whenever dealing with Gustaf."

Karl snatched the dessert plate and stuck it under my nose.

I wanted to be offended, but my heart just wasn't in it. So, with a smile I couldn't keep from taking shape, I gobbled up a dream bar.

◎ ◎ ◎

"Okay," I said to Karl a few minutes later, as I enjoyed my sugar high, "update me on the rest of the investigation."

"Don't push it, Doris."

"Oh, come on."

He sighed, as if he didn't have the energy to argue with me. And perhaps that was the case. As I already mentioned, he looked like he hadn't gotten much sleep as of late. I, on the other hand, was brimming with sugar-induced vigor. "At the moment I'm not involved in anything interesting. I'm checking out the Olafsons, and one of the BCA guys asked me to review inmate records from when Lars did federal time."

My mouth fell open. "You've got to be kidding. Lars was incarcerated decades ago. Besides, he wasn't a hardened criminal. Do they really believe that someone from back then would have reason to murder him all these years later?"

"I'm not sure. They don't share a hell of a lot. Maybe they just want me out of the way, so I won't interfere with their investigation."

"Well, if I were you, I'd say something."

"I bet you would."

I had to laugh, which normally would have gone unnoticed by everyone except Karl, but the place had suddenly gone quiet, and my voice carried.

Karl's mouth formed an "O," as his eyes slid to the doorway.

Tracking his line of sight, I saw why the oxygen had been sucked out of the place. Louise Gustafson, Gustaf's wife, had entered the room.

She failed to express her condolences to Dot, which wasn't shocking given her disdain for Lars and the entire Carlson clan.

Yet it did beg the question, "Why is she here?" Which is what I asked Karl by way of a murmur.

He responded with a grunt, his focus never veering from the woman as she charged around the tables, her pellet eyes glued to Gustaf.

With a helmet-head of blue-rinsed hair and a purple wool car coat that swooshed as she dodged around tables, she called to mind a Minnesota Vikings' linebacker—only way more frightening.

As for Gustaf, he was dressed in a black suit, contrasting with his face, which had lost all color. If lying on his back, he could have been mistaken for a corpse—of a whale.

I held my breath, as did Karl and everyone else in the place except for Etta Wilhelm. She began hyperventilating but waved off all offers of aid, apparently not wanting to draw attention to herself. No need to fret about that. Louise only had eyes for Gustaf.

Upon reaching him, she slapped an envelope against his chest. "You've been served! I'll take every dime you have. And that includes the gambling winnings you've attempted to hide from me. In other words, you're finished."

If possible, Gustaf became even more insipid looking.

"Can she do that?" I asked just loud enough for Karl to hear. "Serve him herself?"

He shook his head. "I don't think so. But it makes for good theater."

"Gustaf Gustafson, you're a wretched loser!" Louise's words echoed throughout the room as she swiveled on her chunky-soled boots and plodded toward the exit.

Dot stepped in front of her before she got there. "What are you doing here?"

Louise stopped and fixed her fists to her hips, akimbo style. "I don't have to answer to you. This is my church. My family has paid for practically everything in here."

"In that case," someone yelled from the far corner of the room, "how about buying a little more heat? It's freezing in here."

A few folks tittered but fell silent when Louise scoured the room, contempt wrenching her face into a scary mask.

"Get out!" Dot pointed to the door, as if Louise had lost her way and needed directions.

"I plan to do just that, as soon as you move your fat ass."

"What did you say?" Dot shuffled closer.

"You really want me to repeat myself? I think not. Now move!"

"Don't you dare boss me around." Dot poked Louise in the chest with her finger. "You and yours have done that to my family for decades. Dad took it. I won't."

"What are you talking about? Your father extorted money from us. He was nothing but a low-life criminal."

That remark must have crossed "the line" because Dot shoved Louise, who staggered backward into the refreshment table, both the lemonade pitcher and the coffee urn crashing to the floor. "Help!" She flapped her arms. "Dot ruined my coat, and she scalded my hands!"

Dirk Dickerson sprang to his feet, his chair tipping over, and the sound reverberating like the pounding of a drum.

I expected Karl to leap into action too. But he only whispered to me, "Let's see where this goes," before mouthing the same to Ed.

"Are you okay?" Dickerson wrapped his arm around Dot.

"I will be," Dot said, while a couple women from the kitchen dashed across the floor with dish towels and cleaning rags, "after I finish her off!"

With that, Dot wormed out of Dirk's embrace and lunged at Louise.

For her part, Louise employed a cracking slap across Dot's face, bringing her to a standstill.

Dot rubbed her cheek. "You contemptible old bittie!" She then shoved Louise with two hands. And, once again, Louise tripped, this time over the kitchen help, the whole lot of them tumbling to the floor.

Most everyone in the room had risen to their feet by then.

Ole Svengaard, the regular from the café, was making book, and Gustaf Gustafson, who never missed an opportunity to place a wager, was among the betters.

As for Karl, he ate up the floor with long strides. "Stop it! All of you!" He waded into the melee, assisting Louise to her feet, while Ed helped the kitchen ladies off the floor.

"You got control of her?" Karl tipped his chin toward Dot.

"Yeah," Dickerson assured him, "she's fine." Dot twisted, and Dirk must have tightened his grip because she let loose a string of utterances not normally heard in church. "It's been an emotional day for her, that's all."

"How about you?" Karl asked Louise, who remained in his grasp. "Have you cooled off?"

"Cooled off? She scalded me!"

Ignoring her grumbling, Karl proceeded to guide Louise from the room, leaving Ed behind.

Everyone else in the hall erupted in chatter. Everyone except for Tweety. She lingered next to the mortician and stared at Dirk and Dot, who cuddled in a corner. If looks could kill….

Having very limited interest in Tweety or the mortician or even Dirk and Dot at the moment, I scouted the room for Rose but didn't spot her anywhere. I didn't see Etta either.

My imagination went crazy. In my mind's eye, I saw Etta pinning Rose to the mat in what could have been billed the second match of the day. My stomach twisted in knots, and I barreled down the hall to the stairway. Climbing two steps at a time, I reached the vestibule, where I found Rose and Etta standing toe to toe, as if in the center of the ring.

"What's going on?" I wasn't entirely sure I wanted to know.

Rose pointed to Etta. "This one here told Tweety that Lars wanted to get back together. But it wasn't true. She lied."

Etta blushed, her half-exposed bosom blossoming color similar to her henna-red hair.

"The truth is," Rose said, too wound up to give Etta a chance to defend herself, "she went to the café with Lars on Saturday mornin' for one reason and one reason only—to make Gustaf jealous. She just admitted it."

Rose gestured toward the gathering crowd, as if to assure me that they'd confirm her account. "She knew Gustaf had a meetin' across the street and would see her, especially bein' she made sure that she and Lars sat in front of the windows."

I bent toward Etta and lowered my voice. No need for everyone to hear what I had to say. "Etta, from the start, I doubted you drove Lars to the cafe to discuss getting back together. But I never would have guessed that you were out to make Gustaf jealous. Why in the world would you want to do that?"

"I'll tell you why," Rose shouted before Etta could open her mouth. "She was countin' on Gustaf divorcin' Louise. But he was draggin' his feet."

I held my hand up, signaling Rose to keep her mouth shut. "Is that true?"

Etta inspected the floor, as if utterly intrigued by the industrial tile. "I only said what I did because Tweety badgered me into telling her something."

"What about Dot?" I wanted to know. "You told her the same thing when she phoned you that evening, right?"

"Well… yeah… but only because she caught me off guard."

"Again, Etta, why?"

"I… umm… wanted Gustaf to be free."

"So you decided to help him along." That was Rose again.

I had trouble making sense of any of this. "Etta, didn't fibbing to Dot and Tweety bother you? Weren't you afraid that Gustaf would find out?"

"I never… I just wanted—"

Rose interrupted. "How about Lars? Didn't you feel the least bit guilty about usin' him?"

Etta raised her chin, signaling she still had some fight left in her. "Did I feel guilty for using Lars? Not a bit. He took my money and had no intention of paying me back. He owed me."

"Well," Rose blurted out, "if that's not a fine howdy-do."

"Why didn't you mention any of this to me when I stopped by your place?" I asked.

Etta clutched her glasses, the chain attached to them partially hidden beneath her jowls, now hanging extra low. "I was ashamed, and I didn't know how to fix what I'd done."

Shifting her attention to something behind me, her features brightened. "I have to go now, Doris. My ride's here."

Glancing over my shoulder, I saw Gustaf approach, only to stop a couple yards shy of his girlfriend. "You wanted to make me jealous?" His voice was halting. "And you didn't mind sneaking behind my back to do it?"

True, Gustaf was in no position to criticize anyone for being sneaky. Even so, I felt sorry for him. His wife had just served him with divorce papers, and his girlfriend had ended up being a stinker in her own right.

Etta reached out to him, but he recoiled. "Were you the one who called Louise? Told her that I was seeing someone?"

A tear fell from Etta's eye and trickled down her cheek, marking a trail through her rouge. "I only wanted us to be together. And you were slow to—"

"Did you also inform her that I'd been spending time with Ed?"

"No!" Etta threw her hands up. "That wasn't me, I swear. I was happy that you and Ed had found each other."

In spite of being packed with people, the hallway fell silent, as if everyone had decided to let Gustaf mark the course for whatever happened next. And, after a few moments, he did just that. He swiveled on the heels of his wingtips and trudged away, leaving Etta behind to sob into her hands.

## Chapter 17

It was six o'clock when I arrived at the café. Because it was closed, I parked in the alley, behind my sister's Jeep, and entered the building through the back door.

"Where's Rose?" Grace sat at the prep table with a crossword puzzle, a carafe of coffee, a cup, and a large bag of M&Ms.

"She's at home in bed. She's a disaster." After helping myself to a handful of M&Ms, I briefed her on everything that had transpired that afternoon between Rose and Tweety and, later, Rose and Etta. "Even though Etta admitted that Lars never asked her to reconcile with him, Rose couldn't be consoled. She's worse off than ever." I retrieved a stool and sat down. "Although she may finally see that Lars wasn't such a good guy."

"He sure fooled me." Grace got up, grabbed a cup, and poured me some coffee.

"Wait a second. Aren't you supposed to be so great at reading people?"

She stuck out her tongue.

I restrained myself from responding in kind. "I gave Rose one of her new pills, and Sophie came over to stay with her." I popped one M&M after another into my mouth, all the while berating my-self for eating sweets. "I couldn't just sit there. I had to do some-thing. So here I am, still unsure what that something should be."

My sister pitched her elbows on the table and steepled her hands as if praying, although I knew better. "Have you spoken with Karl?"

"Not since I left the church." Another M&M. "Why?"

"Well, Allie dropped by here on her way home from the fu-neral. She mentioned that when she went to get her coat, she overheard Dot arguing with Dickerson. I guess Dot thought he had gotten too friendly with Tweety at some point during the day." She waggled her brows.

"And, a bit later," she continued, "out in the church parking lot, Allie heard Tweety giving Dickerson what for. Supposedly, she didn't like how quickly he had rushed to Dot's defense when she went after Louise."

"Interesting." I raised my cup but refrained from drinking. I didn't really want any coffee. Not even hot coffee.

"Oh, it gets better." Grace wiggled around on her stool, scar-ing me into thinking that I was in for another epic story. "Dicker-son attempted to smooth Tweety's ruffled feathers by insisting that he didn't care for Dot and only planned to stay with her until he got Lars's money."

"What?" I bumped my cup, and coffee splashed over the side.

"That's why I wanted to know if you'd spoken to Karl. See, Allie and I called him."

Using a paper napkin, I wiped up my mess. "He didn't say anything about Dickerson confessing, so you must have talked to him after I did."

"Dickerson didn't exactly confess, Doris. Not to Lars's murder at any rate. Still, Karl agreed to pass the information on to the BCA guys right away. They're out of town until later tonight."

I set my coffee-soaked napkin next to my cup. "In that case, I imagine Karl is on his way to Dot's place to pick up Dickerson himself."

"Nope. Karl's at a meeting in Warren. But he texted. Said he called the BCA agents, and they didn't want Dickerson questioned until they could do it. Ed's to set up an interview for them for nine o'clock tomorrow morning."

Still more M&Ms found their way into my mouth. "What about between now and then?"

"Ed's to keep the guy under surveillance until one of the BCA guys can relieve him."

"Really? Ed?"

"The BCA guys don't see it as a problem." Grace sipped her coffee. "They believe that as long as Dickerson doesn't suspect that anyone is on to him, he's unlikely to leave town without Lars's money."

"But the will reading is tonight."

"It'll take a few days for Myrle—that's who Lars hired as his lawyer—to make the distributions. Just like when Mom died. Remember?" Grace's bun had wilted, and she pulled the binder free to rework the knot on top of her head. "In any event, Karl said he left a voicemail for Ed. Told him to get over to Dot's right away. He also said he'd drive back here as soon as he could."

While Grace twisted her hair, images passed through my mind of Rose at home in bed, her own hair a tangle of frizz from snatching at it as we drove home from the church. "She's so vulnerable." No need to say her name out loud. These days Rose was front and center in both our minds.

"Yeah, she's far too old for this kind of strain." Grace's voice quaked. "I don't know what I'd do if… " Finishing that sentence wasn't necessary either. I loved Rose, but she and my sister shared a special bound.

"Grace, Ed shouldn't be in charge of looking after Dickerson." I crunched another couple of M&Ms, swearing to myself that they'd be my last. "Not even for a little while."

"You're right. But what can we do?"

"We agree then," Grace said after summarizing our discussion as I once more drove to the north end of town. "If Rose hasn't improved by morning, you'll take her to the doctor?"

"Of course. I don't relish Betcher doing his whole 'I warned you not to let her go to the funeral' number on me. But I won't let that stop me from getting her the help she needs."

When I turned off the highway, my car bounced over the same pot holes I had encountered during our last trip to Dot's house. Sure, I could have avoided them, but I would have hit others anyhow, so what was the point? Besides, the top of my head was numb.

The sky was dark and glittering with stars. "Gonna be cold tonight," Grace stated while listening to the weather report on the radio. She wrapped her arms around her midsection as if preparing.

"It's ten after seven." I switched off the radio. "Dot should be at the law office." I passed by her house at a crawl. Dot's half of the place was dark. It was difficult to see the guest suite from this vantage point.

"There's Dickerson's truck." I gestured toward the black Tahoe parked along the side of the road. "I don't see a sheriff's vehicle anywhere."

"Even Ed's not dumb enough to drive a cop car to a stake-out."

"Well, I don't see his pickup either. And, with that Packers' decal in the back window, even I'd recognize it."

I drove down a side street. "We can't view the entire guest suite from this angle, but we can see most of it." I slowed. "There may be a lamp or two on in there. Otherwise, it appears dark."

"Dickerson doesn't strike me as the kind of guy who'd go to bed at seven o'clock. At least not alone."

I took a left. "Dot's at the law office, remember?"

"Tweety's not."

I dismissed Grace's comment. I'd had the misfortune of witnessing Tweety in a compromising position once before and couldn't bring myself to contemplate the possibility of a repeat performance.

One more left turn and I had us back in front of Dot's house. "Absolutely no sign of Ed."

To take stock of the entire street, Grace rotated her head in *Exorcist* fashion. "Maybe he's watching from a distance through binoculars."

"You really think so?"

"Naw. He's nowhere around." She squared herself in her seat. "Now what?"

I pulled alongside the curb, across from the Tahoe, and switched off the engine. "We need to see if Dickerson's inside."

"Whoa! You promised we wouldn't leave the car."

"That was before discovering that Ed had gone AWOL." I opened my door.

"Wait." With both hands, Grace pushed against my suggestion. "You said that even though he didn't come right out and admit it to Tweety, Dickerson most likely murdered Lars."

"So? You've believed that from the start."

"But, now that you agree with me, don't you think we should call Karl?"

"Karl already said he'd get back here as soon as possible."

"Okay. Let's wait for him."

"Grace, we don't even know if Dickerson—"

"His truck is here! Where else would he be?"

She had a point. The weather was too icky to go far on foot, especially when a vehicle was available. "Well, he could have walked to the bowling alley. It's only a couple blocks."

Grace rolled her eyes. "Why would he do that? Or is that what killers do in their down time? Bowl?"

The truth was, regardless of what she said, I needed to knock on Dickerson's door. I had to look him in the eyes. Now that I was almost positive that he was responsible for Lars's death and Rose's distress, I had to see if I could spot his wickedness. Had it been there all along? Had I simply mistaken it for arrogance?

"Let's just knock," I said. "If he answers, we'll ask for an appointment for tomorrow to discuss… umm… investing. We'll then say goodbye, drive around the corner, and wait for Karl." I gave her a second to think that over. "If he doesn't answer, we'll call and update Karl, then drive around town in search of Ed."

Grace huffed.

Taking that as a begrudging yes, I eased from the car.

At the same time, my sister mumbled something I couldn't quite hear. Considering her tone, I got the feeling it wasn't nice.

◎ ◎ ◎

Under a bright sky, courtesy of a billion stars reflecting off the snow, we trudged up Dot's driveway and peered through the garage windows. Confirming that she and her car were gone, we climbed the three-step stoop on the side of the house to the guest-suite entrance.

I felt anxious but a little cocky too. Evidently, Dickerson hadn't recognized me in the Olafsons' alley the previous night. If he had, he would have done far more than stare at me at the church. Nevertheless, I inhaled a calming breath and held it to the count of four before exhaling to the count of eight, just like I'd been taught in therapy.

Opening the metal storm door under the dull light from the fixture overhead, I knocked on the wooden entrance door and practically fell inside. "Whoa."

"What's going on?" Grace curled around me from behind, the air escaping her mouth in a cloud of steam.

"The door's open," I whispered before pushing on it and calling out, "Mr. Dickerson? It's Doris Connor and her sister, Grace Anderson."

Neither Grace nor I moved for the next ten seconds. Then, hearing nothing, I patted along the interior door frame until I found a light switch and flipped it on. The tiny foyer lit up. "Mr. Dickerson!"

In front of us, the basement door was closed, as was the door to our right, which led into Dot's portion of the house. The guest suite was to our left. That door stood wide open, revealing a loveseat, a pair of wingback chairs, and a coffee table.

"Mr. Dickerson?" With only the light from the entry to guide me, I stepped into the guest suite's sitting area, despite Grace's attempt to hold me back.

"Let's call Karl right now!" She stomped her foot. "Something's wrong. I can feel it."

"I'm not calling Karl based on one of your feelings. Remember, you also felt that Lars was a decent guy." A couple more steps and I bumped into the corner of the coffee table. "Ouch! Mr. Dickerson?"

"Usually my feelings are right on." Grace tailed me, stepping on my heels. "And I feel trouble."

I shared her unease. Even so, I shuffled farther into the room.

"Doris, what if he really is with Tweety?"

"It's too quiet. Remember how noisy she was last time?"

"I try not to recall any part of that night."

Between the sitting room and a small dining area, I stopped, and Grace walked into my back. "Ouch!"

"Sorry," she said. "Now, please, can we go?"

"But… umm… Dickerson could be hurt. It's not normal to leave the door open like that." As reasoning went for remaining where we were, it was weak.

Grace took notice and pumped her fists against her hips. "What are you suggesting? That he somehow injured himself, crawled to the door, opened it a tiny bit, then crawled off to the bowels of the house?" She pinched her eyes shut. "I shouldn't have said bowels. Now I have to use the bathroom."

"Get a grip!"

"We have no business in here, Doris!" Another foot stomp. "Now, I'm going outside to call Karl. You can explain yourself to him."

"Okay, okay." I intended to follow her—really, I did. But, as I perused the room one last time, I caught sight of a notepad on the dining table. "Wait a second." The pendant light hanging above the table offered only dull illumination. Yet it was enough for me to make out writing of some kind on the pad. I inched closer to read the scrawl across the top. "What the… "

Grace crowded me. "What is it? What does it say?"

"It's… it's my name underlined."

"Your name? Dickerson didn't know we were coming over."

"Exactly." I stretched across the table to get a better look, and my heart crawled into my throat. "Oh, no."

"What?" Grace whispered. "Tell me."

"It can't be." I motioned beyond the table. "It just can't be."

Yet it was. A man's body lay sprawled on the floor.

Grace bent over the table. "He's just drunk. He smells like he was squeezed out of a bar rag." She spoke with the kind of conviction meant to reassure me. It didn't.

I edged around the chairs, and Grace followed, again stepping on the back of my boots. I wanted to yell at her, but I couldn't. I needed to concentrate on my breathing.

I methodically inhaled and exhaled, silently agreeing with Grace that the odor of alcohol was strong. Although the metallic stench of blood was also present. I had smelled it before. Not that long ago. And, like then, it triggered my gag reflex. As a result, I barely registered the broken wine bottle on the floor, the puddle of wine mixed with blood, and Dirk Dickerson's smashed head before I threw up.

# Chapter 18

My sister and I settled into the back seat of the sheriff's SUV, which was parked in Dot's driveway. Even with blankets wrapped around us and the heater running full blast, we trembled.

Grace's head drooped to the left, and what remained of the bun in her hair rested on her shoulder, as if totally spent. I could relate.

Karl opened the front door. "You two doing okay?"

We responded with guttural sounds.

"You've experienced quite a shock." His eyes drifted between us, his features showing both contemplation and worry. "I'll be a few minutes more. Then, I'll take you home. Someone will drop your car off later." He rocked back on his heels. "Anything to add to your statements?"

More grunts from us. These in the negative.

He shut the door and returned to the house.

"It must have been a heat-of-the-moment thing." I gulped water from the bottle Deputy Monson had handed me before stuffing us in here. "If someone had planned to kill the guy, they would have brought a weapon. A gun or something. They wouldn't have opted for a wine bottle."

"You mean it was a crime of passion?" Grace examined the sky through her window, like the stars might provide answers if studied close enough. "A woman? Following drinks?"

"No one had drinks. No glasses in the sink or dishwasher. And the only glass on the floor came from the bottle. The cap was still fastened to the broken neck. The bag and receipt were on the counter in the kitchen."

A disembodied voice uttered an unintelligible command to somebody over Karl's car radio. "I looked in the bedroom," I said following an equally garbled radio response. "Nothing had gone on in there. The covers weren't even rumpled."

"So, what on earth happened?" Grace downed a good portion of her own water.

"I don't know."

"And the killer? What's the story there?"

"Well, according to Ed, he received a call around six-forty from Myrle, requesting that he join the others for the reading of the will. He phoned Karl, who said he could go if he came back here as soon as he was done. So, he took off around ten minutes before the hour."

"Why would Karl allow him to leave?"

I squeezed my eyes shut. Post-vomiting wooziness persisted. "He feels sorry for him. That's my impression anyhow." Once the nausea passed, I blinked them open. "He probably decided that he shouldn't stand in the way if the family—and, by family, I mean Dot—was finally ready to accept him."

"What about watching Dickerson?"

"As you said, Grace, the BCA agents didn't see Dickerson as a problem. Even so, I bet Karl's kicking himself right about now."

Another sip of water to combat my cotton mouth. "Ed said Dot returned home from the funeral just before six. He got here a few minutes ahead of her. She parked in the garage. And since he didn't see her again, he presumed she was still in the house when he took off for the law office."

"How about Dickerson?" Grace asked.

"Ed never saw him but figured he was in the guest suite being his vehicle was out front."

"Well, it's obvious then. Dot killed Dirk Dickerson."

"I'm not so sure." I hesitated to say what was on my mind, although remaining mum wouldn't make it any less likely or troubling. "If Dickerson killed Lars and Dot killed Dickerson, that means we've had two killers roaming around Hallock. Add the one we caught a few months back, and that's a whole lot of murderers for one little town."

My sister pulled her blanket tighter around her shoulders. "Yeah, *Dateline* would have a field day up here."

"On the other hand… " My voice trailed off as I tapped my toes, like that might prime my brain. "If we assume that one person killed both Lars and Dickerson… "

"It had to be Dot."

"I still don't see her killing her own father. When I spoke with her outside the Cenex station, she seemed genuinely distraught over his death."

"What did you expect her to do? Cheer?" Grace angled her head. "In the future, Doris, you may want to avoid criticizing my ability to read people because you're clearly horrible at it."

I blew her a raspberry.

She rolled her eyes. "In the fish house, you saw how angry she got with Rose for supposedly 'encouraging' Lars to spend 'her' inheritance."

She overdid the air quotes, but I didn't point that out. Rather, I said, "She also referred to him in the present tense. She wouldn't have done that if she had known he was dead."

"Why not? She wanted to avoid giving herself away." Grace knocked her empty water bottle against her leg, drumming to the beat of her thoughts. "As for Dickerson's death, she may have gotten livid enough to kill him because of Tweety. You know what they say, 'Beware a woman scorned.'"

"That's not how the saying goes."

"Close enough. Plus, from what I understand, after you commit one murder, the next one is way easier."

In addition to possessing a self-proclaimed knack for reading people, my sister had apparently become an expert in criminal theory. At least she could rattle off related adages. Whether or not they were true was another matter.

Nonetheless, I had to agree that the evidence pointed to Dot, relative to Dirk Dickerson's death at any rate. "Okay. She was a few minutes late getting to the law office, which indicates that something held her up, but—"

"Wait." Grace dipped her head toward me. "How do you know she was late?"

"I listened in while Ed updated Karl."

"Where was I?"

"In the bathroom, losing everything you ate today."

"Yeah, I was really sick."

"No kidding." I sniffed. "You still smell kind of funky."

"Hold on. You vomited too. Maybe you're just catching a whiff of yourself." She clutched her midsection. "Though I will admit I haven't been that sick since I got drunk on Boone's Farm wine with Boyd Ferguson during our junior year."

◎   ◎   ◎

After Karl drove Grace and me back home, Sophie left, I checked on Rose, and Grace trotted upstairs, her phone to her ear. As for Karl, he headed into the living room, where, after I gargled and changed my sweatshirt, I found him seated in the leather club chair.

He contemplated the Christmas tree, while I flipped the switch on the gas fireplace and settled into a corner of the lumpy sofa. "I haven't had time to put it away," I said, excusing my tree's presence in late February.

"At this point, leave it up." The reflection of flames from the fireplace played across his cheek. "Tell everyone you're getting a jump on next year."

I attempted a chuckle, but it fell flat. I was too preoccupied with images of Dirk Dickerson's body and concern for Rose.

To hear Sophie tell it, Rose had experienced fitful sleep throughout the evening. And, while she was now at peace, snoring like usual, I still wrung my clammy hands from worry. "Karl, Rose can't take this."

"I know." He scrubbed his face. "Times like this, I miss drinking."

"Really?" Both my dad and my husband had suffered from alcoholism. So I bristled whenever anyone who shouldn't drink voiced a desire to do it.

Karl must have heard the unease in my voice. "I don't really want a drink, Doris. But this is the kind of night I'd have one—or ten."

Years ago, Karl had served in the army. He was a member of the military police. He never readily discussed those days, but I sensed he had experienced some tough times and often used alcohol to dull the memory.

"You know," he said, eyeing me until I squirmed like a kid in need of a bathroom, "if you and Grace had arrived at Dot's a few minutes earlier, you might have stumbled upon the killer."

I folded my legs alongside me. Although I appreciated his interest in my well-being, I sensed a reprimand on its way, and I wasn't in the mood for that. "Or it's possible that we could have prevented a murder."

He acted as if he hadn't heard me. "First, a few months ago. And, again, tonight. You're making a habit of getting yourself into precarious situations."

It wasn't a reprimand exactly, but it was close enough to irritate me. "I don't do it on purpose."

He narrowed his eyes, wordlessly conveying that he wasn't so sure. "And regardless of what you two claimed in your statements, I don't believe for a second that you planned to meet with Dickerson to discuss investments."

Okay, we might have fudged that part. But Karl would have

had a conniption if he'd found out that we were sleuthing on our own. True, he likely suspected it, but he didn't know for sure, and I wanted to keep it that way. "You saw my name on his notepad," I said, as if that proved a scheduled meeting.

"Yes, I did, which concerns me."

It concerned me too. After all, I had no idea why it was there. But I wasn't about to mention that. Karl had just started opening up to me about his work. If he determined that I was freaked out because a would-be fraudster and probable murderer had written my name on a pad of paper before getting killed, he'd back off.

"No, Doris, it doesn't look good. Your name on a notepad near a murder victim—a victim you just happened to find."

"Huh?" A moment lapsed before I grasped what he was getting at. "You're suggesting that I'm a suspect?"

"Well, it's an issue we'll have to address."

My pulse quickened. I hadn't considered that I might look guilty in the eyes of the law. Maybe not in Karl's eyes. But those BCA agents had eyes too. And who knew how they'd see things? "Karl, I can't be a suspect. It doesn't make sense. I only met Dickerson once. He asked me to invest in his business. That's all."

My voice rose in pitch and volume with every word. "Have you spoken to Dot? She's a far more logical suspect. Remember, the body was found in her house. Or, I should say, her guest suite, which is the same thing, right?" Yes, I had difficulty believing Dot was a killer. But that wouldn't stop me from throwing her under the bus in an effort to save myself.

"No, we haven't questioned her." He sighed. "She's missing."

"Really? Well, there you go. That's pretty darn incriminating if you ask me."

"I don't know. She might just be blowing off steam somewhere. She got really ticked off about Lars's new will. Myrle said that Lars signed it only a few days before he died." Karl wiped his forehead with the back of his hand. He was worn out. He had a hound dog look to him. "After liquidating everything and paying the outstanding bills, Myrle was to divide the remainder of the money equally between Dot and Ed. There wasn't much left to divide, and—"

"That enraged Dot."

"Yeah. She had presumed that her dad was a rich man. Myrle said he'd tried to inform her otherwise—without compromising his client's confidentiality—but she didn't catch on. Or she didn't want to believe it. Whatever the case, when she learned how few assets her father had left, she went ballistic."

The windows rattled from a gust of wind, and despite the heat generated from the gas fireplace, the furnace rumbled to life. "Notwithstanding all of that," Karl went on to say, raising his voice to be heard over the noise, "I have trouble believing she killed Dickerson."

"Really?" I wanted to hear his opinion. After all, he was an actual law enforcement professional, whereas, I apparently was a mere murder suspect.

"I find it unlikely that she could have gone to Myrle's office right after committing such a grizzly act," he explained. "She couldn't have regained her composure that quickly."

My foot had wiggled its way out from under my afghan, and a small hole in the heel of my sock caught my attention. "If she killed him as soon as she got back to the house at six o'clock, she would have had close to an hour to compose herself before heading out again." I pulled at the threads until the hole grew to the size of a quarter. "Along the way, she could have dumped her bloody clothes and stopped at the liquor store for a bottle of liquid courage."

"The liquor store? Where did you hear about the liquor store?" His countenance changed as he put two and two together. "You listened in on Ed and me, didn't you?"

"Well, yeah, a little."

He shook his head. "I thought you told me earlier that you didn't believe Dot was capable of murder."

"I have trouble believing she killed her father. That's a little different." I stood because I was too antsy to sit any longer. "Although, at this point, I'd believe just about anything if it meant wrapping this up." My voice caught. "That is, as long as… ah… Grace and I don't end up in jail."

Karl rose and clutched my shoulders. "I doubt I'll have to arrest you and Grace."

"You don't sound very convincing."

He chuckled, though I found nothing funny about the situation. "Don't worry, Doris. We'll get to the bottom of this."

"How? I finally agreed with Grace that Dickerson most likely killed Lars, only to have Dickerson murdered too."

"He still could have killed Lars."

"Karl, that would indicate we've had multiple killers running around town. And that possibility freaks me out."

The corner of his mouth twitched. "Most everyone is capable of murder."

"Hey, if you're trying to make me feel better—and safer—you're really bad at it."

He drew me into a hug, his arms and his usual scent of pine trees and raw wood enveloping me. "Everything will be fine. Trust me."

I wasn't sure I could. Because of Rose, these murders needed to be solved as quickly as possible. There wasn't time for law enforcement to dot every "i" and cross every "t."

Chapter 19

Given that I was an ugly crier, I stepped out of Karl's embrace before any tears fell. He had to leave, so I could go to bed. I was exhausted.

Still, I wanted to know about his trip to Warren. What was so darn important there that he couldn't have come home as soon as Grace called him? If he had, my sister and I may not have been the ones to find Dickerson's body. Not that I blamed him for that, but…

"So, Karl," I said after deciding I had enough energy to ask one or two questions, "did you finish everything you needed to do in Warren?"

The narrowed his eyes. He knew what I was up to. Even so, he said, "I met with a couple administrators from the Duluth prison camp."

"And?" I leaned against the entry wall, praying it would support me. My bones were too weary to do so.

"Well, I suppose I can tell you. It's public record, available to anyone willing to take the time to look." Yet he vacillated. "It… umm… seems that Arne and Anders Olafson were prisoners in the Duluth prison at the same time as Lars."

"What?" Just like that, the flood gates opened, and adrenaline again swamped my system. "You've got to be kidding!"

"Olson's their real name. Arne and Anders Olson. They look about the same as they did in their prison pictures. Only older. And Anders has that scar." He drew his finger along his jaw, as if I might have needed reminding. Fat chance.

"They were in federal prison back then?" I repeated. "For what?"

"Fraud. One of the BCA agents got wind of something but didn't have time to follow up. That's why he asked me to check the prison records. I'm now waiting to hear where they went and what they did after their release." He looked directly at me. "And, like you suggested, we have to determine their connection to Dickerson."

He reached for the doorknob, only to drop his hand. "I almost forgot." Recovering his notebook from his breast pocket, he flipped through the pages. "Our cursory canvass of Dot's neighborhood yielded nothing. Either folks weren't around or they didn't see anything. So, I've got to ask again if you spotted any unusual vehicles or people when you first got there."

The question baffled me. He was well aware of my lack of car-related knowledge. Last year he'd been forced to perform some fancy footwork to fend off charges against me for grand theft auto and dognapping. "No one was outside, Karl. It's too cold. And Grace recognized all the vehicles."

He clicked his pen several times.

The sound rattled my nerves. Or my nerves may have been rattled already, and the clicking just exasperated the condition. No matter, I needed him to stop. So, to that end, I posed a question of my own, hoping he'd have to quit clicking to mull over his answer. "Have you obtained any useful fingerprints in either case?"

*Click. Click.* My plan didn't work. Unlike a lot of men, he could multi-task—think and click at the same time. "In the case of Lars's death, we're still looking for the murder weapon as well as his phone, wallet, and keys." *Click. Click.* "Hopefully, we'll get prints off one of them." *Click. Click.* "If they aren't at the bottom of the lake."

While his nervous habit of jingling his keys and coins irritated me at times, it was music to my ears compared to the pen click-ing.

"How about in the Dickerson case?" I asked. "Has anyone recovered fingerprints from Dot's place? Other than mine and Grace's?"

*Click. Click.* "It's too early. But we did find Dickerson's phone. And it wasn't hard to access. Like the rest of us old geezers, he kept his password on a slip of paper in his wallet." *Click. Click.*

"Anyway, there were no texts or emails of interest, but he did receive three calls around the time of his death. One from Ed about five-thirty. That's when he scheduled Dickerson's meeting with the BCA agents for tomorrow morning. The call lasted less than a minute." *Click. Click.* "The second one came from Gustaf around six-forty." *Click. Click.*

"Gustaf? I didn't realize he knew Dickerson."

"Neither did I. That's why I'll question him first thing in the morning."

My curiosity piqued. "And the third call?"

*Click. Click. Click.* "From Tweety, a few minutes after Gustaf's. But, like his call, hers went unanswered, and she didn't leave a message." *Click. Click.*

I couldn't take it anymore and grabbed the pen from his hand. "Have you talked to her?"

He snatched it right back. "Why do I always end up question-ing Tweety?"

I grinned. Tweety was the bane of his existence.

"It's not funny. She makes me crazy." He shoved the pen and notebook into his shirt pocket. "Plus, we can't find her."

"What?" I leaned forward and almost fell over. I had to get to bed. "You're kidding. You can't find Dot or Tweety?"

"Do I look like I'm kidding?" No, he looked like his dog had just died. "Now, I really have to go." He groped for the knob before his hand fell to his side again. Yep, he had the "Minnesota long goodbye" down pat. "You… ah… scared me tonight, Doris."

His voice had gone soft, causing a surge of heat to climb my neck. If the furnace had still been running, I would have had an excuse for the warmth I felt on my face. But it wasn't, so… "I was fine. Though it's nice of you to be concerned."

"Yeah, I'm concerned." He wiped an errant strand of hair from my cheek, wrapping it behind my ear. My face tingled, as did a few other body parts. The guy had magic fingers.

Clearly, he also had places to go and people to see because, without another word, he walked out the door. While, once more, I stood there like an unwitting member in the cast of *Groundhog Day*.

# Chapter 20

The sun wasn't up when Grace called and woke me from a dream involving Karl, me, and a spray can of whipped cream. I immediately assured myself that I wasn't responsible for what I dreamt. However, the fact that I couldn't rid my mind of the sexy images once I was awake was another matter altogether. One I'd have to consider some other time.

As I knuckled sleep from my eyes, Grace advised me to get down to the café right away because Tweety was a no-show.

Hanging up, I bid farewell to Fantasy Karl and crawled out of bed. I sifted through the heap of clothes on the floor until I found my cleanest dirty sweatshirt and jeans, threw them on, and brushed my teeth.

When I trudged through the back door of the café, the aroma of fried bacon and fresh coffee greeted me. Given I had forgotten my tennis shoes, I wiped my ankle boots on the doormat before tossing my jacket on the nearby chair. I headed to the sink, where I attempted to clean a smudge of toothpaste from my Hallock Bearcats sweatshirt. Having little success, I tossed the paper towel into the trash, snatched an apron from the cupboard, and wandered over to Grace.

When she noticed me, she ended her call and stuffed her cell phone into her rear pants' pocket. "You could have showered," she said, wrinkling her nose, "and worn clean clothes." Her visual critique of my appearance stalled at my sweatshirt, the toothpaste stain more noticeable now that a dark water mark encircled my entire left breast.

I tugged the apron over my head and tied it twice around my waist. The bib hid most of the problem area. "You said I had to get down here fast. And since Will was able to come right over to stay with Rose..."

"Did you even bother to look in a mirror?"

No, I hadn't. But realizing that wouldn't be a good response, I said, "Most of my clothes are in the laundry, which I had planned to finish this morning. Although, because of your emergency, I had no choice but to grab things off my flo–chair."

Grace, who seldom went anywhere looking less than photo ready, tsked as she plated a stack of pancakes and a side of bacon. "This is for Louise Gustafson."

"Is she still in town?" I accepted the plate, eyeing the bacon.

"Don't you dare eat that!"

"Jeez."

"Yeah," she said, like she hadn't just bitten my head off. "Gustaf lit out of here through the back door the second she came in the front. He almost knocked me over."

Her face turned grim, which confused me. The food on the plate looked... well... good enough to eat, as did everything on the grill. On top of that, I had arrived to help out. "So, what's bugging you?"

"I'm worried about Rose."

"Me too. So, we probably shouldn't mention that we're suspects in Dickerson's murder. She's too shaken up as it is."

"Karl wasn't really serious about that, was he?" She flipped a couple eggs and a patty of hashbrowns on the grill.

"I'm hoping it's just how law enforcement refer to anyone who comes across a murder victim. Even so, Rose didn't sleep well again last night. When I peeked in on her before I came down here, I found her blankets strewn across the floor. That's why I think we better be careful what we say to her."

"Right. Although she might hear from other folks about how these investigations have gone from bad to worse." She grabbed a plate from the shelf above her. "For instance, did you know that Dot's in the wind? And, like I already told you, Tweety's nowhere to be found either."

"Well, Tweety skips work all the time."

"Not the day after a murder, she doesn't."

"Grace, at the rate people have been dropping dead around here, it was only a matter of time."

With a groan, Grace shooed me toward the swinging doors that led to the dining room. "Go before Louise's food gets cold." She wagged her finger. "First, though, you might want to get rid of those mascara smudges. You look like a raccoon." She perused the bottom half of me, from my wrinkled jeans to my scuffed boots. "A raccoon that spent last night in a trash can."

Twisting my lips into a sneer, I spun away from her, licked my finger, and rubbed the area beneath my eyes. Normally, I wouldn't have done anything so disgusting while waitressing, but I felt kind of sorry for Gustaf. Therefore, I didn't care if I passed cooties on to his mean wife.

◎  ◎  ◎

In the dining room, I found the regulars sitting along the counter. Ole saluted me. And, as I grabbed the coffee pot, I saluted him in return. The corner-booth ladies huddled in their usual spot, their heads practically knocking against one another as they shared secrets in the morning sunlight. While Allie, waitress extraordinaire, scurried about, filling cups and delivering checks to patrons who clanged silverware against ceramic plates and exchanged theories about the latest murder.

Louise Gustafson sat alone in a booth along the far wall, her purple wool coat in a rumpled heap behind her back.

"Good morning, Louise."

She sized me up through pinprick eyes. "I didn't realize you worked here."

I set her plate in front of her. "When they need extra help. Always have."

She offered up a sniff, obviously unimpressed by my willingness to lend my sister a hand.

"Can I pour you some coffee?" I asked.

"My cup's already full, as you can plainly see."

For some reason, Louise had always intimidated me, most likely because of her family's stature in the community. That's probably why I often stammered when I spoke to her. "I... ah... guess I only asked about the coffee out of habit."

If wise I would have taken my leave at that point, but wisdom had never been my strong suit. Besides, I wanted to know the latest scuttlebutt about the murders and presumed Louise would be privy to it. She was a lot like her husband in that regard. "Anything else for you?" I asked, ransacking my brain for a segue from talk of food and drink to that of murder. Not surprisingly, I came up empty.

"No. Nothing more." The woman didn't even bother to lift her head.

"Louise, I'm... umm... sorry about you and Gustaf." I wasn't the least bit sorry. But, because I couldn't think of any other way to broach the subject of her and Gustaf's split, I had to lie in an effort to get her to open up.

"Why do you care about Gustaf and me?" A piece of pancake teetered on her lower lip before falling back onto her plate.

"Well... umm... you two are an institution around here."

She slurped her coffee. It sounded like water getting sucked down a drain. "Well, Gustaf should have considered that before sneaking around with his bastard son and Lars. He never expected me to find out about either. Although Dot was only too happy to inform me about Ed. And once she did, I had no trouble dis-covering that Gustaf had been palling around with Lars too." She set her cup down and licked her hairy upper lip. "See, Dot want-ed to do business with me."

"You mean you and Dot are friendly?" In my mind I replayed the scene in the church basement, where the two women had gone for each other's throat.

"Of course, we're not friendly! I can't stand her. She's Lars's daughter. But because she's just like him, she was hell-bent on in-heriting all his money. She didn't want her dead sister's kid to get so much as a dime." She cupped her hand alongside her mouth and lowered her voice. "Little did she know that Lars had already blown most of it." She cackled, exposing a row of coffee-stained teeth.

"At any rate," she added, "Dot tried to manipulate me into giving her a hand. To be exact, she asked me to speak with Lars's lawyer, Myrle Nygaard. He happens to be my second cousin's kid and owes me for getting him a job here in town after no firm in Fargo would hire him. See, he barely passed the bar exam on his third try." Over the end of her broad nose, she uttered, "His head's softer than a two-minute egg."

With a bite of pancakes, she continued, chewing between words. "Lars had mentioned to Dot that he was contemplating changing his will to include Ed, and she wanted me to get Myrle to dissuade him. In return, she promised to keep me apprised of the happenings around here, while I spent time with my mother in Alexandria."

"So, what happened?"

More cackling. "I didn't say a word to Myrle. I'm not doing Dot's bidding."

That didn't shock me. Although it may have explained some-thing. "Did Dot find out? Is that why she was so irate with you at the funeral?"

"Could be. I don't care. I only went there to serve that no-ac-count husband of mine. I wanted to see his face when I slapped him with divorce papers in front of everybody. But I barely escaped with my life. Dot's a lunatic! I've already prepared notes for Myrle, so he can draft a complaint against her for assault."

With that, she picked up her fork and stabbed her pancake with such relish that I stepped back, out of striking distance.

◎ ◎ ◎

The bells on the door jingled as Karl entered the café, crisp air sneaking in behind him. He slid into the booth one down from Louise.

While eager to ask him about a number of things, I hesitated. After all, Grace had more or less accused me of falling from the ugly tree that morning and hitting every branch on the way down. Then, again, why did I give a hoot what Grace—or Karl— thought? At almost sixty-two, I was done seeking the approval of others regarding my appearance. That included Karl, despite what my dreams may have indicated.

With coffee pot in hand and the aroma of the rich brew making my nostrils twitch with pleasure, I weaved around tables until I reached the sheriff's booth. "Are Grace and I still under suspicion in Dickerson's death?" No point in beating around the bush.

"You're off the hook." He obviously saw no need to waste words either. "I explained to the BCA guys that you're nosy and—"

"I am not nosy."

"Whatever." He sipped the coffee I poured him. "I told them how you often get caught up in things that aren't any of your business. But you're no killer."

"Well, by golly, Sheriff. That was mighty nice of you. Yes, sir-ee."

Like everyone else as of late, Karl shrugged off my sarcasm.

"I also indicated that you actually assisted in apprehending a criminal a couple months back." He smiled, like that last comment should appease me. "Still, if I were you, I'd keep my distance. Those BCA guys aren't like me. They can get cranky when folks interfere with their work."

I wasn't about to let him see my relief. Granted, I doubted that he had really suspected me of murder. Yet he had made me a topic of conversation with those BCA agents, which I found a bit humiliating.

Nevertheless, I set aside my feelings, deciding that I'd be best served by not belaboring that point. "So," I said, instead, "Tweety never showed up for work this morning. Do you happen to know anything about that?"

He dropped his head to his chest. "Didn't you hear what I just said about staying out of police business?"

"I'm not asking about police business, per se. I merely want to find out if you have any news on Tweety, Grace's waitress, whose absence has necessitated my waitressing here, which is one of my least favorite activities."

While I rambled, he zeroed in on the right side of my face. And, when I finally stopped for a breath, he said, "Doris, you have a smudge across your cheek." He pointed, as if I might have forgotten where my cheek was located. "You must have missed it while washing up this morning."

"As I said, Tweety's missing." I wasn't about to discuss my hygiene habits, such as they were, with him of all people. "Now, I don't really care where she is, but Grace does."

He lowered his eyes. I sensed he had to or he'd laugh at the sight of me pivoting until I stood in profile so he couldn't stare at my dirty cheek. Okay, what he thought of me might have mattered a little.

"We picked up Tweety early this morning for questioning in Dickerson's death." He spoke to the table. "She claimed she'd been out all night with some guy. But we've been unable to confirm that. So, until we do, she'll remain a guest of the county. You can let Grace know."

I would. Let Grace know, that is. But, first, I had a few questions.

Before I got a chance to ask them, Louise bruised the air with her napkin. "Sheriff! Oh, Sheriff! How are your investigations coming along?" She had cranked up her volume awfully high considering Karl was only five feet away. "It's downright uncivilized to have two more murders in our little town. It may cause folks to think twice about whether the job of sheriff is too much for you."

Karl's neck mottled red. "We've interviewed a number of people and followed up on several leads." He had upped his volume too. He must have decided to satisfy everyone's curiosity at once. "But we haven't arrested anyone."

"Then," Louise said, "you suspect that one person killed both people?"

"I didn't say that." He set his jaw.

"So... we've had multiple killers on the loose for the last few months?"

The place began to buzz like a hive full of bees.

"Mrs. Gustafson," Karl growled, prompting all the bees to shut their little traps, "I'm not at liberty to discuss ongoing investigations. Now, if you'll excuse me... " He snatched a menu from behind the napkin dispenser on the table and reviewed it in spite of knowing it by heart.

"Well, Sheriff... " Louise flung her arms wide. "We're all taxpayers here, so we pay your salary. In other words, you're accountable to us, don't ya know."

Karl dropped his menu and clutched the edge of the table until the tips of his thumbs turned white. "Rest assured I'll brief you as soon as I have something to say."

Louise proceeded toward the door, stopping alongside the sheriff. "Have you interrogated Gustaf?" Her voice remained loud enough for all to hear, if so inclined. Most were.

Karl rocked back, like Louise was an oddity that required scrutiny through a wider lens. "What exactly are you asking? If your husband's a suspect in these murders?"

"Oh, I'm not sure Gustaf even knew that Dirk Dickerson character. But you'll want to add him to your list of suspects in Lars Carlson's death." She let Karl mull that over. "It's why I asked if you were leaning toward one murderer or two. You see, as of late, Gustaf spent considerable time with Lars, even though he hated him, as everyone knew. So, you'd be wise to find out where Gustaf was when Lars got killed."

"What about you, Mrs. Gustafson?" Karl clearly wanted to get under Louise's skin. I could see it in his eyes. "Where were you this past Saturday afternoon and evening?"

She huffed as if to say, *How dare you?* But when Karl refused to blink, she replied, "Well, if you must know, I was with my mother in Alexandria. She had a difficult time managing on her own last week. I had to stay by her side."

"Oh? When did you drive up here?"

She glared. The sheriff glared back. And my eyes volleyed between them.

"Monday," she said after several moments. "I got a motel room in Grafton. On Tuesday morning, I saw my lawyer. And, in the afternoon, I served Gustaf with divorce papers, as you well know. Now, if you'll excuse me…"

## Chapter 21

"What did you make of that?" I asked Karl after Louise Gustafson strutted out the front door of the café, all eyes on her, most likely to ensure that she really left.

"Well, she definitely wants to cause trouble for Gustaf. But, as she mentioned, Gustaf didn't know Dickerson."

"Yet he phoned him just before the man got murdered."

"Gustaf was drunk. He doesn't remember placing the call."

"How convenient." Of course, I didn't really believe that Gustaf had killed Dirk Dickerson. He was a lot of things—obnoxious, self-absorbed, and as useless as a screen door in a canoe—but he was no more a killer than I was. Still, "being too drunk to remember" was a poor alibi. And it bugged me that Karl sounded fine with it.

"What about when Lars died?" I asked. "What was Gustaf up to then?"

Karl sighed with impatience.

"It's a simple question." I was growing perturbed. "But, if you don't want to answer it, fine. I'll ask Gustaf directly."

The sheriff slumped in his seat. "He was in his fish house, getting drunk."

That didn't surprise me. Gustaf was still hungover when I saw him the following afternoon, when Lars's body was pulled from the lake. "And?"

"And, that's it. After spotting Etta with Lars through the window of the café on Saturday morning, Gustaf got it in his head that she planned to drop him and go back to Lars."

With the coffee pot growing heavy, I set it on the table. "Which is exactly what she wanted him to think."

"But rather than demanding a divorce from Louise, he drove out to his Ice Castle and drank himself into a stupor. Ed found him there around seven-thirty that night."

"How did Ed know he was there?"

"He phoned him repeatedly. And when Gustaf didn't pick up, he stopped by his house, then headed to the lake."

"Which means, for most of the day that Lars got murdered, Gustaf was on his own, not communicating with anyone."

An edge crept into his voice. "What's your point?"

I leaned in. "In the Dickerson case, you considered me a suspect because I happened upon the body."

"Being you found him, we had to clear—"

"Yet you seem fine with the fact that Gustaf doesn't have much of an alibi for when Lars got killed. And he hated the man."

Karl pinched the bridge of his nose. "Oh, I get it. You're ticked off."

My teeth clinched. "Well, I'm certainly not thrilled that I was the focus of a discussion down at the station. That a bunch of men sat around, debating whether or not I was trustworthy."

"Doris, we had to look at your connections to—"

"That's what I mean! It doesn't sound as if you and your law-enforcement buddies reviewed Gustaf's connections to either of the deceased men. It's like you didn't see the need because he's one of the guys."

"Oh, come on."

"Did you even bother to check his phone? See how many calls Ed made to him? Or, for that matter, did you examine Ed's phone? See if he really placed those calls?"

"Now you suspect Ed of killing Lars, his own grandfather? Or are you merely suggesting that he covered for Gustaf?" Karl clamped his lips together until they formed a thin white line. "You were at the lake when Ed pulled Lars from the water. You saw how upset he was. How upset he's been ever since."

He was right. Ed seemed to be taking his grandfather's death hard. Even so, I was frustrated by the entire situation and itching for a fight. And Karl happened to be available, so… "That's beside the point. If Gustaf and Ed had been any other people, you would have demanded to see their phones right away."

He glowered, his eyes so black that if I had been an actual criminal, I would have wet my pants. "As a matter of fact," he said with a large serving of attitude, "I did follow up with Gustaf this morning at the station."

"And?"

He mumbled.

"What was that?"

He fingered the rim of his cup. "I had to take a call. And when I got back, he was gone."

◎ ◎ ◎

I placed Karl's order on the table in front of him. "Two eggs over easy, hashbrowns, wheat toast."

"Thanks." He snipped off the end of the word, confirming that he was still miffed with me, which was fine. I wasn't thrilled with him either.

As I refilled his coffee cup, he lifted his head, saw my clean-scrubbed face, and his crow's feet crinkled.

"So I washed. So what?" Both my tone and expression warned him not to tease me.

And he didn't, choosing, instead, to focus on his food.

"Hey," I said after staring at the top of his head until he was done eating one of his eggs and a slice of toast, "why are we even discussing Gustaf and Ed or Louise?" Although crabby and contrary, I didn't want to argue with Karl. At least not anymore. He was a good cop and had been working pretty much day and night to clear these cases. "Didn't we already establish that Dickerson likely killed Lars, and Dot killed Dickerson?"

He spoke around the food in his mouth. "Those are assumptions. We need to look at the facts. Follow the evidence." He swallowed. "That's why we're still tracking down leads and questioning people."

That's also why the folks in town had gotten edgy, complaining that Karl and his BCA cronies were dragging their feet. "Who are you questioning now?" I'm certain I came across as apathetic, and that's exactly what I intended.

Karl dropped his fork on his plate with a clank. "What's gotten into you, Doris?"

I plopped down on the seat across from him. "I want this ordeal over. For Rose's sake. And my own." My voice was hushed yet stern. "But every time I think the end is in sight, you guys go and question another person or examine another piece of evidence. It mixes me up. And it's making me crazy!"

He opened his mouth, no doubt ready to say that I was already crazy or some such thing, but I glared, convincing him to remain silent. Then, my eyes got misty, and my bottom lip trembled.

He had no clue what to do in response to me becoming emotional. "Well... ah... I suppose it wouldn't hurt to tell you that the BCA agents drove down to Alexandria yesterday to interview Louise." Yep, he assumed that giving me a little inside information would make me feel better.

I'm ashamed to say that he was right. "But Louise was up here. And she's still in town."

"They didn't know that."

My mood plummeted again. "Which means they wasted an entire day! And that's what I'm talking about, Karl. It feels like you guys are just flitting from—"

"Doris, we do not flit. And it wasn't a waste. No one wanted

180

to tip Louise off. That's why they went unannounced. And even though she wasn't there, they had an informative conversation with her mother and some of the neighbors." He checked his wristwatch. Being over sixty, he still wore one. "And, in a few minutes, Louise will provide a sworn statement down at the station, possibly committing perjury in the process."

"How so?" Spotting Allie, I slouched farther down in my seat.

Karl glimpsed across his shoulder, saw who I was hiding from, and shook his head. "Well, I really shouldn't say. But being our office leaks like a sieve, you'll find out soon enough anyways." He bent over the table and whispered, "Like Louise, her mother claimed that the two of them were together in Alexandria until Monday morning. But a couple neighbors insisted that Louise left town several days before then."

"Why would Louise and her mother lie about that?"

He leaned back, picked up his cup, and replied over the rim, "That's what we need to find out."

Hmm. Karl and his colleagues had now added Louise's mother to their list of persons of interest. The woman was older than Rose, for God's sake. While I wanted to be supportive of law enforcement, I returned to the kitchen exasperated.

⊙ ⊙ ⊙

Approaching Karl again a little while later, I handed him the bill for his breakfast. "Grace wants to know if you'd let Tweety out on work release. And, trust me, she's not kidding. She says she needs the help."

He sipped the last of his coffee before indicating with his thumb and forefinger that he'd appreciate a speck more. "Tell her that Tweety will be out shortly. I just got a call. Her alibi checked out. Besides, no one really believed she killed anyone. Although it does seem as if every time a guy of dubious character comes to town, she gets mixed up with him, and I'm left to scare her straight."

I placed the pot on the table with a smile. "So, you're telling me that I won't have to work for her anymore after today? At least for a while?"

"Doris, with all due respect, you haven't done a lick of work since I came in." He gestured toward Allie. "She, on the other hand, has run herself ragged."

I took a quick look in Allie's direction. Sure enough, she caught me in her sights. She looked more than a little peeved, prompting me to sit down opposite Karl and scoot over until she was out of view.

Karl acted as if he might say something about me sitting down on the job. But, in the end, he decided against it. Smart decision considering my present mood. "Anyway, that call I just got?" he said, instead. "I was also told that Dot got picked up a while ago by the highway patrol. They brought her into the station—for drunk driving."

"What?"

"From the sound of it, she's been doing nothing but drinking since last night. But she passed out before telling us anything of consequence. So, now, we have to wait for her to sober up."

"Dot was driving drunk? I can't believe it."

"Neither can anyone else. Well, no one except Ed. He's the one who called. He's also pretty sure he smelled alcohol on her breath when she arrived at the law office last night."

"Karl, I really doubt that Ed could distinguish the smell of booze from that of mouthwash or breath mints."

"Oh, come on, Doris. Ease up on him. He's a good kid. He's had more tough breaks than anyone deserves. Granted, he's not the best cop, but he'll get better. Just like your daughter did."

That hurt. I didn't appreciate him comparing Ed to Erin. But what could I say? She had done some dumb stuff on the job. Heck, she was currently on probation. Nevertheless, as her mother, I had to stand up for her.

Before I got the chance, though, Gustaf distracted me.

He stood outside the café's glass entry door in profile, as if that way no one would see him. Never mind his inner tube belly protruding well beyond the narrow door trim.

"Gustaf must want to make sure that Louise is gone." I motioned toward the entrance.

Karl barely glanced over his shoulder. "He's meeting me. Contrary to what you said, I had every intention of questioning him more about his whereabouts last Saturday as well as the call he placed to Dickerson just before the guy died."

The bells on the door jingled when Gustaf lumbered in. Heading our way, his footfalls sounded like rolling thunder. If it had been summer, all the farmers in the place would have hurried over to the windows to examine the sky.

# Chapter 22

"Hey, Gustaf!" I vacated my spot on the bench seat. "Coffee?" Admittedly, I felt embarrassed for criticizing Karl for what I had erroneously claimed was his lack of interest in getting the truth out of Gustaf. Still, I wasn't embarrassed enough to return to the kitchen and miss out on whatever the two of them had to say.

"Just a half cup, Doris. I'm only staying a minute." Gustaf flipped his thumb in Karl's direction. "Then, he's either hauling me off to jail, or I'm heading back to the bank."

"Give it a rest," Karl growled. "It's not like I'm investigating these cases alone. The BCA guys also have a say in how we proceed. And I can assure you that they'd be furious if I gave you a pass just because we're friends." He eyed me sideways. That admonishment was meant for me too.

Gustaf tossed his jacket onto the bench seat before sliding in after it.

I nudged his shoulder. "Move over."

He and Karl creased their foreheads so hard that they looked like they'd have to screw their hats on going forward.

"What?" I emulated them. "I'm not leaving. Besides, Gustaf would tell me everything later anyhow. So think of it as me merely streamlining the process."

Knowing I was right, Gustaf shuffled over, and I sat down, careful not to extend my scrutiny beyond our booth for fear of Allie.

"Okay, Gustaf," Karl began with a dismissive glimpse my way, "what did you do after you spotted Etta and Lars in the window of the café on Saturday morning?"

"I already told you. I got to thinking that she might go back to the buzzard, so I went out to my Ice Castle and got drunk."

I raised my index finger. "You told me that you and Etta were just friends. If that's true, why would you care if she reconciled with Lars?"

Gustaf scowled, and Karl shot me a look that said, *be quiet or leave.* He apparently wanted to conduct his own interview. Who knew?

"That was around ten-thirty in the morning," Karl said as a matter of fact. "Kind of early in the day to start drinking, eh?"

"What can I say?"

The café was busy and noisy. No one could hear Gustaf or Karl. Even so, they kept their voices low.

"What did you take out there to eat?" the sheriff asked.

"Huh?" Gustaf blinked. "Umm… nothing."

"Oh, come on. I've known you since we were kids. There's no way you spent the entire day in your fish house without eating."

"I… ah… already had some stuff out there."

"No, you didn't. Not in the mini-fridge or the cupboards. I checked the place out on Sunday, after we pulled Lars from the lake."

"You what?" Gustaf attempted to sound incensed, although, like always, it came across as whining.

"Just tell me about the food," Karl said.

Gustaf wrestled a hanky from his pants' pocket and wiped sweat off his forehead. "Before I left Hallock, I… umm… picked up a few snacks at Cenex."

"I'm not buying that either." Karl shook his head. "You can't go eight hours without a hot meal."

"I… ah… was too distressed to eat much."

"Give me a break. You do some of your best eating when you're distressed."

Gustaf swiped at the sweat dribbling down his temples.

"Listen here." Karl reached across the table and grabbed Gustaf's mitt of a hand. "You already lied to me about Lars spending time with you out at Lake Bronson. Don't try it again, or I'll run you in, friend or not. Now, what really happened after you spotted Etta with Lars in the café?"

Gustaf let all the air out of his lungs. "I already told you."

"That's it." Karl went to stand.

But Gustaf motioned him back down. "Fine! Someone will probably blab to you anyways." He flashed me the stink eye. "I didn't go to Lake Bronson right away. I waited until Etta and Lars left the café, then I followed them." He swallowed hard, both of his chins getting involved. "Etta drove Lars back to his apartment. I parked down the street. And, after she left, I went inside and confronted him."

"Oh?" The unusual expression on Karl's face portrayed his surprise. "And how did that go?"

I pulled a few napkins from the table dispenser and handed them to Gustaf. Right away, he put them to good use.

"We didn't talk long. He had to get ready for the shuttle to Thief River." After rubbing the top of his head with the napkins, Gustaf wiped the back of his neck. For a second, I thought he might lift his arms and wipe his pits too. "I asked what they were doing together." Thankfully, he kept his arms to his sides. "Lars laughed. He could see how upset I was, and he got a kick out of that. He was such an ass."

When neither Karl nor I commented, Gustaf went on. "He wanted to know how much I'd pay him to stay away from Etta. I told him I'd already agreed to give Etta the money he had borrowed but refused to repay." He wadded his soggy napkins and tossed the wet ball onto the table, only a few inches from me.

Because I preferred to maintain a healthy distance from all things Gustaf, I scooted farther down the bench, stopping only when my right butt cheek spilled into the aisle.

"He called me a sucker." Gustaf's face had gone red. "I wanted to slug him. But I didn't. I didn't kill him either. I just left. I decided that if Etta preferred that snake in the grass to me, fine."

Karl didn't appear happy. He set his jaw, and his lips barely moved when he asked, "Why'd you lie to me?"

"I didn't lie exactly." Gustaf squirmed, the vinyl seat answering with a series of burps. "After I left Lars's place, I came here and ate lunch. The special was Crescent Roll Taco Bake. I was so shaken up that I ate two orders of the stuff. Afterwards, I picked up a bottle of whiskey at the liquor store and drove out to the lake."

"Again, why didn't you tell me that initially?"

Gustaf stared at the sheriff as if he couldn't believe his ears. "Well, duh. I didn't want you to suspect me of killing Lars. I hated him. Everyone knew that. And I hated him even more after he tried to get close to Ed."

Gustaf waffled. "Not... ah... that I was jealous or anything. I just didn't like how he treated the kid." He appeared to be choosing his words carefully. Given the look on Karl's face, I couldn't blame him. "One day he'd thank him for finding us. The next, he'd ask him for money." His gaze swung between Karl and me. "You didn't know that, did you?"

I couldn't speak for the sheriff, but I certainly had no idea. And, once more, I wondered how Rose could have allowed herself to get involved with such a horrible man.

As I pondered that, Gustaf and Karl drank their coffee, while Ole shared one of his pitiful jokes with the guys up at the counter. Naturally, his buddies razzed him loud and long when he got done.

As a result, Gustaf had to speak up when he told Karl and me, "Lars actually said that Ed owed him financially for supporting his mother over the years." He shook his head, and a drop of sweat hit my cheek. I gagged a little and wiped it away. But that's all I did. I couldn't move any farther away from the guy, or I'd fall on the floor. And I wasn't about to go anywhere.

"When I heard that," Gustaf added, his voice gruff, "I got pissed off because Lars never gave Janice a dime. For years my dad and Louise's family supported Janice and the baby. The first baby. My daughter."

Karl leaned across the table. "Gustaf, I understand why your family provided Janice with money. But why would Louise's family contribute to the cause?"

"Her father wanted Louise and me to get hitched. But, like I already told Doris," he continued, glancing my way, "given that Louise couldn't have kids, she wasn't crazy about Janice and the baby living around here. So, being her father didn't want to jeopardize any future business opportunities with my old man, he was more than willing to chip in to keep Janice far away and Louise happy."

Gustaf's face remained a deep, angry red. "Lars, on the other hand, never offered up a cent in support of Janice. His own daughter." He hesitated. "The fact is, my dad and Louise's father paid Lars too."

Karl grunted. "Why on earth would they give Lars money?"

At the counter, Ole told another joke, followed by more noisy laughter and groans.

Gustaf took the opportunity to retrieve the napkin wad from the table and wipe a sweat ball from the tip of his nose. Again, I gagged. "Well, at first," he then said, "they gave the support money to Lars to pass on to Janice. But after I discovered that none of it ever made it to her, I told Dad he'd have to pay her directly."

His eyes darted from Karl to me and back again. "When Lars found out, he blew a gasket. He warned my old man. Told him that if he didn't keep getting checks too, he'd drag Janice and the baby back home, where everybody would see them all the time."

189

Once again, Gustaf appeared to think twice before proceeding. "I suppose you should know," he eventually said, "I mentioned all of this to Ed. And he got furious. Said he was gonna track Lars down."

"When was that?" Karl wanted to know.

"Oh..." Gustaf halfway raised his arms, exposing basketball-sized sweat stains. "Several days ago."

◎   ◎   ◎

I caught a glimpse of Allie when she whizzed past our booth. She looked busier than a moth in a mitten, as Rose would say. For a second, I considered getting up and giving her a hand. But when Karl began a new line of inquiry, I decided to stay put next to Gustaf.

"Gustaf," the sheriff said, "did you see anyone out on the lake on Saturday?"

"You mean anyone other than Ed?"

"I mean anyone."

"No, I don't think so. I stayed indoors. I'm sure most folks did. It was cold." He appeared to think about that. "Although, being it was Saturday, there were a lot of folks out there. At least I saw a heck of a lot of vehicles."

Gustaf drank more coffee, and when he set his cup on the table, he pointed a finger at Karl. "Hold on."

I hadn't eaten all day, and I must have been starving because, in that moment, Gustaf's finger resembled one of the corn dogs served at the Minnesota State Fair. I had to blink repeatedly to rid myself of the image.

"I did see someone" Gustaf said. "At least I think I did."

"What do you mean?" That was Karl.

"Well, ah, just after dark, I went out to my vehicle to grab a couple rolls of toilet paper. The Ice Castle was fresh out, but I always keep a spare roll or two in my SUV." He waited, as if he expected us to compliment him on his preparedness, like he was some kind of overgrown boy scout.

When we didn't, he continued. "I took my Lumen flashlight with me—the high-powered one." He smiled, clearly proud of himself regardless of what we thought. "Anyways, after I got the toilet paper and closed the hatch on my SUV, I caught sight of movement in the brush along the shoreline a ways down from me. A person, I—"

Karl interrupted. "Man or woman?"

"I dunno."

"What were they doing?"

"I dunno that either. And since I couldn't understand why anyone would be out there, among all those weeds, I chalked it up to me being three sheets to the wind and went back inside. I didn't give it a second thought until just now."

"Interesting." Karl wiped his hand down his face.

"You don't believe me?"

"I don't know what to believe. I suppose we can take a ride out there and see what we can find."

As Karl grabbed his jacket from beside him, his cell phone rang. He dug the phone out of his pocket and grunted "uh-huh" into it twice before disconnecting. "I have to go back to the station. Why don't you follow me, Gustaf? We need to examine your vehicle." He pulled his jacket on. "You don't mind, do you? Then, after I finish up what I have to do, we'll head out to the lake."

"Why do you wanna look at my car?" Gustaf's whine had mushroomed into a full-blown whimper.

"Because I can't trust a word you say without verifying it. You lie too much."

"What are you implying, Karl? That I killed Lars?" Gustaf's face had turned burgundy, a color I'd never seen on a face. "Then, what? I threw him in the back of my SUV, drove around the lake, and dumped him in some open water before returning to do some more fishing and drinking? Is that what you think of me?"

Spittle flew. Thankfully, none of it landed near me. "Well, I don't know if I can do that, Karl—I mean, Sheriff. I don't think you can examine my vehicle without a court order."

"Really?" Karl frowned. "You're going to make this difficult?"

"Umm… well… no." Gustaf must have grasped the futility of arguing. "It's just that I don't feel so good all of a sudden."

"What's that got to do with anything?"

"Karl… " I couldn't keep quiet any longer. "I'd be careful if I were you. The last time Gustaf insisted he didn't feel good, he proceeded to puke all over the inside of my car."

# Chapter 23

About fifteen minutes later, when Gustaf felt like his old self again, he and I drove to Lake Bronson in his vehicle. He was determined to see if any evidence existed to support what he thought he had seen on Saturday night. Considering the sheriff's mood, Gustaf worried that if he couldn't confirm his story, he'd get thrown in jail for sending law enforcement "on a wild goose chase."

I had volunteered to go with him because I was determined to get some answers of my own. While Karl and his buddies looked at this, that, and the other, Rose was at her wits' end.

I also tagged along because Grace didn't trust Gustaf to keep from doing something stupid if left to his own devices. According to her, Gustaf was a doofus, but he was our doofus. As such, we were obliged to watch out for him. Especially now that Louise and Etta were out of the picture.

On top of that, Grace figured it might be best if I left the restaurant for a while. Allie had complained to her that as a waitress, at least on that day, I'd been as worthless as the gum on the bottom of her shoe.

When Gustaf and I approached the area by the lake where he had purportedly seen someone milling about in the snowy brush on the night of Lars's death, we spotted one of the sheriff's SUVs parked along the side of the road.

"Karl beat us out here?" Gustaf wondered out loud. "Didn't he have to get back to the office?"

"He did. What's more, you never mentioned exactly where you planned to take him."

"I didn't, did I?" He looked at me. "Odd, huh?"

"Yeah. Odd."

Gustaf slowed until I warned him off. "Don't park here." I cast my eyes around our surroundings: flat and ruddy snow-swept fields, wire cattle fences, and bare trees. Farther down the road a plowed driveway about a quarter-mile long led to a farm site. "Park over there. Along that drive." I considered the location of the patrol car. "Hopefully, we can still see what's happening."

With one eye on the road, Gustaf reached into the back seat. "Lately I've had the feeling that someone's been following me, so I put these in here just in case." He handed me a pair of binoculars.

"Are we being followed now?" I craned my neck but spotted nothing but a half-dozen crows, their caws sounding through the bare trees.

He let up on the accelerator as he neared the approach. "I haven't sensed anything since I was out with Etta the other night."

Now that he had invoked Etta's name, I couldn't avoid addressing the subject of their relationship. "Gustaf, I'm sorry about what happened with her." While unsure how I truly felt, the down-and-out look on his face indicated that he was heartbroken.

He turned the car around and backed onto the gravel drive before stopping next to a metal mailbox riddled with bullet holes. He shifted the car into park. "Her phoning Louise on the sly to blab about us seeing each other was a rotten thing to do. True, I haven't always been honest with Louise, but I really wanted things to be different with Etta."

I got the impression he meant it, although... "Wait a second, Gustaf. You say you wanted a more honest relationship with Etta, yet you expected her to deceive Louise?"

"Yeah, well… "

"You must have realized that she was after more than a supper companion." In my mind's eye, I saw myself climbing onto my high horse. "Even so, you had no intention of divorcing your wife. So you weren't honest with Etta either."

He took a turn with the binoculars. "For Pete's sake, I'm sixty-two, and Etta's seventy-five. That's a huge age difference. What's the point of us getting married?"

"I happen to agree. But you didn't make your feelings clear to her."

With the binoculars still pressed against his eyes, he stumbled over his words. "Well… umm… wouldn't she have realized it on her own after a while?"

"I don't know, but she obviously wanted you to fish or cut bait and decided a phone call to your wife might push you to do one or the other."

"Well, I'll be."

"Huh?" I gawked at him, astonished. "Seriously? You're only now realizing why she did what she did?"

"No. No. I'm not talking about that." He handed me the binoculars. "Look who's headed to the patrol car."

I pushed forward in my seat and leaned across Gustaf. He unzipped his jacket, and the odor of sweat permeated the air.

Refocusing the binoculars, I kept my inhales to a minimum. "Well, I'll be darned. That's not Karl, it's Ed. What's he doing out here?"

"I don't know." Gustaf shifted his SUV into gear. "Let's go find out."

"No!" I tracked Ed as he crossed the highway, seemingly unaware of our presence. "He has something in his hands." I lowered the spy glasses. "Are you sure you didn't mention anything to him about what you might have seen out here?"

"Doris, like I said, I didn't recall any of it until earlier today." He relieved me of the binoculars and pressed them to his face. "He's put whatever he had in his hands into a plastic bag. Now can we go?"

"No!" I grabbed the binoculars, raised them to my eyes, and watched Ed ease himself behind the wheel of his vehicle.

"Doris, that might be an evidence bag. And whatever he stuck in it could prove I wasn't seeing things."

"In which case, we'll find out soon enough. In the meantime, I'd like to ask Karl how he knew to send his deputy to this exact location."

◎　◎　◎

An hour later, I walked into the sheriff's office at the court-house with lunch. Grace had a contract to provide "prisoner meals," although no one usually spent much time in the holding cells. On the rare occasion when one of the cells was occupied during mealtime, Tweety jumped at the chance to make the de-liveries. Today that task had fallen to me.

"Hi!" I raised my chin to greet the only deputy in the bullpen, where a half dozen utilitarian desks lined the walls. I didn't rec-ognize the guy, but that may have been because he appeared to be about twelve years old. Then, again, over the past few years, most folks around town looked too young to do their jobs.

"I'm here to deliver lunch." I raised my Styrofoam cooler. "Can I go on back?" The fluorescent lights replied with a hum, but the deputy only nodded as he hurried about, dropping files onto desks already piled high with paper.

The corridor leading to the holding cells smelled like the ath-letic bags my kids left around the house when they were young. Ode to jock straps and sports' bras. I passed the first cell. Empty except for a cot, a thin mattress, and a green surplus blanket. Next to the cot stood an aluminum sink and toilet combination.

Not a great setup, but after the facilities I had used in Will's fish house, I envied it.

In the second cell, Dot sat on her cot, legs crossed and head against the beige cement-block wall behind her. She appeared to be asleep. Her glasses rested on top of her head, in the rat nest that was her hair.

"I brought you lunch."

Without moving, she opened her eyes, which were red where they should have been white, and smacked her lips. "I'm not hungry." She spoke in the shaky voice of someone with a horrific hangover.

I gestured toward the empty cell. "Your jail mate's gone?"

"You mean Tweety? Yeah."

Perfect. I placed the cooler on the concrete floor and leaned my forehead on the bars of her cell. "Dot, what happened?"

Her own head remained against the wall. She probably couldn't have raised it if she had wanted. "Why should I tell you?"

"Because I don't get it. You drinking? Then, driving drunk?"

A tear escaped her eye and trekked down her cheek, the light catching it. "I was such a fool. I assumed he liked me. Maybe even loved me." No need for her to identify the cause of that tear.

"How'd you realize he didn't?"

She picked up the bottle of water lying next to her and twisted the cap on and off. "When I got back from the store on Saturday, ready to make my special supper, Dirk told me that Dad had called to ask what kind of wine to bring. He also said he—Dirk— had to drop by a potential investor's house. He asked to borrow my car. Said his wasn't working right, and he didn't want to risk breaking down on some country road and missing Dad's visit."

"He couldn't see the investors the next day?"

"They were headed to Arizona the following morning and wouldn't be back until spring. So it was a now-or-never kind of thing." For some reason, she tossed her head from side to side but abruptly stopped. It must have hurt something awful. "The whole thing felt off. Even so, I gave him my keys."

She sipped from her bottle. "After he left, I checked my phone and discovered that Dad hadn't called Dirk. Dirk had called Dad. So I phoned Dad, but he didn't answer. That's when I decided to walk over to his place. Among other things, I wanted to find out what he and Dirk had really talked about on the phone. The wine story didn't ring true."

"Huh? At Cenex, you acted like it—"

"Yeah, well, I lied."

"You also told me that you didn't go anywhere once you got home from the store that afternoon."

"So I lied twice." She didn't seem the least bit bothered by it.

"Why?"

"Why do you think? I didn't want anyone suspecting me of killing my dad. See, we didn't always get along. But I never would have murdered him." She stopped for a beat. "Anyways, I went to Dad's apartment but—"

"When did you get there?"

She cradled her head in her hands and peered through her fingers. "About five-thirty. Why?"

"No reason." It wasn't my place to inform her that a tenant had seen her car turn into the parking lot at five-fifteen. If she was being truthful with me, Dirk Dickerson had been behind the wheel.

"Even though Dad's car was there—it's hard to miss his red Caddie—he didn't answer his door. That's why I assumed he was with Rose." She lifted a shoulder as if to say, *It was an honest mistake.* "In any event, I walked back home and started supper, still assuming he'd arrive on time."

"Did you happen to recognize any of the other cars in the parking lot at your dad's place?" If Dot's SUV had been parked anywhere near her father's vehicle, she would have noticed it. Granted, I had a tendency to confuse cars, but Dot wasn't me. What's more, she had those hard-to-miss fuzzy dice hanging from her rear-view mirror.

"No, I didn't. Why?"

"No reason." By that time, her dad had obviously left in her SUV, Dirk Dickerson doing the driving. She must have just missed them. "How about while walking home? Did you see any familiar vehicles then?"

"It was dark, Doris. I only saw headlights."

She dropped her head against the wall, and it landed with a thud. She winced. "Dirk got back to my place around seven-thirty. I demanded that he tell me where he'd been, but he refused. Then, on Sunday night, when law enforcement began questioning people, he asked me to lie and say he had never left the house."

"Didn't that make you wonder?"

She turned her bloodshot eyes on me. "Of course, it did. But he claimed that if he disclosed the names of the investors, they'd back out of the deal. See, they didn't want anyone to know what they had planned until they had all their financing in order."

With a shiver, she pulled the scratchy-looking green blanket over her lap. "He also argued that being a stranger in town, he'd automatically become a prime suspect." Her voice grew haunting. "Then, he said he had fallen for me. Said he only needed a little more seed money and his dirt company would become a reality—a reality he wanted to share with me." She closed her eyes. "I was such a fool."

It didn't seem appropriate to agree with her, even though the catty part of me wanted to do just that. "Have you reported any of this to Karl?"

Her eyes snapped open. "Well, of course, I have. You don't think I'd only confide in you, do you?"

I refrained from answering. After all, she was right. We weren't close. Not in the least.

"The sheriff stopped in here an hour ago. I had just woken up. I told him everything."

"So, why repeat it all to me?" Not that I minded, but it did seem odd.

"I guess I needed to say it out loud again to get it straight in my head." She massaged her temples. "I'm not thinking clearly." More massaging. "Anyway, you happened to be here."

"What about your family? Have they been around?" I scanned the area like I might find little Hannah, her granddaughter, hiding in a corner.

"Are you kidding? I make a good babysitter now and again. But that's about it."

"Dot?" Two questions weighed heavily on me. "Do you think Dirk Dickerson killed your father? That's what people are saying, but you knew him best."

"I didn't know him at all. Not in the end. And, of course, he never said anything to me about harming Dad. Although, now, it seems likely that he did." She thrashed around on her cot. Her butt must have been sore from sitting on that thin mattress. But she couldn't do anything about it. She wasn't steady enough to stand. That much was plain to see.

"When I mentioned to the sheriff that Dirk washed my SUV early Sunday morning," she went on to say, "he got all excited. They're examining it right now for evidence. Plan to check his Tahoe too."

She sized me up. "I bet you can't wait to blab this all over town."

The story would make for juicy gossip, that's for sure. Yet the retelling of it held little appeal to me. "Your story will get out. That goes without saying. But no one will hear it from me."

I picked up the cooler. "I better get back to the café." I took one step before spinning on my heels. "Dot?" I had almost forgotten to ask my second question—the most important one. "Did you kill Dirk Dickerson."

"Are you nuts? Like I said, he wanted me to lie for him. But I didn't kill him. Why would I? I had no proof that he had done anything to Dad." She cradled her head again. "Not until yesterday."

"Well, Dickerson got murdered yesterday, so…"

"So nothing. I didn't kill him."

She pushed her glasses down onto her nose before returning them to the top of her head. Her hangover apparently prevented her from seeing with or without them. "I spotted him cuddling up to Tweety at the funeral, in the hallway next to the bathroom. I saw you and Rose there too." She snuggled farther under her blanket. "And, later, when I followed them, I heard him tell Tweety that he didn't really like me. He only pretended to, so I'd hand over my inheritance."

Her voice cracked. And wouldn't you know, a part of me felt sorry for her again. Granted, it was the dumb part. The part that never learned. Still...

"All the pieces fell into place then." She stared at the block wall opposite her. "I went home and—"

"What time was that?"

"Umm... six o'clock. Anyways, I wanted to kick him to the curb. I knocked on the door to the guest suite. I figured he was in there because his truck was parked outside. But he didn't answer."

"The door to his suite was shut?"

"Of course, it was shut."

"So, what did you do?"

"Well... " She wiggled around some more, the springs of her cot squeaking like they were getting pinched. "I wanted to phone him from my side of the house, but I was afraid that Tweety might be with him. I was afraid she might answer. Yet, after a few minutes, when I didn't hear talking or noises of any kind from over there, I decided that they must have gone somewhere in her car."

A safe assumption, given my memory of Tweety's antics with men. If they had been in there, Dot would have heard them. "And?"

"And, that's when I changed clothes and went—"

"Wait! You changed clothes? Why?"

She looked at me like the question was irrelevant. Nonetheless, she answered. "Because my clothes got stained with lemonade and coffee when I had that run-in with Louise Gustafson at the church."

"Okay." I twirled my hand for her to proceed.

"I left the house and—"

I motioned for her to stop again. "When was that?"

She huffed. "Six-fifteen. Now, can I finish?"

"Yeah, go ahead."

She stared, daring me to interrupt. "I hunted all over town for Tweety's car. I even went out to the distillery because Dirk liked that place. But nothing. Although, eventually, I spotted it behind the church. I went inside, but no one was around. And that's when I realized I was late for the reading of the will."

"So you drove to Myrle's office. What time did you get there?"

"Five minutes after seven. I walked in just behind Ed." The noise she uttered next was part laugh, part cry. "I imagine you've heard all about what happened there. My dear old dad had nothing in the end. Even his land was encumbered to the hilt. Just another ruse. And, once again, I was the victim."

"That's why you stormed out?"

She blinked as if she wanted to cry but wouldn't give me the satisfaction of seeing her do it. "I drove to the liquor store, bought a bottle, and headed out of town."

"Huh? You stopped at the liquor store after you left the law office?"

"Yeah. Ed rode my bumper the whole way. He even waited. Then, when I came back out, he followed me until I made my way to the highway."

"You never went back to your place?"

"Nope. Still haven't been back there." She appeared bemused. "I've always done what's right. Yet I've ended up with zilch time and again. Even my husband left me with nothing. He was a butthole too."

"Dot, do you have any idea who might have killed Dickerson?" I set the cooler back down on the floor. Like Karl, I could also stretch out a goodbye.

"Tweety," she replied.

"What makes you say that?"

"Well, when I eavesdropped on them at the church, I heard Tweety ask Dirk how long it would be before they'd get my money. From what I gathered, she had planned to move to Min-neapolis with him. It sounded as if he had agreed to let her stay at his place until she found one of her own."

She curled her upper lip in disgust. "That's probably how he got her into bed in the first place. Yesterday, though, he did his best to weasel out of the deal, which made Tweety furious."

"Dot, according to the police, Tweety's alibi checked out. She couldn't have killed Dickerson."

She slumped against the wall. "Are they sure?"

"Sounds that way."

"I just can't catch a break."

# Chapter 24

I returned to the café at one o'clock. Grace was alone in the kitchen. She had removed her chef's smock. Her bright green t-shirt read, *If you think I'm short, get a load of my patience.*

After placing the cooler on the prep table, I patted the cover. "All the food's still in here. Tweety's been released, and Dot's hangover prevented her from eating. But she did get chatty with me."

"Really? She must be going stir crazy. Why else would she talk to you?"

I would have considered that remark rude if I hadn't already come to the same conclusion.

"Where's Allie?" I skimmed the room.

"I sent her home because it's been slow in here due to Manny Baker's funeral." She shook her head. "Boy, she was grinding her teeth over you."

"Yeah, yeah. I'll apologize the first chance I get."

Grace pulled the lid off the cooler and retrieved the wrapped foam plates from inside. Each plate was divided into sections. One held Egg Roll Hot Dish, the second was mounded with Orange Jell-O Salad, and a cupcake filled the third. "I haven't eaten all day."

"Neither have I," I added. "And I was starving hours ago." Images of Gustaf's finger came to mind, and I shuddered.

"You okay?"

"Just a little chilled," I lied. "That's all."

Emptying the rest of the cooler, I passed my sister a set of plastic flatware and a bottle of water. "Now, let me tell you what happened at the jail."

I had barely sat down, when Tweety barged through the back door, slamming it behind her. "What those law enforcement guys did to me was a fragrant violation of my rights!"

Grace chuckled. "You mean flagrant, don't you?"

"That's what I said."

Yep, if Tweety's brains were ink, she wouldn't possess enough to dot on "i."

"They picked me up at the VFW in Kennedy last night, and they've held me ever since. They said they had to 'verify' my alibi before they could release me." She used her air quotes properly, and I almost fell off my stool.

"If you were at the 'V,' why didn't they just confirm it with the bartender?" Again, that was Grace.

I kept quiet. Tweety hated me. She wasn't crazy about my sister either. But, because Grace had re-hired her and allowed her to move back into the apartment above the café, she got a pass.

"Well, I... umm... didn't get to the bar until ten o'clock." Tweety's cheeks flushed.

"Where were you before then?" I blurted out.

She wrinkled her beak of a nose. "I'm not gonna tell you. Besides, it don't matter. They let me go."

After towing another stool out from under the prep table, Grace patted the seat, and Tweety sat down. "You must be beside yourself," Grace said, while wordlessly warning me to let her handle her wayward waitress. "Why don't you have a little something to eat and tell us about it? You'll feel better."

Tweety coveted the Lemon Cupcake on my plate, drool forming at the corners of her mouth. From all my time working with her at the café, I knew she loved lemon. Grace's cupcake was chocolate.

"I need to go upstairs and shower." She wouldn't get any argument from me. She smelled ripe—even riper than me. "I couldn't very well do it at the sheriff's office." She scraped the remnants of last night's lipstick from her lips with her teeth. "But, I suppose, a little something to eat might settle my nerves."

Realizing I had no choice, I handed over my cupcake, and she peeled its wrapper away without so much as a thank you. "They haven't arrested anyone for either murder," she said, "although the talk at the station is that Dickerson killed Lars."

Grace tsked. "Then, afterwards, he got murdered himself. That sure was awful."

"Oh, I don't know." Tweety smacked her lips as she ate. "He probably deserved it."

"Huh?" I wrenched my head so hard that I almost got whiplash. "I thought you liked the guy."

"He ended up being a schmuck. Certainly not worth fixin' my face for."

Grace shot me a look, but I wasn't about to comment on Tweety's face. The thought had never even occurred to me.

"You know," Tweety said, "he promised that I could go to Minneapolis with him. But, yesterday, he renegaded."

"You mean reneged?" That was me.

She ignored me.

Grace, however, frowned at me again before saying, "Tweety, that must have really ticked you off."

"It did. But I didn't kill him. Like I already told you, I was with someone else at the time."

"Who?" Grace pressed her, demonstrating once more that she was every bit as nosy—I mean, curious—as I was. Still, I alone had been tagged with that label.

"Nope." Tweety shook her head until I heard her brains rattle. "That's a secret. No one knows except those BCA guys and Karl."

"Oh, come on," Grace pleaded. "We'll find out soon enough anyway. You know how this town is."

Tweety pretended to zip her lips.

Although that didn't stop my sister. She enjoyed a challenge. "Was it Ed? Did you hook up with Ed again?"

"No!" A knot formed above Tweety's nose. "I won't ever go out with another law man."

That's when it occurred to me. "You went home with Nils Lund, didn't you?"

Grace pounded the table with her fist. "The mortician?"

"Yep. I saw her hanging all over him just before Rose and I left the church."

"Tweety! He's got to be thirty years older than you." Judgment echoed through my sister's voice, which stunned me. Age differences had never held her back.

"He's not so old. He's younger than Dirk. And he's in pretty good shape. Must be from moving all those bodies and caskets and things."

◎ ◎ ◎

Tweety had barely left the café when Rose wandered through the back door.

"Hey! What are you doing here?" Grace asked.

Rose wiped her boots on the rug and tossed her jacket on the nearby chair before shuffling to the prep table. "Sophie wasn't feelin' too great, so Will's takin' her in for a checkup." She squinted at me. "He said he'd call and update you once they get back home."

I pulled a stool out for her, and she sat down. Grace did the same. "You don't seem all that busy." Rose surveyed the kitchen. "Everyone at Manny's funeral?"

Grace nodded.

"I considered goin'." Rose wiggled around on her stool, attempting to get comfortable. "But I just wasn't up to it. I didn't sleep too good last night."

Grace squeezed her hand. "Have you been takin' your pills?"

"Oh, yah." Rose hooked a thumb my way. "The warden here makes sure of that."

"Although I can't get you to eat much, can I? And that's not good. You'll get too weak."

Grace stood, her stool squeaking as she slid it backwards. "Let's see what I can find you for lunch."

"I really don't want anything. I don't have much of an appetite."

Grace nevertheless checked the refrigerator. "I have some chili I can heat up. That is, if you don't want any of the wild-rice soup that's already on the stove."

"I mean it." Rose waved a bent finger. "I don't want anything."

With that, she went to stand, swayed, and almost hit the floor before I caught her.

❂ ❂ ❂

Rose pulled her oxygen mask down to scold me. "You shouldn't have called the ambulance. I'm fine."

While crouching next to Rose, I inspected the two women who, along with the guy in the driver's seat, comprised the volunteer ambulance crew. The woman who replaced Rose's mask over her nose and mouth worked at the post office, right across the street from the ambulance garage. The guy driving was a local farmer who seemed to be on call all winter long.

I didn't recognize the middle-aged woman with the permed ink-black hair, although I liked her as soon as she told Rose, "Listen here, you should be glad she called. You're no spring chicken. And your blood pressure is way too high, dontcha know."

Having no response to that, Rose closed her eyes.

⊚ ⊚ ⊚

Grace arrived at the hospital an hour later to pick me up. Dr. Betcher had insisted that Rose be admitted. He said he needed to keep an eye on her.

"How's she doing?" Grace asked, as I slid into the passenger seat of her Jeep.

"I'm not sure. But, like I said over the phone, Betcher won't let anyone sit with her because she needs her rest, and he doesn't think she'll get it if she has company. Naturally, I wanted to argue with him, yet I didn't because he's probably right."

Another thought came to mind. "Oh, by the way, I caught Will and Sophie on their way out. Sophie's fine. Just some Braxton Hicks contractions."

Grace bumped over a couple ice ridges before coming to a stop at an intersection near downtown, a pile of snow fifteen feet high filling the middle. After plowing the streets, city main-tenance workers routinely dumped the snow in the center of the four-way stops, and there it remained until they had time to scoop it up and haul it by truck to a location outside of town. As a result, we had temporary roundabouts every winter.

Grace circled the perimeter of the mammoth snow pile. "I phoned Will a few minutes ago and suggested that we postpone tomorrow night's gender reveal party."

"Oh, shoot! I forgot all about that."

"I assured him that since we hadn't started decorating the café and the food would keep, it wouldn't be a problem to set another date."

"And?"

Grace smiled. "He said no way. He insisted that the party go on as scheduled. Sophie's parents just arrived from Fargo, and he's already sick of them."

"Really?"

"Yeah. He said they started irritating him before they even got out of the car." She turned down the alley between the library and the gazebo. "Being a snow storm is expected for the day after tomorrow, he doesn't want to wait. He's afraid they'll end up stranded here for a week."

A part of me was pleased that my son didn't care for his in-laws. Granted, it was the petty part. And, yes, my therapist would have been delighted to explore those feelings at length. But because I had quit therapy, she wouldn't get the chance.

"Well," I said, "from the sound of it, Rose won't be going any-where for days, so there's no point in delaying the party on her account. And being Betcher thinks we're too distracting to sit with her, we may as well go ahead with it."

"Okay. Let's go home and finalize the plans. Then, after closing time tomorrow, we'll get the food ready, decorate, and throw a party."

"And maybe between now and then something will break in the murder investigations, and we'll have another reason to celebrate."

Grace came to a stop behind the café. "We can only hope."

I opened my car door, and the cold was quick to find my neck. I hunched my shoulders. "I keep going over everything in my head, but I still don't know anything for certain.

"I get upset with Karl and those BCA agents because they seem to suspect pretty much everyone in town. But, truth be told, I'm no better. Each person I've spoken with has had a motive for killing Lars, Dickerson, or both."

◎ ◎ ◎

Once we drove our respective cars back home, we met in the kitchen, where Grace fetched a beer for me and a bottle of white wine for herself. "Doris, write 'pick up more beer and wine' at the top of our to-do list for tomorrow."

I sat down at the table and scribbled a note to that effect. Afterwards, I sucked down a fair amount of my beer. "I know she's old," I said, referring to Rose. "And she can't live forever. But her life shouldn't end like this. I always imagined her going out while hang gliding or in a bar brawl."

Grace filled a tall water glass with wine. It was going to be one of those nights.

"Maybe," I added with a pang of guilt, "we should have listened to Betcher and insisted that she return to assisted living after her high blood pressure diagnosis. If we had, she wouldn't have gotten involved with Lars."

"He was a degenerate for sure." Grace took a long drink of her wine. "But Rose enjoyed his company. And, at her age, that's gotta count for something."

"You sound like Karl."

"Well, you know what they say: Great minds… "

"No comment." I meant to sip the rest of my beer but gulped down almost half of what remained in the bottle. "I guess I shouldn't have said that. But I get so tired of him reminding me that he's a law enforcement professional, and I'm not. That solving crime is his business, not mine. I want to shake him and yell, 'Then, do it already! Solve these crimes!'"

"It takes time, Doris."

I pushed back my chair. "I've got a horrible feeling that we don't have a lot of time. Betcher said all of this has been way harder on Rose than any of us realized."

Setting my empty bottle on the counter, I grabbed another from the fridge and plunked back down on my seat. "I also hate to admit it, Grace, but I… ah… probably should have listened to you."

My sister grinned. "I'm sure you're right. But what are you talking about exactly?"

"Well, I should have pushed Karl to interview Dickerson as soon as you shared your suspicions about him with me."

She lifted her glass, only to set it down again. "Don't be too hard on yourself. You spoke with the guy outside the medical center just a day or two after Lars's body was recovered."

"True." I twisted off the cap on my beer bottle. "But, as Karl would say, I haven't been trained in investigative techniques.

Consequently, I wasn't sure what to ask him and probably wasted a lot of time."

I gestured toward my sister's full glass of wine. "Why aren't you drinking?"

"Oh, I don't know. It's just not going down very well."

I took another pull from my bottle. "I'm not having any problem whatsoever."

"And that's fine. You don't have anywhere to be, right?"

Right. So I drank more while further contemplating our current situation and my role in it. "Grace? Why do I insist on being in charge all the time? Why do I have such a hard time letting anyone else have a say, even when they might know better than me?"

Grace got up and scrounged through the cupboards until she found a partial bag of M&Ms next to the chocolate chips. Sitting back down, she pushed her glass of wine aside and placed the open bag of candy in the middle of the table. "Probably because you're used to being in charge."

She pitched a few M&Ms into her mouth. "If you hadn't taken control out on the farm, the place would have gone back to the bank. Then, where would you and the kids have been?" She stopped for a beat. "Scratch that. Where would you and the kids and Bill and Bill's parents have been? Bill certainly wasn't going to do much."

Condensation trickled down my bottle as I scraped the label with my thumbnail. "Still, I think I might be too pushy at times. I know Karl, for one, doesn't like it."

"Oh? Has he said something?"

"Not in so many words, but he—"

"Then, don't worry about it. I've never known Karl to be shy about speaking his mind. Besides, it's really not any of his concern."

"True enough."

Grace grinned. "What's more, it's just your nature. You're a pain in the ass sometimes. And, at your age, you're probably not going to change, so everybody better get used to it, Karl included."

I kicked her under the table. "I am not a pain."

She kicked me back. "Are too."

"Am not."

My cell phone rang, and I grabbed it. "Hello? Yeah. Okay." I offered the caller only staccato responses, while I held my gaze on Grace. "Really? Okay. Right away." I rang off.

"Grace, that was Dr. Betcher. Rose woke up and is asking for us, but he only wants one person in with her at a time." A riot of emotions rose inside of me, causing my voice to quiver. "She's so agitated that he had to put her on oxygen and a heart monitor." Grace went pale. "Being I've already been up there," I told her, "you should go."

# Chapter 25

Answering the front door, I found Karl on the porch, the Olafson brothers standing behind him.

One look at me and he asked, "Are you okay?" He stepped closer and chuckled. "You've been drinking, haven't you?"

"I had two beers."

"I thought one was your limit."

"Well, after the day I've had, I deserved two." I relayed everything that had happened, finishing with, "Grace is at the hospital now."

Karl glanced over his shoulder at the twins. "This was a bad idea. We should leave and let you be. Although I'm not sure it's a good idea for you to be alone."

"Why? I'm not drunk."

"But you are upset. And you have been drinking, so—"

"Enough! Now, what do you need?"

Karl fidgeted with his cap. "I need to question these two. But they don't want to do it at the sheriff's office because the BCA agents are there. They won't go to their house because they think the agents have bugged it. The café is closed. And my place is way the heck out of town. So, I was wondering…"

"If you could question them here?"

"Yeah. At your dining room table. It wouldn't take long."

I shrugged. "I suppose. You've done it before. Although, like last time, I'm not going anywhere. I'm waiting for Grace."

"That's fine. I wouldn't let you leave anyways." His crow's feet crinkled. "You're probably over the limit."

"You think you're hilarious, don't you?"

"Well, I've been told that I'm kind of funny. In fact, I think you said I—"

"Yeah. Yeah." I opened the door, and all three men stepped into the entry, taking turns wiping their boots on the rug.

"Would you like some coffee?" I led them through the foyer and into the dining room.

"Sure," Karl said. "If it's no bother."

"How about some Earthquake Cake? Grace brought some home from the café the other day."

"Don't go to any trouble."

"It's no trouble at all."

Arne and Anders hung their jackets on the back of their chairs at the round oak dining table that had been in my late husband's family for close to a hundred years. Though it had hosted all kinds of conversations during that time, I was positive that it hadn't been the setting for law enforcement interrogations until recently. One such gathering had occurred a few months back. Now, another.

In the kitchen I started the coffee. While it brewed, I pulled a Tupperware container from the fridge and cut four large pieces of chocolate-peanut butter cake, placing each on its own plate. When the coffee was ready, I filled three mugs, arranged everything on a tray, including forks and napkins, and served my company.

On my next trip from the kitchen, I carried my own mug of coffee as well as my own plate of cake. But, rather than stopping in the dining room, I went on to the living room, where I flipped the switch for the fireplace with my elbow and plopped down in the leather club chair.

As I situated myself, I heard Karl say, "I know when and why you two did time in federal prison in Duluth, but tell me in your own words what you did after you got out." Both twins sputtered until the sheriff added, "Fill in the blanks right here and now, or I'll escort you down to the station, where the BCA agents are camped out. Who knows? They might even call in the feds."

That loosened Arne's lips. "Well… umm… after we got released, we traveled east. One thing led to another, and we soon became the accountants for… ah… family."

"A mob family." Karl sounded like it was an indisputable fact. "I read about them in the report I received overnight."

"You can call them whatever you want." That was Arne again. "We only did their books. Nothing more. True, we may not have done everything kosher, money-wise, but we didn't get involved in the violent stuff. And when the feds dropped the net over the family's operation and offered us a deal, we took it."

"A deal that required both of you to testify against the whole lot of them in federal court, right?"

"Yeah. And, afterwards, we entered the Witness Protection Program."

I felt like I was listening to an old-time crime drama on the radio, where I had to imagine the actions of the actors.

Karl: "You didn't remain in the program though, did you?"

Arne: "No. It wasn't to our liking, so we walked away from it. But we kept our new names. Then, we moved up here."

Karl: "Why here?"

Arne: "Look around, Sheriff. Who's gonna come searching for us way the hell up here?"

Glancing out the window, I had to agree. The wind howled and the snow swirled through the woods behind the house as well as along the little-traveled road out front. No, most folks wouldn't come up here on a whim.

"Plus, we were familiar with the area. We spent time just east of here when we were kids."

"Really?" No doubt, Karl wrinkled his forehead. Something he regularly did.

"We've told you that before, Sheriff. That's why we reckoned we'd be safe from… umm… anyone who might feel we done them wrong."

Hearing that, I got to thinking. How many people were living on the lam in Kittson County? Sure, most of the farm families had resided in the area for generations. But, what about the others? The ones who, over the last few decades, had moved here to open stores or work in factories? What were their real stories?

Karl interrupted my musing to ask Arne and Anders, "Were you aware that Lars lived here?"

"No," Arne answered. "We just learned about that."

"When?"

The brothers remained tight-lipped.

"Fine." Karl scooted his chair back. "Let's head down to my office."

"Okay! Okay!" Arne shouted. "Lars brought up the whole prison thing on our way home from the casino on Saturday."

"No good little weasel," Anders snarled, as a fork clanged against a ceramic plate.

"Care to elaborate?"

"He threatened us," Arne answered for his brother. "We didn't recognize him. He had to tell us who he was. Then, he said we'd have to pay him… ah… insurance money if we wanted to keep our identity a secret from the folks around here and the guys back east."

"Did that make you mad?" I envisioned Karl tilting his head, like he often did when he posed a question that he knew the answer to.

"Darn right!" Anders hollered before Arne added, "He wanted $10,000, and he only gave us a couple days to get it. But… "

"He died before it was time to pay up," Karl finished for him.

"Well, yeah. That's the long and short of it."

"Fortunate for you, eh?"

My eyelids had grown heavy. Beer—even just a couple bottles—always made me sleepy. I set my coffee mug and dessert plate on the end table, noticing the dust and trying to remember the last time I had cleaned. I couldn't remember, so I gave up, laid my head back, and closed my eyes.

"That's why we didn't say anything," Arne said. "It looked bad for us. But we had nothing to do with his death. Really, we didn't. We just drove him to the casino and back again."

The guy sounded sincere. Although my now deceased husband had also sounded sincere whenever he claimed that the women he ran around with were "only friends."

"Okay," Karl said. "What happened after you dropped Lars off at his apartment? Where did you go?"

"We don't wanna say."

"I don't care. Tell me."

"Okay. Okay," Arne replied. "We went to the Dell in Argyle for supper." He hesitated. "We had… umm… a couple women with us."

"And I'm sure they'd be happy to verify your story."

◎ ◎ ◎

"Don't mind me." I shuffled through the dining room and back into the kitchen. "I'm just refilling my cup." I reappeared in the doorway, clutching the pot. "More for any of you?"

Anders lifted his cup, but before he spoke, Karl said, "No more for us, Doris. We're almost done here." Anders frowned and set his cup back on the table.

At the same time, Arne handed Karl a sheet of paper. Apparently, it listed the names and contact information for the brothers' dinner companions on the night in question.

"Thanks." Karl folded the paper and tucked it in his breast pocket. "Now I have just one last thing to ask you two."

I leaned against the kitchen counter and sipped more coffee while listening in on the conversation in the dining room and wondering when exactly I had become such a slob. The setting sun shined through the window over the sink, but the streaks, dirt, and water marks on the glass wrecked my view. For years, I had been such a conscientious cleaner.

Karl's voice broke through my thoughts. "What's the deal with you two and Dirk Dickerson? You knew him from before you moved to Hallock, so don't lie. I'll check everything out. And if I find that you've been less than forthcoming, I'll make you regret the day you moved here."

"Well, Sheriff," Arne said, "we weren't well acquainted with him before he showed up here. But we knew his step-father, Byron Tillis, from our time in the pen."

I pictured Karl scribbling that name in his notebook. "Did you pull con jobs with the guy? This Tillis?"

"No. Never. We only got to know him in Duluth. He was released ahead of us. So, when we got out, we went to see him in Minneapolis before heading out east. He was a good guy."

"A real good guy." Anders sounded like his mouth was full of cake.

"Yeah," Karl muttered, "a real gem, I'm sure."

"He was well into his eighties by then and sick with the big 'C,'" Arne continued, dismissing Karl's snide remark without comment. "Didn't have much time left.

Arne went on. His stepson, Dirk, was around a lot and always sucking up to him, angling for a job, even though he was closing in on retirement age himself. Yeah, he wanted to be Byron's wingman, but Byron said he didn't have the right stuff."

"How'd he end up here?"

"Well... " Arne said on the end of a slurp of coffee. "He showed up out of the blue. I guess before Byron died, he mentioned that we lived up here."

"And?"

"And he told us he wanted to prove Byron wrong. Prove he was just as good as him at cons." Arne stopped for a minute. I suspected he was choosing his words carefully, determined not to incriminate himself or his brother. Or, he might have been eating cake. Like everything else that Grace made, her earthquake cake was hard to resist. "Dickerson told us he planned to pull Byron's favorite con. See, Byron liked to bilk rich, lonely women out of money. But we said we wanted no part of it."

Karl asked, "How'd he decide to target Dot?"

"He'd met her on the Internet." Arne slurped more coffee. "One of those sites for lonely hearts. She wrote that she was the only surviving child of a Red River Valley farmer. Said she owned a bed and breakfast and hinted that she'd soon have access to a whole lot of money." Forks scraped across plates. "She told him she lived in Hallock. And that's when he hatched his plan."

"His plan entailed what exactly?" Karl's tone remained impassive.

"Well, Dirk supposedly came to visit Dot after 'falling' for her online." Arne's voice was thick. Clearly, he was attempting to eat and talk at the same time. "He pretended he couldn't get a room at the motel and told her he'd hafta head back to Minneapolis."

He then said, "Of course, Dot wouldn't hear of that. She gave him the guest suite at her place and didn't even charge him." A fork pinged as it hit a plate. "I guess he had more charm than any of us gave him credit for."

At that, Anders chuckled. "Yeah, charm."

"What about that whole dirt business?" Karl asked, not waiting for Anders to finish yucking it up.

"Dirk called Dot 'easy pickings,'" Arne said. "On top of being lonely, she was money hungry. So he asked her to invest in his dirt business. Said he had done all kinds of research, and the dirt thing was a winner. But, the truth was, he hadn't done any research. And, of course, he didn't intend to start any business. He just made it all up on the spot. That's why Anders and I were sure that no one would believe it. At least no one with half a brain."

Even though I was alone in the kitchen, I blushed. After all, I had believed Dickerson's story. I had considered his dirt business idea innovative. I, evidently, had less than half a brain.

As I contemplated the depths of my gullibility, Arne said, "When Dirk discovered that Dot really didn't have access to much cash as long as her dad was alive, he went crazy. That's why Byron never allowed him to be part of any of his capers. Dirk was a hot-head who didn't do his homework."

"So… " Karl picked up the conversation from there. "Dickerson killed Lars to speed up Dot inheriting his money?"

The brothers hemmed and hawed before Arne finally replied, "He never actually admitted that."

"I don't buy that for a minute."

"Well, what do you expect me to say, Sheriff?"

"Try the truth! Either here or down at the station."

"Okay! Okay! We're… umm… pretty sure he killed him. But he never came right out and confessed it to us, so you can't get us for withholding information or nothing like that."

"Explain this then." Karl's tone was laced with annoyance. "If Dickerson was only after Lars's money, why'd he try to convince other people around here to invest in his dirt business?"

"Greed, plain and simple," Arne answered. "Once he discovered that he'd have to wait for Dot to get her inheritance, he decided to use the time to see how much money he could con out of other folks. He didn't realize how frugal they were. That's why he ended up—"

"… asking you to pretend to be investors." Karl sounded as if he knew exactly where this story was headed.

"That's right." Arne said. "He wanted us to talk up his business while carting folks around in the senior van. But, of course, no one around here was gonna invest their hard-earned money on our say-so. It's not like our family has lived here for generations." He paused for a two count. "Besides, we wouldn't have done it. That kind of stuff is behind us now."

Karl didn't speak for a while. And, when he did, he simply said, "Where were you two last night between five-thirty and seven-thirty?"

"Oh, come on." Arne groaned out the words. "We already gave you all kinds of information."

"And I appreciate it. I'll also check it all out. Meanwhile, I need to know where you were when Dickerson got murdered."

"We were… umm… eating in Argyle."

"Again, Arne?" There was a note of misgiving in Karl's voice.

"Yeah. What can we say? We really like the food there."

# Chapter 26

Karl spoke into his phone. "Yeah, Uh-huh. You don't say. Umm… okay." He disconnected and told the Olafson brothers, "I have to get back to the station. But I'll want to talk to you guys again, so don't do anything foolish, like hightail it out of town."

Arne assured him, "We won't because we didn't do nothing wrong." He hesitated. "Although we do have an appointment In Stephen later today. We'll be gone a couple hours."

"An appointment?"

"Yeah, some… ah… family business. We'll come right back after we're done."

"What kind of family business?"

"Well, we can't really say."

"Then, you can't go. I mean it."

Hearing chairs scuttle along the wood floor, I peeked out from the doorway that led into the dining room. I saw Arne and Anders lumber toward the entry, grumbling.

Once they left the house, I emerged from my hidey-hole. "Karl, what was that all about?"

"Who knows?" He bent from side to side. Not far from Medicare age, Karl dealt with occasional back issues. "I don't have time to put up with any of their nonsense."

"They lied to you." I reconsidered my words. "Or they lied to me. In any case, they lied."

"Huh?" He placed his hands on his lower back and arched against them. "What are you talking about?"

"Well, they just claimed that they ate in Argyle on the night Lars died. But, when I spoke to them outside the medical center, they told me they'd eaten in Karlstad that evening."

I allowed him a second. "People don't get confused about where they went right after someone they were with is murdered." No, Grace wasn't the only one who could spout home-grown theories regarding criminal behavior.

"Are you sure you heard right?"

I nodded.

"Well, I have to get back to the station."

"You think they might have killed Lars?"

"I don't know." He looked to the ceiling, as if seeking divine insight. "Maybe. Maybe not." Obviously, the entity in charge of insight—divine or otherwise—was not on duty.

"What about Dickerson's death? Could they have killed him too?"

"I suppose that's possible." He shoved his hands into his pants' pockets and jingled his keys and coins. "I better ask Ed to keep an eye on them until I get done at the office and can check out their alibi."

"Umm… speaking of Ed, did you happen to send him out to Lake Bronson around eleven o'clock this morning to follow up on what Gustaf told you?"

He stopped jingling. "What Gustaf told me about what?"

"That he may have seen someone along the shoreline on Saturday night?"

The sheriff's expression indicated a need for more information.

So I obliged. "Gustaf and I drove out there before he brought his car to the station."

"Oh, that explains why it took him forever to get there. I was waiting."

"Well… ah… Grace suggested that I go with him to keep him out of trouble." Whenever possible, blame Grace.

Karl glimpsed at me out of the corner of his eye, like what I had just said was so absurd that it didn't even warrant a direct look.

Nevertheless, I pressed on. "You see, Gustaf wanted to make sure he hadn't imagined the whole thing."

"Doris? What does any of that have to do with Ed?"

"Well, Ed was out there, in that exact area."

He pressed his fists to his hips. "Oh, so we're back to suspecting Ed of killing Lars, are we?"

Karl could be extremely obnoxious. "I'm just passing on information that I thought might be of interest." I used my best "I don't care" voice.

"Did you speak to him? Ask him what he was up to?"

"No. We only saw him come back from the shoreline with a clear bag in his hands. Maybe an evidence bag."

"You identified it as an evidence bag? How close were you?"

I wasn't about to admit that we had watched him through binoculars.

"I don't know what to tell you," Karl said. "He may have been following up on a lead for one of the BCA agents. I haven't spoken to him in a while." He started for the door. "Now, I really have to go."

"Wait. What's got you in such an all-fire hurry?"

"Doris… " He dragged my name out. "Both Dot's car and Gustaf's car are being examined, as is Dickerson's."

"And?"

"And now I better make sure that the twins' van gets scrubbed too."

I stared at him. There was more.

"Okay, okay. I also got conformation that Louise Gustafson has been cleared in Lars's murder. I didn't mention it because I knew you didn't like that we even took the time to investigate her."

"Well, she wasn't much of a suspect."

Karl massaged his forehead. "Doris, she had motive and op-portunity. Plus, she lied to us. Even so, we verified that she was with Myrle in her Grafton hotel room Saturday afternoon, draft-ing her divorce petition. And when they finished, the two of them went out to supper."

"Then, why did she lie and say she didn't come to Hallock until Tuesday?" The furnace kicked in, as if to underscore my question.

"Well, she insisted to the agents that she didn't really lie because she never technically set foot in Hallock until Tuesday, when she showed up in the church basement."

"Still, why—

"She didn't want anyone to discover that she had been fol-lowing Gustaf and Etta on Thursday and Friday."

I stepped back. "You mean she stalked them?"

"She was after evidence to use in the divorce. Like Gustaf said, she didn't really care that he and Etta were running around together. But, once she found out about Ed, she decided she'd had enough."

"Yeah, well, I hate to admit it, but I can see her point. Her hus-band had a son with another woman. And that was after he'd already had a daughter with her."

Karl leaned against the front door. "Anyways, she figured that proof of a girlfriend on top of out-of-wedlock children would give her the best chance of a huge settlement. But after she learned about Lars's death, she hid the fact that she was anywhere near here for fear of becoming a suspect in his murder."

"Wait. You just said she had an alibi. She was with Myrle."

He retrieved his leather gloves from his jacket pocket. "Yeah, well, since everyone knows that Myrle will say and do whatever Louise wants, she decided that her alibi might be problematic."

"And Dickerson's death?"

"Like she said, she never met the man." With that, Karl pulled on his gloves and left.

As for me, I sat down on the staircase that led to the second floor and thought things through. Tweety was in the clear. So was Louise Gustafson. But the Olafson brothers were another matter.

At some point during Karl's questioning, they had rocketed to suspects number one and two in my mind. The way I figured it, the twins probably killed Lars for trying to blackmail them. It would have been easy for them to dispose of his body in Lake Bronson on their way home from the casino late Saturday afternoon.

As for Dirk Dickerson's murder, Arne and Anders certainly had motive to kill the guy. They hated him. They also had opportunity. No one knew for sure how long he was alone in the guest suite before Dot returned home from the funeral. Arne and Anders could have killed him during that time.

It was a solid theory, yet something still scratched at me like a pesky cat. But I shooed away my uncertainty because I wanted these cases wrapped up and life in Hallock to return to normal. Then, Rose would regain her heath. I was positive of that.

After mulling over everything a few more minutes, I concluded that I had been befuddled all week because I had suspected the wrong people. But now I was certain that Arne and Anders were the bad guys.

Ex-cons themselves, they had killed Lars, another ex-con. Then, they killed Dirk Dickerson because he had the power to put their lives in danger if they refused to assist him in his latest scheme.

Emptying my coffee cup in the kitchen sink, my fingers and toes tingled. I had solved both murders. Now, I just needed to prove it—and find time to clean the house.

## Chapter 27

It was right after five o'clock when my sister returned from the hospital. Between Karl's departure and her arrival, I had showered, downed several more cups of coffee, and dusted. Yep, I was again firing on most—if not all—cylinders.

"How's Rose?" I asked, meeting Grace at the door.

"Sleeping peacefully, which is also what I plan to do right after I eat some supper."

I took her by the arm and pulled her into the living room. "First, you've got to hear this." I pushed her down onto the couch. "I've changed my mind."

"About what?"

"I'm pretty sure that the Olafson twins killed both Lars and Dirk Dickerson."

"Oh, brother." She flopped back.

"Hear me out. Karl ended up interrogating Anders and Arne here. Don't ask me why." Owing to my highly caffeinated state, I paced around the room. "But because they got questioned around my dining room table, I heard everything."

Grace leaned forward, placing her elbows on her knees and cradling her head in her hands. "Slow down, Doris. You're making my head hurt."

"I can't slow down." Like a record playing at chipmunk speed, I proceeded to relay the Olafsons' motives and opportunities as well as Karl's plan to have Ed watch the two men until he finished whatever he had to do at the office. "As we know… " I stopped to catch my breath. "Ed's incompetent, which is why we need to keep an eye on them too."

"Dickerson killed Lars," Grace said, like she was refreshing my memory. "And Dot killed Dickerson."

"None of that's been proven. Not officially."

"Doris, you were pretty sure of it not that long ago. At least as far as Dickerson killing Lars."

"But, then, I heard from the Olafsons. Not only were they in prison at the same time as Lars, but they lied about where they were after Lars got murdered."

Grace yawned. "Well, I think you're wrong. And I'm exhausted. So, whatever you have planned, I refuse to be a part of it."

◎ ◎ ◎

Ten minutes later Grace and I took off in my SUV. "Okay, I'm here," she complained from the passenger seat, "but you can't make me get out of the car. I don't care how much you threaten me. Whenever we leave the car, we get chased, stumble upon a dead body, or–"

"Fine. We'll stay put." I slowed as we passed the Olafson house. The senior citizen van idled out front, but neither brother was in the vehicle.

Coming up on the intersection just beyond the house, Grace whispered, "Don't look now, but Ed's parked around the corner."

"I'm driving, Grace. I have to look."

"Trust me. No one's coming. Just keep moving."

I did as she said because I felt like I owed her. After all, I had bullied her into coming along. Then, again, if the tables had been turned, she wouldn't have thought twice about doing the same to me.

Once through the intersection, I turned down the alley behind the gas station and parked alongside a snow-covered hedge.

"We should have brought snacks," she said, as I shifted into park. "This stakeout business is boring." Two seconds later, she added, "How long do we have to sit here?"

"Longer than a minute." I strained to see down the street. "I wish I had Gustaf's binoculars."

"Binoculars won't help. It's getting dark." Grace wiggled in her seat.

"Why are you so antsy?" No need to wait for an answer. "I wasn't the only one who drank too much coffee today, was I?"

"I have to cut back. I think I'll walk over to Dollar General and buy a snack." She reached for the door handle. "Want anything?"

"Hold on." I gestured toward the window. "It's Arne and Anders. They're getting into the van."

Grace offered only a quick glance in their direction. She didn't strike me as all that interested.

"Let's follow them." I slipped the car into gear. "See where they're headed."

"Why? They're probably just off to give someone a spur-of-the-minute ride. They wouldn't leave town. Not after Karl's warning."

"Well, let's find out."

Grace sagged in her seat. "I really wanted a Diet Coke and some red licorice."

"You just got done saying that you've already had too much caffeine." Though some licorice did sound good.

As the senior van headed our way, Ed fell in behind it, tailing so closely that the twins must have noticed him. After all, they were crooks. Watching for tails was part of the job description.

I backed my car up until it was completely hidden. And, once they drove by, I counted to twenty before taking off after them.

By the time I reached Highway 75, a two-lane road that served as the primary route out of town, both vehicles had turned south. "I think you were wrong, Grace."

"Not necessarily. Their rider may live in the country."

We drove past the oil company as well as a couple other industrial sites. Then, while I maneuvered what we locals called the "s" curves, Grace said, "Okay. I might have been wrong."

Because I was a mature adult, I didn't say, *I told you so.* Although I did add a check mark to my mental list of "Times I've Proven my Sister Wrong."

◎　◎　◎

Given that the Red River Valley was flat—no hills or even humps—cars could be seen for miles. Because of this, I kept a healthy distance behind Ed. If he spotted us, he'd immediately phone Karl.

Our drive was peaceful. We shared the road with few other vehicles. The sky was dark yet full of stars. And fresh snow stretched across the stubbled fields, all the way to the horizon.

"Oh, come on, Grace. Aren't you the least bit curious about what the twins are doing? Why they ignored Karl?"

My sister laid her head against the headrest and closed her eyes. "Not curious enough to spend the evening playing Cagney and Lacey."

"What's gotten into you? In the beginning, you were all gung-ho about me solving these murders."

She rocked her head my way and squinted through her slitted eyelids. "As far as I'm concerned, the murders are solved." She waved her hands. "Which makes all of this a complete waste of time."

I checked my side window. Seeing no oncoming traffic, I flipped on my blinker and passed the car ahead of me. It was traveling fifty miles per hour. Sure, during the winter, drivers had to watch for patches of ice, particularly black ice. But fifty? Really?

"Well… " I returned to my own lane. "How can you be so sure after everything I told you about Arne and Anders?"

"That's nothing but chatter. It only confuses things. And delays the inevitable."

"A few hours ago, I would have agreed with you. But, now, I think we need to consider—"

"Doris, stick a fork in me. I'm done. I'm emotionally exhausted from my visit with Rose. I hate hospitals. You know that." She again closed her eyes. "If you want anything more from me, you'll have to buy me a coffee or a Diet Coke."

"Fine." I slowed as we entered the town of Stephen, population 575. "We'll get something here."

◎ ◎ ◎

After parking a couple blocks from the Stephen Community Arts Center, we watched Arne and Anders enter the building.

"A meeting at the arts' center?" Grace momentarily squeezed her eyes shut. "I must be really tired because I don't understand that at all."

Ed had parked up the street, only a few cars back from the Olafsons' van. A dumb thing to do in my opinion. Even for a rookie. Which led me to get irritated with Karl all over again. How could he possibly compare Ed's police work to that of my daughter?

While I stewed over that, Grace shoved her stocking cap on her head. "Ed probably wouldn't recognize me if I walked right up to him. But disguising myself seems like the appropriate thing to do when running for snacks while conducting surveillance." She donned sunglasses, then opened her door. "I'm getting coffee and a treat or two." Her voice was resolute, so I didn't bother to suggest that she order decaf. "You want anything?"

I agreed to a cup of coffee but declined all offers of food. I'd eaten nothing but junk all day.

When she returned, she tossed a share pack of M&Ms, a

bag of red licorice, and a container full of mini brownies on the dashboard. "Maybe surveillance isn't so bad," she said, her lips ringed in chocolate frosting. Obviously, she had consumed an iced donut too.

She handed me a Styrofoam cup of coffee and kept one for herself. An hour later the coffee was gone, as was half the licorice, most of the mini brownies, and all of the M&Ms. My jeans barely stretched across my waist. To breathe, I had to unbutton them. I also silently berated myself for wearing jeans rather than leggings.

With both of us hyped up on sugar, we went on to debate whether or not to run into the center to see what was keeping the twins. We ultimately decided against it because we didn't want Ed to spot us. At least that's what we claimed. In truth, our stomachs ached too much to run.

At eight o'clock, Arne and Anders emerged from the arts' center, a dozen men and women tagging along with them. They all laughed and chatted until peeling off to their respective vehicles.

As soon as the twins drove away, heading north again, Ed followed. We waited a minute or two before I put my car in gear and took our place at the rear of our truncated caravan.

# Chapter 28

Passing through the towns of Donaldson, population 20, and Kennedy, population 174, we noted that, as usual, they were closed up for the night. Hallock was also quiet.

We turned right onto Birch Avenue, passed the medical center, and finally came to a stop in the alley behind the twins' place. They had parked the van out front. And, for all we knew, Ed had pulled in directly behind them.

After I argued that we had no choice but to see what the brothers were up to, Grace said, "I knew it. Even though you promised that we wouldn't, we're about to do the exact same thing we did the other night."

"No, we aren't." With my stocking cap pulled over my ears, I unfolded myself from behind the wheel. "Then, we nosed around their garage," I whispered against the squeak of their backyard gate. "Now, we're gonna nose around their house."

"You're so funny."

I grinned. "Thanks! But save your compliments for later, when I have time to revel in them. Right now, we have work to do."

Grace glared. "What if the twins see us? Hell, what if Ed sees us?"

"First of all, I'll wager that Ed's already fast asleep in his car. As for Arne and Anders, if they come after us, and we can't outrun them, we deserve whatever we get." Bold talk coming from someone who waddled down the sidewalk because of everything she'd eaten.

A light burned in the rear corner of the house, prompting us to climb onto the back deck. It, like the sidewalk, was free of snow, no doubt courtesy of the shovel leaning against the railing.

Because of the mammoth gas grill in the middle of the deck, it was evident that the twins enjoyed wintertime grilling, something I'd always wanted to try, but Grace had refused to do.

Having a look-see through the window to the right of the back door, I spotted a light over the kitchen sink but no people anywhere. Thus, I tiptoed off the deck, Grace trailing me, and slinked along the side of the house.

That sidewalk was also clear of snow. The twins must have been obsessed with shoveling, something I couldn't imagine. The best Christmas gift I had ever received was a snowblower. The fact that I had gifted it to myself didn't bother me in the least.

Reaching another lit window, I stopped. A three-foot snowdrift banked the foundation of the house and acted as a barrier to seeing inside. Still, it didn't block the sound of music—Latin music. Grace and I shrugged. Arne and Anders didn't strike us as lovers of salsa tunes. The soundtrack to *The Godfather*? Perhaps. But not salsa.

I motioned to Grace that I'd lift her in my cupped hands, so she could see what the two men were up to.

She whispered, "For the millionth time, why?"

"I don't know." I copied her tone. "But they lied—"

"They may have just gotten mixed up."

"No one gets mixed up about where they eat following a murder." Of course, I had no idea if that were true or not. But, given that my sister routinely stated as fact whatever she wanted, I presumed she'd be hard pressed to argue with me for doing the same.

Grace sighed and stepped into the snowbank, and I did the same—minus the sighing. She settled her right foot in my inter-locked hands and grasped my shoulders. I hoisted her up, my arms wobbling. She was far heavier than I had expected.

"Steady," she said.

Easier said than done.

Attempting to distract myself from my exertion, I added up all the calories I had consumed that day. It made me so depressed that my hands gave way, and Grace tumbled into the snow.

Ignoring her groan, I asked, "What did you see?"

She rose to her feet, shaking herself like a wet dog. "They're dancing. Together. Just the two of them."

"Huh?"

"Yeah." She brushed snow from her pant legs. "They're doing the tango."

"You're kidding."

"No, she's not," uttered a deep voice.

Grace and I jumped and somehow hit each other mid-air. We landed on our butts, snow up to our ears.

"What are you doing?" Arne demanded, as he and his broth-er emerged from the shadows.

"Well…" I wasn't at all sure how to respond. "Umm… you see…" Because the scar along Anders's jaw appeared even more disturbing than I remembered, I gave Arne my full attention. "You two… umm… must have gotten mixed up when you spoke with Karl." No way was I coming right out and accusing them of spin-ning tales. They had worked for people who fed their enemies to the fishes. Come to think of it, Lars had become fish food. At the thought of that, I forgot to breathe. I swayed. And almost fall over.

Grace steadied me before assuming my role as interrogator. "We need clarification," she reiterated. "And… ah… we're sup-posed to report back to the sheriff by… ah… ten o'clock, which is only a little while from now. If he doesn't hear from us by then, he'll stop over here himself."

Impressed with the story she had woven, her eyes glinted.

"You'll then have to justify to him why you went to Stephen after he warned you against it. And, trust me, no matter what you say, he'll be angry. So, you'd be better off just telling us what we want to know."

"How did you—"

"We followed you," Grace said. "We were on our way to… umm… Dollar General when we saw you head out of town."

Anders bent his head toward his brother. "You swore that the idiot deputy was the only one tailing us."

Arne waved him off. "What do you want to know?" His voice was seasoned with suspicion and trepidation.

Grace and I stepped out of the snow bank and stomped our feet to loosen the clinging snow. And, when done with that, I pulled up my big-girl panties, literally and figuratively, and returned to posing my own questions. After all, if I intended to lure these guys into a confession, I had to be assertive. "Now… umm… where exactly did you two go after you dropped Lars off at his… umm… apartment on Saturday afternoon?" Okay. The assertive thing needed work.

Even so, the brothers exchanged weary glances before Arne replied, "We already said."

"No, you didn't. You told me that you went to eat in Karlstad. But when Karl interviewed you, you claimed you took your dates to dinner in Argyle."

"Well, I'll be," Anders muttered, eyeing his brother with what appeared to be disillusionment. "You screwed that up too? And here you're always telling me that I hafta let you do all the talking because you're the smart one."

"Shush!" Arne pivoted back to me. "What I meant to—"

"Don't lie," I warned him. "Karl will find out, and he won't take kindly to it."

"Oh, all right. Come inside and we'll talk. It's too cold out here."

"No way!" Grace stepped out from behind me. "We are not going anywhere with you. Certainly not inside. You can tell us what we need to know right here."

I concurred. As long as we remained outside, we had a chance of running away, if it came to that. But, once in the house, our chances diminished greatly. "Remember," I said, "we have to get back to the sheriff's office, so…"

Arne squinted at me through the lenses of his thick glasses, the bifocal lines seemingly slicing his eyes in half. I swallowed hard.

"We were at the same place we were tonight," he finally uttered.

"The Stephen Community Arts Center?"

He nodded, while Anders studied his feet.

Wondering what he found so interesting, I dropped my eyes and noted Anders's unusual footwear. Although black with laces, they weren't wing tips. The toes were patent leather, and the sides were suede.

"Okay," Arne said, as I eyed his shoes too. Sure enough, they matched his brother's. "We take ballroom-dance lessons there."

"What?" I jerked my head, certain the words had gotten mixed around while routing their way through my brain.

"We're practicing for a Latin dance competition coming up next week in Minneapolis."

"Really?" I fought the urge to look around to see if we were getting punked.

As for Grace, she clamped her teeth down on her bottom lip, no doubt to keep from laughing.

Arne didn't seem to notice our reactions. "On Saturday, we had to get to practice by five-thirty. That's why we rushed off after dropping Lars at his door."

"Still, we were late," Anders grumbled. "Our partners were none too happy. Damn Lars."

"Huh?" Granted, it wasn't much of a follow-up question, but it was the best I could do under the circumstances.

"Lars slowed us down," Arne explained. "He didn't get back to the van on time at the casino. He said he had to recoup his losses."

"But he didn't," Anders added. "What a lousy gambler."

I had never heard Anders speak as much as he had in the

past two minutes. Obviously, he had decided that he couldn't do any worse than his brother. Or maybe it had nothing to do with Arne and everything to do with the silver flask he repeatedly pulled from his pants' pocket. He took another nip and slipped it away.

"Anyways," Arne said after giving his brother the side-eye, "we went to Stephen yesterday too, following the funeral. Practice started at five-thirty, same as always, and finished just before eight, like tonight."

"So, you were there at the time of Dirk Dickerson's death?"

"Yep. We headed out from the church shortly before five. Didn't you see us? Lots of folks did."

Grace's bottom lip had turned white from biting it. Undoubtedly, it was numb. She wouldn't be asking any more questions tonight. It was all up to me.

I shifted my gaze from brother to brother, not sure where to direct my next remark. I settled on a branch in the tree behind them. "Why didn't you report this to the sheriff?"

Arne stepped toward me. "We take ballroom dancing," he repeated, as if that was reason enough to stay quiet. And, if the look on Grace's face was any indication of how others might react to the news, he was probably right.

"What about the women who supposedly went to dinner with you? You gave the sheriff their names and phone numbers. Were they—"

"Our dance partners," Arne cut me off to say. "I called them when we left the café earlier today, and they agreed to cover for us. It was a lot to ask of them. But they're nice ladies."

"Yeah," Anders said. "Real nice."

# Chapter 29

Thursday morning, after a breakfast of oatmeal and berries to compensate for all I'd consumed over the last several days, I considered walking on the treadmill in the back porch but decided it was too cold out there. Instead, I showered, brushed my teeth, pulled on black leggings and a pink tunic, and left the house after donning my winter gear. I was eager to see Rose, although my mind was revving with thoughts of other things too.

After finishing up at the Olafson house the night before, I had phoned Karl to tell him what Grace and I had done. He wasn't happy with us for interfering in his investigation. No surprise there. But because the information we had obtained was potentially significant, his growl wasn't accompanied by much of a bite.

Before disconnecting, he had assured me that he'd check the twins' alibi. And, if verified, he'd cross them off the suspect list in both murder cases.

After hanging up, I had gone to bed, tossing and turning all night, unable to escape various theories regarding Arne, Anders, and the murders. Most likely, they had killed both Lars and Dirk Dickerson. But, if I was wrong, only Dot and Gustaf would remain on the suspect list, at least in the case of Dirk Dickerson. And while they both caused me consternation, I doubted that seeing them on wanted posters would make me feel any better.

Shaking my head, I returned to the moment and headed down the hospital corridor until I spotted Rose's room. I plastered a smile on my face, unsure what to expect.

As I walked through her door, she opened her eyes, like she had sensed my presence. "Hi," she whispered, her pale face and hair half hidden among the white sheets and pillowcases.

"How you doing?" I gently squeezed her hand, careful to avoid her IV paraphernalia.

"Pretty rotten." She scrunched her nose, the oxygen lead clipped to her nostrils seemingly itching her.

"Is Betcher taking good care of you?"

"Oh, yah. He and the nurses are great. They say I'll be fine, regardless of what I feel like now. I just hafta rest." She inhaled a shallow breath. "I guess everything got to be too much for me, Doris. My innards started shakin' something fierce. I kept gettin' dizzy. And the idea of eatin' made me sick."

"You should have told me."

She pursed her lips. "I thought it would stop. And when it didn't, I got nervous you'd send me back to assisted livin'."

"Rose, you never have to go back there unless you want to."

"Good. Because I like livin' with you and Grace." Another shallow breath. "Although I don't mind tellin' ya that this nerve thing scared me spitless. Dr. Betcher says we've gotta watch it from here on out." She shook her head. "In all my born days…"

"Well, just rest and don't worry about a thing. You'll always have a home with us. And we'll do whatever is necessary to keep you healthy."

She smiled, and the back of my eyes stung. I turned away.

None of the flowers we'd ordered had arrived yet, rendering her room stark and sterile. "You should receive some deliveries today," I said. "So you have that to look forward to."

"Okay." Her eyelids drooped.

It was time for me to leave. "Is there anything Grace or I can bring you later?"

"No. I'm just tired. I think I'll take a nap." She closed her eyes.

"That's fine. You rest." I patted her hand. "I love you, Rose."

◎ ◎ ◎

When I reached the café, I parked in the alley, next to Grace's Jeep. Exiting my car, I skated across the icy pavement, entered the building, and snagged an apron from the cupboard.

As Grace turned my way, the doors that separated the dining room from the kitchen slammed open, and Tweety barged in, an order slip in her hand. "Grace, you'll never believe what I just heard!" Seeing me, she clamped her mouth shut.

"Go ahead and tell us," Grace said. "Doris isn't going any-where."

Tweety's nostrils flared. "I don't—"

"Oh, come on." Grace enticed her with a wiggle of her finger. "Just tell us."

"Well," Tweety began, unable to hold back, even though she obviously wanted to deprive me of her news. "Dot just got re-leased from custody." When neither Grace nor I said anything, she added, "They found plenty of Lars's fingerprints in her car, but they figured that didn't matter being he was her dad and all. They said they needed something more, like blood or pieces of his brains or what not."

Yep. Tweety had a way with words.

"Believe it or not," she continued, "Dirk's fingerprints weren't anywhere in the car. That means he either wiped them away or never used Dot's SUV in the first place. The police said it's too bad they didn't get to interview him before he got his head bashed in with that wine bottle."

◎ ◎ ◎

Soon after Tweety returned to the dining room, Karl trudged through the back door. "Morning, ladies."

I didn't waste any time with pleasantries. "We just heard that you let Dot go."

"For now. She's still facing a drunk-driving charge."

"So," I said, "does that mean Arne and Anders murdered Lars and Dirk Dickerson?" In that case, this entire mess would be cleared up soon.

A sense of relief washed over me, which bothered me on some level. After all, how could I be relieved that two people I knew had murdered two other people? When had I become such a ghoul?

Karl sat down on the stool catty-corner from me. At the same time, Grace ambled over, her spatula in one hand and a pot of coffee in the other, three mugs dangling from her fingers.

"No, Doris, they didn't kill anyone." Karl rescued the cups and passed them around. "Their alibies checked out. They told the truth about where they were both nights."

"Really?" Hearing that, a stab of disappointment pierced my chest. Yep, I was one sick woman. "I guess I thought they might have gone over to Dot's house and killed him before Dot got home from the funeral. And that's why, when Dot got there, Dickerson didn't answer her knock on his door. He was already dead."

Karl nodded. "A decent theory. Just one problem: The door to the guest suite was closed when Dot arrived but open when you and Grace got there an hour later. So someone else visited Dickerson—and likely killed him—in the interim."

"Or Dot lied," Grace said. "You know, I've suspected her—"

"At any rate, Karl…" I raised my voice to drown out my sister. "You're saying that the Olafsons didn't kill him."

"No, they didn't. Their alibi checked out. They were out dancing at the time of Dickerson's death."

"Hmm." I screwed up my lips. "No wonder something bugged me about my theory. I had forgotten about the whole open-door, closed-door thing."

❂ ❂ ❂

Tweety again pushed her way into the kitchen. As soon as she saw the sheriff, however, she spun toward the door again.

"Wait!" Karl shouted. "I have a few questions for you."

She circled in his direction. "I'm really busy."

"No, you aren't." Grace plucked the order slip from Tweety's fingers. "We're all caught up. So go ahead and talk to the sheriff." She reviewed the slip. "I'll start in on this Denver omelet order."

If looks could kill, Tweety would have been arrested on the spot for the murder of my sister.

"It'll only take a minute," Karl said, although he didn't appear too excited about speaking with her either.

"Sheriff, my alibi already checked out." Her whine was every bit as annoying as Gustaf's.

"Tweety, you're not in any trouble. I simply need to pick your brain." His eyes immediately locked with mine, his warning me not to make any wise cracks.

Mine said, *Wise cracks? Who? Me?*

"So, Tweety," he proceeded, "did anyone go with you and Nils to the Eagles after Lars's funeral?"

She poked her nose into the air. "Why do you wanna know?"

"Because it's my job." He scrubbed his face with his hand. Yep, he'd rather bust up brawls at the Eagles every night of the week than deal with Tweety. "Now, tell me."

She gnawed the nail on her right middle finger. Like the others, it had been chewed to the quick. "No one went with us, but Gustaf did meet us there." She patted her yellow yarn-like hair. "We happened to leave the church at the same time, and Nils asked if he wanted to join us for a drink. Nils is a nice guy, and he reckoned that Gustaf could use a drink or two after what Louise put him through, serving him divorce papers in front of every-body."

"Why didn't you mention Gustaf when we first discussed your alibi?"

"Like I said, Sheriff, he didn't go with us. And he wasn't the only guy I talked to when I was there." She scowled at me. "Unlike some people, I have lots of friends."

I sat on my hands to keep from reaching across the table and wringing her neck.

And Karl? He watched both of us until certain he wouldn't have to break up a fight. "But, Tweety," he then said, "you and Nils did sit with Gustaf, right?"

"Yeah. Most of the time. Except for… well… when we didn't."

The sheriff squeezed his eyes shut. I had seen him do it many times. He was counting to himself, in hopes of regaining his cool. "When you were seated with him," he said once he was all done, although he didn't look any calmer, "did he phone anyone?"

Grace shuffled closer, willing to risk burning the omelet to hear Tweety's response.

"Besides Dirk?" she asked.

"You heard him call Dirk?"

"Of course. He was sitting right next to me. And he called him for me. Though he used his own phone." She stopped for second. "But I told you all that before."

"No, you didn't."

She covered her mouth with her fingers. "Oops. My bad. Well, I meant to. See, Gustaf called because I didn't dare. Still, I wanted to give Dirk a piece of my mind."

Again, Karl shot me a warning look.

And, once more, I said nothing, though this time I had to bite my tongue until I swore I tasted blood.

"Sooo," Karl went on, exasperation oozing through the word, "Gustaf phoned Dirk, but he didn't answer, so you called him?"

"How did you know that?" She didn't wait for an answer. "I called him a few minutes later, after I got my courage up." Tweety fluttered her spider-like eyelashes. "There were a few things I wanted to get off my chest."

Karl cut his eyes my way, but I only shrugged. Jokes about Tweety's massive bosom were overdone. She couldn't help that her boobs were so big that her feet had barely grown to a size five because of all the shade. "What exactly did you intend to tell him?" Karl asked.

"Well, Gustaf and I both planned to say that he didn't have any right to be a… nincompoop to me. Though we were gonna use way worse words."

Karl inhaled deeply. "Okay, Tweety, one last question: At any time, did you get the impression that Gustaf might have been acquainted with Dickerson beforehand?"

Tweety offered up a deer-in-headlights look, prompting Karl to try again. "Do you think Gustaf knew Dickerson before he called him?"

"Nope." She pumped her fists against her hips. "But that didn't mean he couldn't tell him off." Once again she raised her big-bird beak into the air. And, for a moment, I pondered the likelihood of her drowning if she ever stood like that out in the rain. "Gustaf's not so bad," she added. "Although Dirk ended up being a louse."

Because Karl had been reviewing his notes, he was distracted when he asked, "When was that exactly, Tweety?"

"Well," she answered, "he's probably always been a louse. But I only realized it yesterday."

"No!" Karl appeared as if he wanted to punch something. "I meant… when did you and Nils and Gustaf leave the Eagles?"

"Oh. Around seven. But only me and Nils left. Gustaf stayed." She shook her head. "Sheriff, I swear I told you all this stuff before. Are you sure you didn't just forget? Are you getting too old for your job?"

From the immediate look of regret in her eyes, I knew Tweety wanted to take those words back. But given she couldn't, she doubled down on them. "In any case, being I don't feel like repeating myself, I'm not gonna answer any more of your questions. And I don't hafta. It's my continental right, dontcha know."

"Trust me," Karl said. "I don't want to ask you anything else. Nor do I want to trample on your rights—continental or otherwise."

⊚　⊚　⊚

After Tweety left the kitchen with her Denver omelet order, I turned to Karl. "Let me get this straight. The Olafsons are in the clear for both deaths. Gustaf has an alibi for Dickerson's murder, and you're convinced that he was in his fish house, getting drunk, when Lars got killed. So that only leaves Dickerson and Dot as suspects in Lars's murder. But Dickerson's dead, and you let Dot go."

"You aren't surprised, are you? You never thought Dot was capable of murder anyways, right?"

"Since when do you listen to me? Besides, even though I've had trouble believing Dot could have killed her father, I've had no problem with the possibility of her killing Dickerson. He could have driven anyone to murder."

The sheriff stared at me over the end of his nose.

"Well, you know what I mean, Karl."

He sipped his coffee. "Doris, in the case of Lars's death, a tenant in his apartment building who's been out of town on business since Sunday morning came home last night and contacted us right after a neighbor updated him on everything that transpired in his absence. He—this new witness—confirmed that Dot's car was in the parking lot at five-fifteen, just like the earlier witness claimed. He recognized it from the big fuzzy dice hanging from the rearview mirror. But he's positive that Dot wasn't behind the wheel."

Grace returned to the prep table, sat down, and drank some of her coffee. "How can he be positive?" she asked as she set her cup down. "It had to be getting dark."

"It was," Karl said. "But the parking lot has lights. And after the Olafsons dropped Lars off and left, the person in Dot's SUV flashed their headlights. So, naturally, Lars went over to the car. And when he opened the door, the car's interior light flicked on. And that's also when this latest witness saw the driver. He'll swear it was a man."

Grace and I gaped at each other. "A man?" we said in unison.

"Did he recognize him?" I asked.

"Nope," Karl answered. "Said he had never seen him before. Though he was certain he had dark hair and a slender face."

"Sounds like Dickerson," Grace said.

"Yep." Karl glanced my way. "And not a bit like Gustaf."

Grace rose from her stool. "So Gustaf's truly in the clear in both cases?"

"That's right. Dickerson killed Lars." Karl glanced my way. There may have been a bit of "I told you so" in his tone. "But Dot's still under suspicion in Dickerson's death. Although we're looking at a few other possibilities too."

"Such as?" Of course, that was me. Always digging for more.

"Nothing I can discuss."

# Chapter 30

At two o'clock sharp, Grace locked the front door of the café, while I phoned the hospital from the kitchen. Rose had become more agitated, prompting Betcher to administer a stronger sedative. She was now sleeping peacefully.

As I dropped my phone back into my purse, I called Betcher a "poophead," not because he was a rotten doctor. He wasn't, regardless of what I said or thought about him as a human being. But I wanted Rose to get better, not worse. So, who else could I blame?

Determined to distract myself from worrying about Rose, I bent over to retrieve the boxes of party decorations from beneath the prep table. As I pulled on one of them, my butt high in the air, I heard the back door open and close. Because Grace was out front, I peered between my legs to see who had let themselves in. It was Karl.

I leapt as if goosed and hit my head on the corner of the table. "What are you doing here?" My tone was much harsher than I had intended. But that wasn't my fault. My head hurt. I was worried about Rose. And, as of late, my butt had felt way bigger than normal. Sure, I had meant to start exercising, but the back porch was freezing, and murder had gotten in the way.

Karl didn't strike me as particularly bothered by the tone of my voice or the size of my butt. He looked me up and down, his lips forming a crooked grin and his crow's feet doing their crinkly thing.

"What do you want?"

He dragged his eyes up to my face. "The temperature's dropping fast. That storm may get here a lot sooner than forecast." He stuffed his gloves into his jacket pocket.

"You didn't answer my question."

"Oh, I spotted your car. I wanted to find out how Rose was doing. I'm surprised you're here and not at the hospital."

"Betcher won't let us stay. He said Rose needs to rest. So Grace and I came back here to prepare for Will and Sophie's party. Grace is in the dining room."

Karl lifted the boxes for me, one at a time, from the floor to the table. "I figured the party would have been canceled."

"Not with Will's in-laws bunking at his house until afterwards."

Karl dropped down on a stool and unzipped his jacket. "I also wanted to thank you for what you and Grace got out of Arne and Anders last night, even though I'm not crazy about your methods."

I was about to argue that point when Grace strolled into the kitchen, the swinging doors squawking.

"Anyways," Karl said, switching topics, most likely to avoid arguing with both of us, "since Lars's murder case is pretty well wrapped up, the BCA will send out a press release tomorrow."

"Feels kind of anticlimactic." Yep, I had become a first-rate ghoul. "I wanted to look Dickerson in the eyes."

"I know, but–"

Grace interrupted. "Was Dot involved in any way?"

"No. It appears as if Dickerson planned and executed Lars's murder all by himself."

"That surprises me." Grace spoke slowly, as if reviewing things at the same time. "I would have sworn that she'd had a role in it. After all, she and Lars didn't get along."

"True enough." Karl said. "But she didn't wish him dead. Or, at least, she didn't want him murdered."

"How about Dirk Dickerson's death then?" Grace asked. "What led Dot to kill him? Did she somehow discover that he had killed her dad, so she murdered him in revenge? Or did she kill him because she was jealous of his relationship with Tweety?"

"We can't comment on Dickerson's death at this time."

"Oh, come on, Karl." Grace scowled. "Dot's your culprit. Everyone knows it. And, believe me, most folks around here are getting a little impatient with you and those BCA agents for not charging her." She stopped for a beat. "Hell, not only haven't you charged her, you've released her from jail!"

"Grace, we have no physical evidence against her." Karl pressed his forearms against the table. "No prints were left on the broken wine bottle. As for the rest of the crime scene, it's bound to have Dot's prints all over it since it's her house. Furthermore, because she and Dickerson were an item, it won't be surprising if her DNA is found on his body."

"So, what happens now?" I asked, not trying very hard to keep my aggravation with him and his colleagues from seeping into my tone. "We just forget about the whole thing?"

"Of course, not," he replied. "Like I said, we're working on a few things."

"But you can't share them with us."

"Doris… "

◎  ◎  ◎

After Karl left to handle a domestic dispute and Grace ran to the store, I lugged the boxes of decorations into the dining room and taped up a sign that spelled "congratulations" in pink and blue letters. When I climbed down from my chair, I realized that I'd put it up backwards. "Ugh!"

Concentrating was tough. My mind was overflowing with questions: *How was Rose doing? Why were Karl and his law en-*

*forcement buddies so slow to arrest Dot for Dirk Dickerson's murder? Why hadn't I pressured Karl to pursue Dickerson sooner? And, what had kept me from believing Grace about Dot's guilt, at least in the Dickerson case?*

While rehanging the sign, I zeroed in on Dot because I couldn't do much about anything else at the moment. Regardless of what Karl had said or hadn't said, Dot had killed Dickerson. Although I really couldn't blame her. True, I didn't like that she had lied to me. But I probably would have lied too if I had killed someone.

What's more, Dickerson was an evil man. He was a no-good criminal, who had murdered Dot's father and attempted to steal her inheritance. He had also played her for a fool. And I knew firsthand how angry that could make someone.

Many times over the years, I had daydreamed about different ways to do away with Bill. Not that I ever would have followed through. But I did enjoy thinking about it on occasion.

After climbing down from my chair and ensuring that the sign now hung properly, I sat down. To my way of thinking, every aspect of this ordeal had to be resolved if we wanted to see Rose return to her old self. That included arresting Dickerson's murderer. So, I had no choice. I had to come up with a plan to get Dot to confess. I couldn't wait for law enforcement.

A knock at the front door of the cafe jolted me out of my trance. Ed Monson stood on the other side of the glass.

"Yes?" I said, throwing the bolt open.

"I'm looking for Gustaf. Have you seen him?" Dressed in blue jeans and a brown Carhartt jacket rather than his uniform, Ed seemed different. Even less sure of himself than usual. His eyes darted around the room. And once he had completed that circuit, he examined the floor. "I really need to talk to him."

"No, I haven't seen him. Is there something I can do?"

"Umm… well… umm… no. He's supposed to assist me tonight. That's all. With the pyrotechnics and such."

"The what?" I gulped cold air but still kept Ed outside the open door. "You plan to use explosives at tonight's party? Inside the café?" That sounded dangerous and foolish on so many levels.

"Not real explosives," he assured me. "I just jerry-rigged some sparkler-like cones to shoot blue or pink confetti, depending on what kind of baby Will tells me they're having."

"You know how to do that?" I had my doubts. Extreme doubts.

"It's not hard. There are tons of how-to videos on You-Tube."

"You-Tube videos?" My voice climbed in direct proportion to my increasing anxiety. "Your training with explosives is limited to You-Tube videos?"

"Like I said, they're not true explosives. They don't pose any risk." He twisted his lips. "As long as they're packed right."

"And you packed them?"

"Well, yeah, earlier today. Six with pink confetti and six with blue confetti. Now, I just have to wait to find out which six to light."

No question about it. This was a bad idea. And I'd make sure to let Will know exactly how I felt as soon as Ed left. "Well, like I said, I haven't seen Gustaf."

"Okay, then. I'll keep looking for him."

That comment caught my attention. "Ed, you really watch out for Gustaf, dontcha?"

"What do you mean?" He looked at me as if leery about what I might say next.

"Well, for example, on the night Lars died, you went searching for him. That's what I heard anyhow. And that's how you found him in his fish house, drunk."

Ed shuffled his feet on the cement landing. "Yeah, well, as you probably know by now, he's my dad. And, that day, just before the café closed, I stopped in, and Tweety told me how Lars and Etta had been in earlier. She said they planned to get back together." He paused. "Anyways, I knew that would hurt Gustaf something terrible. See, he really likes Etta. So I wanted to find him and make sure he was okay."

"That was nice of you."

"Yeah, well, I better go."

"No, wait. Come on in here for a second, will you?" Grabbing the sleeve of his jacket, I didn't give him much choice. I yanked him inside and closed the door, shutting out the cold. "I have a question for you."

He shifted his weight from one foot to the other but never met my eyes. Karl was right. I made the kid uncomfortable.

Not knowing how to broach the subject of what he'd been doing along the shoreline at Lake Bronson, I once more jumped right in, not bothering to test the water. "Umm… speaking of Gustaf… He and I were out at the lake yesterday and saw you walking up to your squad car from the shore. Has he said anything about that?"

Ed's nervousness was replaced by caution. He pulled his head back, as if to distance himself even farther. "I haven't talked to him for a couple days. Why?"

"Well, since you were in uniform when you were out there, we figured you were on duty. And we were just curious what you were up to."

He vacillated. "Umm… doing some police business. That's all."

I found myself wringing my hands. "The thing is, that's approximately where Gustaf thought he saw someone in the brush on the night Lars got killed. Did you know that?"

"Umm… yeah…of course. He mentioned it to me that night, after I picked him up at his fish house."

"Really? That's interesting. He told me he couldn't remember saying anything about it."

Irritation crossed Ed's face like a storm cloud. "Of course, he couldn't remember. He was fricking drunk."

"I'm confused then. Why were you only checking out his story today? It's been almost a week since Lars got killed."

He shifted from one foot to the other. "It's the first chance I've had. We've been kind of busy—and short-handed."

"Still, I can't imagine Karl—"

"Karl doesn't know." He fisted his hands. The young man's patience was waning. "I wanted to investigate it myself first.

258

Make sure that Gustaf hadn't been seeing things. Like I said, he was really drunk. I didn't want him to get embarrassed, him being my dad and all."

Given Ed's growing agitation, I proceeded with caution. "Yeah… well… when you came back to the road from the shoreline, you put something into a clear plastic bag."

He practically jumped on my words. "How did you see that?"

"That's not important." If he learned about the binoculars, so would Karl and everyone else, and my reputation as a busybody would be forever cemented. "Anyhow, Gustaf got all excited that you may have uncovered evidence to prove his recollection accurate."

"Well, I really can't say."

"Oh, come on."

"No, I can't. It's part of an investigation. I'd get in a lot of trouble. It's happened before."

"But you can tell me. I'm the mother of your partner. She's a deputy too. On top of that, whatever it is, it's bound to become public knowledge soon enough."

A strange expression overtook his face. "No wonder he said you might be a problem."

"Huh? What was that?"

"Never mind." Ed's cheeks flushed, and he looked away. "Now, I really have to go and find Gustaf." He turned toward the window, as if he might see Gustaf outside.

"But… "

"No. I have to go."

## Chapter 31

Following Ed's departure, I intended to review our conversation. After being wrong about the Olafson twins because of the open-door, closed-door thing, I was determined not to gloss over anything else. First, though, I had two calls to make.

"What is wrong with you?" I asked Will before he even had the chance to speak. "You're letting Ed light fireworks in the café?"

He chuckled. "Calm down, Mom."

"Don't tell me to calm down."

"He's lighting a few sparklers, that's all. The table will be covered with a fire-retardant cloth. And Grace has approved it all. So, relax. It will be perfectly safe."

"It doesn't sound safe. And I didn't get the impression that he planned to limit himself to a 'few sparklers.'"

"I'll talk to him. But, trust me, it'll be fine."

He paused while listening to someone in the background. "Mom? Sophie wants to know how Rose is doing. What's the latest?"

I filled him in. He said something about wishing he could share a room with her at the hospital until his in-laws went back to Fargo. Then, he disconnected.

Next, I called Gustaf. I got his voicemail and left a message for him to call me or stop by the café as soon as he had a chance.

Then, I pushed three tables to the front of the room, near the service window. I covered them with pink and blue paper table-cloths, littered them with pink and blue confetti, and adorned them with one-foot tall, pink and blue stuffed bears, mylar bal-loons clasped in their paws. The serving dishes would sit among the bears.

I shoved another table to the center of the room, where the "reveal" would occur. Because I couldn't find anything in the boxes that resembled a fire-retardant cloth, I left the table bare and moved onto the booths.

"I can't understand it," I complained to the universe. "Who in their right mind would let Ed light fireworks inside the café?"

"What was that?" Gustaf asked from behind me, as I jumped out of my skin.

Spinning around, I spotted him staring at me from over the swinging doors. And when he opened the doors, I saw Ole standing beside him.

"You guys ever think of letting someone know when you're sneaking up on them?"

"Wouldn't that defeat the purpose?" There was a snicker in Ole's voice.

"Anyways, we did say something." Gustaf waved away my complaint. "You were just too busy talking to yourself to hear us."

"So, what's going on?" Ole wanted to know. "I convinced Gustaf to take a couple hours off work to go fishing, and we were coming back into town when we got your call. But the big man here"—he gestured toward Gustaf—"couldn't get his phone out of his pants' pocket until after the call had already gone to voice-mail."

They walked toward me in something less than a straight line, both of them giving off the odor of fish and booze.

"Do you know what Ed plans to do tonight?" I had set a pink and blue stuffed bear on the table in each booth, per Grace's instructions. They'd go home as door prizes at the end of the evening.

"Yeah, but don't worry." Gustaf waved his massive hand. "Ole and I are gonna help him."

"Oh, well, that makes me feel a whole lot better."

My sarcasm wasn't lost on them. Not on Ole at any rate. He slapped his thigh and chortled until his laugh morphed into a hacking cough. Whipping out his hanky, he spit in it.

"I suppose you two have heard that Rose is in the hospital?" They nodded before I added, "Have you also heard that Dot's the prime suspect in Dickerson's murder?"

Gustaf groaned. "Jeez, Doris, of course, we've heard. We were fishing. We weren't out of the country."

"Okay. Do you have any idea how we can trap her into confessing?" With my box of bears empty, I took a break and sat down in a booth.

"Whoa! You want her to confess?" Gustaf's squished his sweaty, alcohol-flushed face. "Doris, I was no fan of Lars, as everyone knows. But Dickerson was… well… a dick, so I'd be more apt to pin a medal on Dot's chest than cuff her wrists."

"But until she's arrested, things around here will remain chaotic, which won't be good for Rose. And she's my priority."

"I understand." Gustaf nodded. "But I just don't think… "

"What did you have in mind?" Ole's gold-flecked eyes shined through his driftwood face. "I'll do whatever I can for Rose."

Ole had always had a soft spot for Rose. Why the two of them had never gotten together was a mystery to me. Then, again, perhaps they had, and I was simply unaware.

"Well," I said, "being we'll all be down here tonight, I thought I'd invite Dot. Tell her she needs to get out, or folks will think she's guilty. Then, once she's here, I'll press her into opening up about what she did–"

"She hit that Dickerson fellow over the head with a wine bottle. That's what she did," Ole said. "I'm not saying he didn't deserve it. But there's no denying what happened."

I raised my hand, palm out. "But, when I spoke with her at the jail, she swore up and down that she had nothing to do with his death."

Gustaf snorted. "What did you expect her to say?"

"I don't know." I needed more time to think. "Grace is getting groceries and booze for tonight. She should be back soon. I'll see what she thinks."

"And Karl?" Gustaf asked. "What does he have to say about you trapping Dot into confessing?"

"He doesn't know. He's not crazy about me getting involved in his business." An understatement if there ever was one.

"I wonder why?" Ole said with a snicker.

I placed my hands on my hips. "Regardless of what he thinks, I won't sit by and do nothing while Rose lies in a hospital bed, hooked up to oxygen and a heart monitor because of everything that's happened around here."

That got Ole to take a step closer. "She's that bad off?"

"Well, Betcher's administering heavy-duty sedatives, and she can't have visitors."

Ole kicked at the floor with the toe of his rubber overshoes, the loose buckles tinkling with each knock against the wood. "I hafta go home and shower." He pointed a crooked finger at Gustaf. "He has to do the same. After fishing—even for a couple hours—we both stink like fish guts."

"Really?" Gustaf sniffed under his jacket sleeves. "I don't stink."

"Your nose ain't working then. Anyways, Doris, we'll get cleaned up and meet you back here in a little while. Then, we'll make a plan. Okay?"

I smiled despite my bad mood. "Okay."

As they turned to leave, I remembered that I had a message for Gustaf. I grabbed his arm. "Hey, Ed's looking for you. It sounds like he's recovered some evidence to support your contention that you saw someone by the lake the night Lars got killed. Not that it will change anything. Dickerson killed him. It's official."

Gustaf sighed. "Still, I promised myself that if we discovered I had imagined it all, I'd cut back on my drinking. So, this is a relief because I like to drink." He clicked his tongue against the roof of his mouth. "Although… since I don't recall mentioning anything about it to Ed, maybe I should taper off on the alcohol anyways. What do you think, Doris? Is not remembering what you did or didn't tell someone as bad as questioning what you saw?"

Oh, brother. "I don't know, Gustaf. But, either way, drinking less wouldn't be the worst thing in the world." I thought about that. "As long as you're drinking, you won't ever ride in my car again. That's for darn sure."

# Chapter 32

When Ole and Gustaf returned to the café, all shaved, show-ered, and nearly sober, I was with Dot and Grace in the kitchen, arranging food on serving platters at the prep table.

After the men threw their jackets on the chair by the back door, they motioned me over to the counter near the stove. There, they loudly complained about the stormy weather and the slick roads.

"Okay, what's our plan?" Gustaf asked afterwards in what I assumed was his quiet voice.

"Pretty good diversion, huh?" Ole added. "Talking about the weather to throw her off?"

I shushed them both. "Why'd it take you so long to get back? It was tough to convince Dot to come down here in the first place. I don't know how much longer she'll stay. She doesn't like Grace or me."

Gustaf shook his head. "It wasn't my fault. Ole drove. And being his eyes are bad, he won't cross traffic, which means he'll only make right turns." Another shake of his head. "You have any idea how long it takes to get anywhere when you only turn right?"

"Oh, shut up. You're more annoying than a box of mosquitoes." Gustaf dismissed his friend with a flick of his wrist. "So,

Doris, what are we going to do? Lock her in the cooler until she confesses?"

"That won't work." Ole scowled. Or so I thought. With all his wrinkles, I had difficulty distinguishing his scowl from his happy face. "She could die of exposure before telling us anything."

"Yeah, I think we can do better than that." I bobbed my head toward the shelf above us. "Don't look now, but Grace set a small video camera on that shelf. We'll be able to capture everything Dot does. It even has audio."

Of course, both men right away rubbernecked in that direction.

"I don't see it," Gustaf whined.

"You aren't supposed to. But, trust me, it's there. And it's on. Grace says it has several hours of battery life."

"Where on earth did she find something like that around here?" Ole wanted to know. "I've never seen nothing like it in the hardware store, and they have prit' near everything."

"She already had it." I prayed they wouldn't ask any other questions. But, of course, they did.

"Why on earth did she have a gadget like that?" Gustaf wondered out loud.

"I refuse to say."

Ole snickered some more. "Oh, to be young again."

"Wait a minute. Now, I see it." Gustaf motioned to the shelf.

I swatted his hand and once more shushed him. "You two go into the dining room, like you're regular guests. Grace and I will get Dot talking. And when she says something incriminating, we'll signal for you through the service window. That's when you'll come back in here and detain her, while I call Karl."

"That could pose a problem," Ole said. "On my way over to pick up Gustaf, I saw Karl leaving town. He was in his personal car, and he didn't have his uniform on."

Gustaf responded with a grunt. "Why would he take time off during the middle of a murder investigation? That doesn't make sense."

I had to agree. Karl had been working non-stop all week.

"Doris?" Ole leaned toward me. "Don't you think you should let him in on your plan?"

"Naw." Why should I? He wouldn't tell me what he and his law enforcement buddies were up to. "He'll find out soon enough."

"Oh, brother." Gustaf wiped his sweaty face with the sleeve of his sweater. "You're lucky we both like Rose so much."

Ole had shifted his eyes in Dot's direction. "Say, Doris, just how long do you suppose we'll hafta keep her subdued after we take hold of her?" He looked back at me. "What I mean to say is, how fast do you reckon Karl can get here, especially since you have no idea where he is?" Dot carried an industrial-sized casserole dish from the walk-in cooler to the prep table. "She looks kinda strong. Not as strong as Tweety, mind you. But strong just the same."

Gustaf dismissed Ole's concern with a snort. "If we need help, Ed's here."

"No!" I hollered, which led both Grace and Dot to spin my way before I assured them with a hand and a smile that all was fine. "I don't want to involve him."

"Why not?" Gustaf appeared confused. "He hasn't done anything wrong."

"I didn't mean it like that." How could I suggest that Ed was more of a hinderance than a help without offending Gustaf? He was Ed's newfound father, and I needed his assistance. "It's just that... umm... I don't want Ed to get in trouble with Karl. You know how the sheriff can be about his deputies following police procedure."

Gustaf nodded. "Yeah, I suppose, you're right."

◎　◎　◎

I stepped over the cords I had duct taped to the floor behind the serving table in the café's dining area. Grace had prepared Crook Pot Cube Steak, a slow cooker full of Spaghetti Hot Dish, and a casserole dish full of Mexican Tater-Tot Hot Dish.

At the end of the table, just beyond the Raspberry Jell-O Salad and the bar platters, sat the cake Grace had baked and decorated. It mirrored the stuffed bears elsewhere in the room, although it measured two feet tall from the tips of its ears to where it sat with its legs outstretched. It was covered in pink and blue buttercream frosting. The inside featured alternating layers of chocolate and vanilla cake with raspberry filling.

My dearest wish was that everyone would eat so much hot dish that they'd end up too full for dessert. Then, there'd be lots of leftover cake for Grace to bring home. That is, if I could convince her not to serve it in the café tomorrow.

Close to fifty people mingled in the room to the soft strains of lullaby music, which probably explained why everyone whispered, and lots of people yawned. The corner-booth ladies had claimed their usual spot, their ranks swelling by one after Tweety joined them, her plate heaping.

Etta Wilhelm and several other current and former teachers were there to celebrate Sophie, a teacher herself.

And many of the farmers who normally lined the counter in the morning had returned, some with their wives. Most of those men claimed their regular stools, as if magnetically drawn to them, leaving their wives to fend for themselves.

Ed manned the "reveal" table, now covered in a heavy-duty silver tarp, ostensibly the fire-resistant cloth my son had mentioned on the phone. The deputy checked and rechecked the tops and bottoms of a half dozen gold cones and a half dozen silver ones, while I prayed that he did so out of an abundance of caution and not because he couldn't determine which end to light.

After assuring that everyone was satiated with food and drink, I drummed up an excuse to exit a conversation with Sophie's parents regarding the advantages of private schools. I had to agree with Will that Sophie's folks were full of themselves and a bit out of touch. After all, what was the point of advocating for a private education for their grandchild when he—or she—would live here, where Will farmed? The only school in this area, while highly touted statewide, was small and public.

As I zigzagged around the tables, heading back to the kitchen, Gustaf and Ole caught my eye. Each of them engaged in various gesticulations, yet I couldn't make sense of any of them. Even so, I nodded, presuming they were code of some kind to advise me that they were ready to take on Dot.

"Break time," I announced to Dot and Grace when I re-entered the kitchen.

I sat down next to Dot at the prep table.

She poured me a cup of coffee and slid it my way. "Now, tell me, Doris, why did you really ask me down here?"

Nothing like getting straight to the point. "Umm... as I said, you'll look guilty if–"

"Why do you care if I look guilty? We don't even like each other."

I couldn't disagree with her there, so I stalled by sipping coffee while attempting to come up with a plausible explanation for her invitation. "Well... umm... Dirk Dickerson was a horrible person. I'm sure any judge or jury would take that into account. That is, if his killer were to confess."

Dot stared at her reflection in the prep table. "The sheriff told me earlier that Ed discovered more evidence against Dirk out at the lake."

"Really?"

"Yeah, the sheriff said he found Dad's wallet, so that'll be a feather in his cap."

I could only repeat to myself, *Even a blind squirrel...*

"Dot?" Grace stood directly beneath the shelf that supported the hidden camera. "What about Dirk's murder?" She spoke louder than necessary and carefully enunciated each word. "Did Karl mention anything about that?"

Dot smiled. "You mean, did he ask me why I killed him?"

My sister and I exchanged wide eyes.

"Umm... no one is accusing you of killing anyone," Grace

said. "Although most folks wouldn't care if you had killed Dick-erson. He was a rotten man, and everyone came to realize that. Some of us sooner than others."

I rolled my eyes. If there was an opportunity to crow, Grace would take it, regardless of the circumstances.

For her part, Dot teared up behind her glasses. "Since I got out of jail, my daughter won't even answer my calls. I phoned her at least four times this afternoon."

"I'm sure that once you explain everything, she'll come around." An idea occurred to me, and before thinking it through, I blurted out, "Want to practice on me?"

Dot lifted one corner of her mouth. "You're really something."

Uncertain if that was a compliment or not, I refrained from reacting.

"You actually believe that I killed Dirk, despite everything I told you at the jail."

"Well… umm… the evidence does point to you."

Dot looked past me, a strange expression taking over her face. I, in turn, glimpsed over my shoulder to find Gustaf and Ole leaning against the service window, doing an awful job of pre-tending not to listen to us. As soon as they discerned that we were on to them, however, they announced that Ed was ready with the gender reveal.

# Chapter 33

Will whispered in Deputy Monson's ear, and Ed removed the six silver cones from the reveal table, placing them at his feet. Apparently, the gold ones contained the appropriately colored confetti.

Grace, Dot, and I watched from the kitchen, propping our elbows on the ledge of the service window, while Will rejoined Sophie, both of them sitting on decorated stools about ten feet in front of Ed.

"No," Dot said, "I still can't believe you two. Even the police have given me the 'all clear.'"

"What?" My elbow slipped off the ledge, and I almost face-planted on the counter. "Then, why were you hiding in your house?"

"I wasn't hiding. I was mourning the death of my father and seething over my daughter's reaction to everything."

"But why haven't you spoken up for yourself?" Grace's voice was shrill. "Publicly, I mean."

"Because the sheriff asked me to give law enforcement a little more time—at least through tonight—to wrap things up."

"Wrap things up?" It took me an extra moment to process that. "They know who killed Dickerson?"

"Yep. And it wasn't me."

"Then, who was—"

"They didn't say."

I felt deceived by both Karl and Dot. He had known all of this—or some of it, at least—when he stopped by earlier. Yet he didn't offer me so much as a hint. He insisted he couldn't discuss it. Still, he went all Chatty Cathy with Dot.

And speaking of Dot, she had come down to the café under false pretenses. She knew she wasn't a murderer. "So, Dot," I said, more than a little ticked off, "if what you're telling us is true, why'd you agree to join us?"

She chuckled. "I wanted to see what you two dimwits were up to." She eyed Grace. "The hidden camera was a nice touch."

Grace's mouth dropped open, but someone saved her the embarrassment of rationalizing her use of the camera by clinking their knife against their drink glass until Will and Sophie stood and kissed.

Afterwards, Will said, "Oops, wrong celebration. In fact, that celebration was what caused our current situation." He patted Sophie's baby bump. "Anyways," he continued, as everyone politely laughed, "thank you all for coming out on such a stormy night." He eyed the plate-glass windows at the front of the cafe.

Even though the sky was dark, the swirling snow remained visible around the streetlights, like the inside of a snow globe. "And I'm sure you all want to head home before the roads get any worse, so let's not waste any more time." He raised Sophie's hand in his. "On with the reveal!"

Hearing that, everyone clapped and cheered.

Everyone but me, that is. I was obsessing over something. "Dot?" I said, drawing our guest's attention back to my sister and me. "Tell us again about your arrival at the law office for the reading of your father's will."

"Why?"

"I'm not sure. I'm just troubled by something." I was quick to add, "Nothing you did. It's something else."

She leaned against the pass-through window. "Well, like I've already said a zillion times, I got there just after seven. I followed Ed inside. But I sat across the room from him because he had drenched himself in enough aftershave to drown a duck."

Her eyes skipped between Grace and me. "He was all cleaned up. Fresh uniform. Hair still wet from his shower." She snorted. "But it didn't matter. He got next to nothing, just like me."

That didn't help. Whatever had been niggling at me continued to do so.

"Dot?" I needed to let whatever it was come to me in its own time. Meanwhile, I'd ask the question that had been plaguing me since the first time I met Dirk Dickerson. "What did you ever see in the guy? I only met him once, but I found him to be a complete ass." Granted, I didn't consider Dot much of a catch either. But that was beside the point.

"Well, Doris, he wasn't crazy about you. After I spoke to you at the Cenex station on Monday, I mentioned to him how nosy you were. And—"

"I am not nosy."

"Whatever. Then, after running into you at the medical center, he wanted to know more." She eyed me sideways. "And, trust me, it wasn't because he considered you cute. You're way too old for him."

"Dot, not that it matters, but I'm only two years older than you and Grace."

She looked at me like I was one bubble short of plumb. "Really? You seem way older."

I fisted my hands, pressing my fingernails into my palms until the pain was so great that I forgot all about popping her a good one.

She went on, oblivious to how angry I was. "Anyways, once we got done discussing you, he said something about how you 'might be a problem.' That you probably 'needed watching.' I asked him what he meant by that, but he wouldn't say."

"He said that?" My anger was replaced by ripples of concern. "Those were his exact words?"

"Yeah. I remember because I thought they were strange things to say."

Recalling my name on the notepad in his suite, I wondered what, if anything, he had planned for me? And, why? Sure, some people may have considered me a pain. But "a problem"? Not really. And I certainly didn't warrant "watching." I seldom did anything interesting or exciting. Grace could attest to that.

"Hey, you two," Grace said, "this isn't going to end well, is it?" She bobbed her head toward the reveal table, where Gustaf joined Ed, while Ole slunk to the back of the room.

Gustaf and Ed each grabbed a long-neck lighter, clicked on the flames, and lit the wicks on the six gold cones. At the same time, someone turned off the overhead lights.

As the wicks burned, curling smoke and the strong smell of sulfur filled the air. The cones sizzled. Then sputtered. And when it appeared that Ed's fireworks' show was a dud, the cones fell over, onto the floor, igniting the ones under the table. Just like that, all the cones took off like rockets, pink and blue confetti shooting from them around the room.

# Chapter 34

Folks ran every which way to evade the projectiles ricocheting off the ceiling and the walls. Because the lights remained off in the dining room, it was difficult to see anything until one of the flaming cones whizzed by.

From the safety of the kitchen, Grace called the fire department, while I watched Will lead his pregnant wife and his in-laws out the front door before returning to join others in their attempt to capture and extinguish the flying canisters.

As Grace headed out the back door to wait for the fire truck, Dot made her way through the swinging doors to offer assistance to some of the senior center ladies huddled behind the counter. The farmers remained on their stools, as if watching a floor show. While Gustaf located Etta, and Ole pulled his trusty hanky from his pocket to cover his nose and mouth.

As I took in everything from the kitchen side of the service window, I noticed Ed speaking with Tweety. And, when they were done, he beelined in my direction. With hot dish and Jell-O strewn all over, it wasn't easy to cross the floor without slipping and falling, but he managed.

Reaching the swinging doors, he appeared to yell at Ole, although I couldn't be sure given all the other shouting, not to mention the hissing and buzzing of the cones. In any event, Ole stood his ground, prompting Ed to flail his arms before shoving Ole aside. Ole stumbled but caught himself. Although Ed didn't stick around to see if he was okay. Instead, he barreled into the kitchen.

"What was that all about?" I shouted at Ed the second he was in front of me. "No one pushes Ole."

Ed said nothing. He merely tried to shuffle away from me, yet I stayed right with him. Eying the back door, he made a second attempt to dance around me, but I followed his lead, step for step.

"Where do you think you're going?" I asked once he finally stood still. "You can't leave. The fire fighters are on their way. The police too. And they'll want to speak with you. After all, this is your doing."

"I know. I know. But it'll be... umm... easier to talk to them outside. It's too chaotic in here."

"Grace is out there. She'll let us know when they get here."

Nevertheless, he started for the door.

"Wait." I followed. "I need to ask you something."

He spun around. "What?"

"Who told you that I 'might be a problem'? According to Dot, it was Dickerson. But that can't be because you didn't know him. You never even spoke to him, right? So how would you have any idea what he had said about me?"

Ed swallowed hard. "What are you blabbering about?"

"Earlier today, Ed, when you stopped by here, you mentioned that someone thought I 'might be a problem.' Then, a little while ago, Dot told me that Dickerson had said that exact same thing. He used those very same words."

"You're nuts." He pivoted back toward the exit.

I slipped past him and pressed my back against the door. "Yeah, I might be nuts. But I know what I heard. So, when did you talk to Dickerson?"

"I never did. Except to schedule his interview for tomorrow."

"And while scheduling that meeting, my name happened to come up?"

"Of course, not."

"I didn't think so. That wouldn't make any sense. Which means, you spoke to him at some other time too." The notion that had been nagging at me finally revealed itself. "Perhaps after Dot left the house to look for Dirk and Tweety."

"What?"

"You claimed you left Dot's house at ten minutes to seven to go to the reading of the will. And since you hadn't seen Dot come back outside, you assumed she was still inside. But when I spoke to her at the jail, she told me that she left the house at six-fifteen in hopes of finding Dickerson and Tweety before going to the law office. So, you would have seen her leave."

"She's lying."

"I don't think so."

"Yes, she is."

I shrugged. "Okay. Let's say you're right. She lied. But what about you?"

"Huh?"

"Ed, you didn't arrive at the law office until five after seven. Why'd it take so long? It's less than a five-minute drive from Dot's house. Heck, everywhere in Hallock is less than a five-minute drive. You know that."

"I… ah… went home. I showered and changed clothes. I wanted to look decent."

"You already looked decent. I saw you a few hours earlier at the funeral and actually commented on your appearance. Your uniform was pressed. Your shoes, shined. Your hair, clean and trimmed."

"I don't need to stand here and listen to this."

"Anyhow," I said, ignoring his protest, "it makes me wonder what could have happened? Why'd you have to clean yourself up again?"

"Move." He pushed me aside, but I came right back to block the door, my arms and legs spread eagle.

"And what about the booze, Ed? You told Karl you smelled booze on Dot's breath at the law office. But she followed you in, then sat on the opposite side of the room. You couldn't have smelled her breath. Besides, she didn't go to the liquor store until after she left the law office."

He grabbed me by the arms and wrestled me away from the door.

"You killed Dickerson, didn't you?" My subconscious had taken a leap, and I felt compelled to announce it. "You waited until Dot left her house, then you killed him. And you tried to pin it on her."

He had heard enough. He threw me against the chair by the door, my head smacking the edge of the thick wooden seat. Touching the area, I felt an egg forming at my hairline. Although taking my hand away, I saw no blood. I had the hardest skull around.

"No one will believe you," he hollered, yanking the door open.

"Don't be too sure." I nodded toward the far side of the kitchen.

He jerked around to find Dot, Gustaf, and Ole.

Nonetheless, after only a second of hesitation, he ran out the door, right into the arms of two firefighters. He struggled out of their grasp, no doubt intending to find another way out. But when he spun around, Dot, Gustaf, and Ole were there, blocking his path.

"Is that true, Ed?" Gustaf asked, his eyes wet with tears. "Did you kill that Dickerson fellow?"

Ed began to sob. "I didn't mean to, Dad. Really, I didn't."

# Chapter 35

"You missed all the commotion," I told Karl a while later, as I finger combed pink and blue confetti from my hair. "And what's with the snazzy outfit?" I didn't often see him out of uniform. He looked good. Dark blue jeans and a blue-plaid flannel shirt under a black leather jacket. He was clean-shaven too.

"I worked this afternoon, and I'm off tonight. But one of the BCA agents called and asked that I stop by and try to get Ed to open up." He wiped a piece of confetti off my shoulder. And even though I had worn a turtleneck, topped with a heavy cardigan, I quivered from his touch. Again, pathetic.

"You okay?" He raised his eyes to the bump on my head.

"Yeah. I fell against a chair."

"Really? I heard you got shoved."

I shrugged. "Whatever."

When it became clear that I didn't want to talk about my ugly bruise or what had caused it, he surveyed the room. "How bad's the damage?"

"They didn't have to hose anything down." I looked to the buffet table. Several fire fighters were eating smoke-flavored hot dish and blackened cake. "But, of course, the place will need to air out. And the walls will have to be repaired. Some of those cones were like warheads."

He wiped my check with his index finger. "You had some Jell-O there."

"Yeah." I fidgeted, my emotions running high. "When the cones launched, almost everyone heaved their plates into the air."

He smiled.

And I checked out those fire fighters once more. "So, Karl," I said, my eyes still on those at the buffet table, "what… umm… did you get out of Ed?"

"Well, it sounds like he just lost it. Last night he called Dickerson to schedule the meeting with the BCA guys. And because he had spoken to Tweety shortly after the funeral, he knew that Dickerson was after Dot's inheritance, but he didn't want her. Or Tweety, for that matter."

It was his turn to scan the room. "Well, that got Ed thinking. He became suspicious of Dickerson and drove over to Dot's. He got there just ahead of her and hid his truck behind the school."

"Oh. That's why no one in the neighborhood noticed anything out of the ordinary."

"Exactly. Then, after Dot left the house at six-fifteen, Ed knocked on Dickerson's door, and Dickerson let him in. Ed said the guy had been drinking. I guess he had stopped at the Eagles and was about to open a bottle of wine."

Karl looked over his shoulder yet again as if searching for something or someone.

I tracked his eyes. The senior center ladies had already scooped up most of the broken dishes and were now mopping squished hot dish and cake from the floor., The place smelled like burnt toast.

"He—I'm talking about Dickerson—knew that Dot had overheard him bad mouthing her at the church." Karl turned back to me. "And he suspected that she planned to kick him out. So, apparently, he was hiding in the guest suite, hoping she'd calm down."

"That means he was there when Dot got home from the funeral."

"Yep. But he knew better than to answer the door when she knocked."

While no one got seriously hurt by the flying canisters, a couple people sustained minor burns, and one of the corner-booth ladies had to go to the hospital for an x-ray after slipping on Jell-O.

"Anyways," Karl went on to say, "Ed started asking questions, and Dickerson was just drunk enough to answer a lot of them. That's how I know all this. Dickerson also said that when Lars was on his way home from the casino with the Olafson brothers, he—Dickerson, that is—called him. That's when Lars told him he'd never invest with him because he didn't trust him."

I rolled my eyes. "Pot meet kettle."

"Yeah. Well..." Another glimpse over his shoulder.

"Hey, are you looking for someone, Karl?"

"Ah... umm... no, not really." His cheeks flushed, but I couldn't imagine he was blushing. He had never struck me as the type. "Now, what was I saying?"

I wasn't used to Karl talking so much or so rapidly. It was out of character, like he was anxious about something. What? I had no idea. "Umm, Lars swore he'd never invest with Dickerson."

"Right. So that's when Dickerson decided that Lars had to die. Remember, Dot had assured him that she stood to inherit a lot of money. And he figured he'd be able to persuade her to give him much of it."

Once more glancing around the room myself, I noticed that Gustaf, Ole, Dot, and Etta were seated in a booth, munching on chips and looking more than a little shell shocked. The murmer of their voices, along with everyone else's, created a hum that was oddly comforting. I turned back to Karl. "So, he borrowed Dot's SUV and..."

"He told Ed that if the cops were to find evidence in a vehicle, he'd prefer it be Dot's."

"A real charmer, huh?"

"Yeah." He waited a beat. "He then fed Lars some cock-and-bull story about Hannah being hurt out at Lake Bronson and Dot needing his help. But, once they got there, Dickerson hit Lars over the head with a shovel and dumped him and the shovel into some open water he had heard somebody talk about."

I had trouble taking it all in. It was unbelievable in so many respects.

"Oh, yeah," Karl said, "I almost forgot. Dickerson also mentioned to Ed that Lars's phone had fallen out of his pocket, but he found it again and threw it to the lake. Ed said that's why he went out there. He thought he might uncover more evidence against Dickerson. And, sure enough, he found Lars's wallet."

"But he had already killed Dickerson."

"Yeah, I think he mostly wanted to ease his conscience. You know, if Dickerson had so brutally murdered Lars, it wasn't so bad for Ed to kill Dickerson."

I shook my head. "You're right, Karl. Ed truly lost it." I paused. "So, what about Gustaf?"

"Well, Ed told me that Gustaf had never mentioned anything to him about seeing someone along the shore. He only said that in hopes of keeping you from poking around."

While all of that was interesting, we still hadn't touched upon the subject that most directly impacted me. And, even though I wasn't sure I wanted to learn the details, I knew I had to ask the questions. "Karl, did Ed say why my name appeared on Dickerson's writing pad?"

"Eh?" Karl twisted his lips. "I thought your name was there because you had a meeting with the guy?"

I intended to say something snarky, but my eyes got watery, and my lips quivered.

"I'm sorry." Karl stepped closer. "I shouldn't be teasing you. It's been a rough night." He clasped my arms but right away dropped his hands again. "Ed told me that when he noticed your name on the pad of paper and asked about it, Dickerson called you nosy and—"

"I'm not nosy."

"Whatever. Anyway, he said you might be a problem and needed watching or something along those lines."

A wave of nausea flowed through me. "Did Ed say what Dickerson had in store for me? What he planned to do?"

"No. But you don't have to worry about him anymore." He bent his head and met my eyes. "He can't hurt you."

I inhaled a deep breath. "You know, Ed stopped by here earlier."

"Yeah, he told me. He was looking for Gustaf. He knew he was losing it, and he needed to come clean. He wanted his dad's help."

"He obviously changed his mind."

"Like I said, he snapped. He's a mass of contradictions right now. When I asked why he tried to implicate Dot, he said he did it because she wasn't nice to him. She wouldn't accept him into the family. But he also told me that even though Lars was a bad person, he had to stick up for him because he was family."

Karl skimmed the room. "Umm… yeah… after he realized that the guy was dead, he panicked. He needed to leave and get cleaned up. His uniform was blood splattered. So he called me to say he had been invited to the reading of the will. Of course, that wasn't true. I spoke to Myrle earlier today. He said he didn't invite Ed to join them because he didn't want Dot to go all Rambo on him. Besides, there wasn't much to inherit."

"So, why did he go?"

"To establish an alibi of sorts. And to plant seeds of suspicion about Dot."

I needed a break to allow my mind to work through everything. So, with a flick of the collar on Karl's flannel shirt, I said, "Now, tell me again, why did you get a night off?"

"Well, we were on to Ed. We had spoken with Myrle, among others. And the BCA guys planned to stop over at Ed's house later tonight." He stuffed his hands in his pants' pockets and jingled his keys and change. "But they thought it might be best if I wasn't involved."

"Why? Don't they trust you?"

"Doris, it's not always a matter of trust. Sometimes, it's just how things have to be. But none of that matters because you decided to take him down first." He playfully chucked my chin. "From what I understand, you even have audio and video."

"The tape was Grace's idea. And, in truth, we had Dot pegged as Dickerson's killer. Gustaf wanted to stick her in the walk-in freezer until she confessed."

An attractive blonde in her early fifties sashayed up to Karl and snaked her hand through the crook in his arm. "Hey, Karl, do you have to stay here much longer? I'm getting hungry." She motioned to the buffet table. "And I'm not eating that."

Karl's jingling picked up. "Oh… umm… Natasha, this is Doris." His eye twitched like he was winking, but I knew better than that. I had never felt like vomiting when Karl winked at me. "We… umm… were on our way to dinner," he said, "when I got the call to stop by here."

My mouth went bone dry. Yet I somehow squeaked out, "Well, don't let me keep you."

"Yeah, I suppose, we should go."

And, with that, Karl and what's-her-name left the building.

# Chapter 36

The cafe had emptied out except for Grace and me. We pulled a couple chairs up to the buffet table and ate cake without benefit of plates. Finishing off the bear's legs, we started in on its face.

After a while, I said to my sister, "I don't even taste the smoke anymore." I swallowed another forkful of buttercream frosting.

"I think all the sugar has deadened our senses."

"I wish that were true. I really don't want to feel a thing."

Grace tore off the bear's right ear and nibbled on it, frosting oozing between her fingers. "Now, tell me, what was Karl doing with Natasha Bagstad?"

"Is that who that was?" I made an effort to sound disinterested. "I don't think I know her."

"She just moved here from Fargo. She's the new court administrator, which means her office is right down the hall from the sheriff's office."

"Good for her." I kept up the pretense although I realized that Grace knew better.

"What did you expect, Doris?" She licked her fingers. Some were blue from the frosting, a couple were pink, and the bandage that covered her latest burn was an odd shade of purple. "It's clear that he's interested in you. He's asked you out a million times. But you keep turning him down."

"I went to a fish fry with him."

"Months ago."

"Well, I can't run around willy-nilly all the time. I have things to do. Obligations."

Grace groaned.

"Besides," I said, "I don't want anything to happen between us."

"Which is good, since it now appears as if that's unlikely."

I punched her in the arm. "It probably wouldn't have worked anyhow."

"Well, it certainly won't if you don't try."

"I mean it, Grace." I forked more cake. Unlike my sister, I had class. I used plastic silverware to eat the bear. "Most relationships don't last. And they're hard to get over. I'm better off with just friends."

"Like Dot?"

I shrugged. "I suppose I could try. After all, I'm getting used to Gustaf."

"How about Tweety?"

"Let's not get carried away."

She chuckled. "I wasn't talking about mere friends, and you know it."

"Yeah, Rose recently mentioned something like that."

"You're kidding."

"Nope." I scooped up another glob of frosting. "You know, Grace, I blame Walt Disney for all of this."

"Huh? You blame Walt Disney for what?"

"Well... " All the sugar I'd eaten made me dizzy, and I had to wait a moment before I could see straight again. "Remember how you told us about the guy who sued the Smart Water people because he didn't get smarter from drinking their water?"

"Yeah."

"Well, I think we should file a class-action lawsuit against the Disney corporation."

"What are you talking about?"

"Grace, for our entire lives, Walt Disney and his company have promised us 'happily ever after.' But that's a bunch of hooey. Most of us only get 'Is that all there is?'"

"You need a drink."

"It won't change the fact that Walt Disney is a liar. A fraudster."

"We have champagne." She stood. "Will was going to make a toast after the reveal. But with the—"

"No. I don't want champagne. I'm doing just fine with sugar. Fact is, I've got quite a buzz going."

"Okay." Grace sat back down. "Now, if you can put aside your animus toward Walt Disney for a minute, I'd like to ask a few questions. Do you mind?"

"Fire away." I looked around the scorched room. "Sorry. Poor choice of words."

"Don't worry about it. I have insurance." She pulled off the bear's nose and gobbled it down. "Oh, this is so good. It's tastes like black licorice." She licked her lips. "I don't understand why Ed didn't just admit what he had done right away. It sounds as if Dickerson drove him to it."

"I suspect that his thinking's been screwed up ever since it happened. Although I'm sure Karl will help him all he can."

"Okay. But what got him spooked tonight? Why did he try to run out of here? Did he somehow find out that the police were on to him?"

I picked at the bear's left foot with my fork. "From what I understand, Tweety told him something was up. I saw the two of them talking just before he ran into the kitchen."

"How did she know?"

"I guess she heard something from the corner-booth ladies. One of them had spoken with a cousin who works in the sheriff's office, who had, in turn, heard it from one of the deputies. Or something like that."

My phone rang.

It was Will. "Hey, Mom, have you made it home yet?"

"No. Grace and I are still... umm... cleaning up the café. Why?"

"Well, the roads are terrible, and visibility is practically zero."

"Did you and Sophie get home okay?" Panic set in.

"Yeah, although we're back in the car again."

"What? Why?" More panic.

"We're headed to the hospital. The baby's coming. Fast!"

Sophie hollered in pain from next to him, while her mother and father complained that she should have given birth in Fargo.

I disconnected, and Grace said, "I heard everything. Do you want to go to the hospital now or wait a bit?"

"Let's go now. We can check in on Rose." I dropped my fork on the table.

"Yeah." Grace glanced around the room. "This mess will still be here tomorrow. What's more, I don't plan to reopen for a few days. Maybe even a week. I need a break. Hell, we all need a break. Maybe we can help Rose escape from the hospital and take her ice fishing again."

"No way! Are you nuts?"

Grace laughed.

I went to stand, only to drop back down in my chair. "I just thought of something."

"What's that?"

"We still don't know if Sophie's having a girl or a boy. All the canisters more or less exploded at once."

My sister shook her head. "Well, as Rose would say, 'Isn't that a fine howdy-do."

## The End

All recipes capitalized in the first instance in the story are detailed in the Recipes section.

## Scotcheroo Bars

1 cup white sugar
6 cups Rice Krispies
1 cup light corn syrup
1 cup (or similar-sized bag) semi-sweet chocolate chips
1 cup creamy peanut butter
1 cup (or similar-sized bag) butterscotch chips

Pour Rice Krispies in a large mixing bowl and set it aside. In a saucepan, combine the sugar and corn syrup and cook over medium heat until the sugar dissolves. Then, bring the mixture to a boil. As soon as it boils, remove the kettle from the heat and stir in the peanut butter. Next, pour the mixture over the cereal and stir.

Press the cereal mixture in a greased 9x13" pan. After that, melt the chocolate chips and the butterscotch chips. Spread the mixed chocolate over the bars. Let the bars cool and set. Cut into squares and store in an air-tight container. (If you overcook the syrup mixture, the bars will be extremely hard to cut.)

## No-Bake Chocolate Oat Bars

1 cup butter
3 cups quick-cooking oatmeal, uncooked
½ cup light brown sugar
1 cup semi-sweet chocolate chips
1 tsp vanilla extract
½ cup peanut butter

Grease a 9" square pan. Melt butter in a large saucepan over medium heat. Stir in brown sugar and vanilla. Then, mix in oats. Cook over low heat until ingredients are well blended—about 2 to 3 minutes. Press half of the mixture into the bottom of the greased pan. Melt chocolate chips and peanut butter over low heat until melted. Spread that mixture over the crust with a spoon. Crumble remaining oat mixture, gently pressing down on top of chocolate mixture. Cover and refrigerate for at least 3 hours. Bring to room temperature before cutting.

## Spanish Chicken Hot Dish

3 cups crushed tortilla chips
1 10-oz can of Rotel
1 15-oz can black beans, drained and rinsed
2 cups shredded medium cheddar cheese
2 cups chopped or shredded cooked chicken
1 tomato, diced
1 21-oz can cream of chicken soup
1 small bunch cilantro, rinsed and chopped
1 tsp ground cumin
Jalapenos, optional

Preheat oven to 350 degrees. Lightly crush chips and sprinkle 1 cup of them across the bottom of a greased 9x13" baking dish. Layer the chicken and the black beans over the chips. Stir cumin into cream soup and gently spread mixture over the chicken and beans. Next, spoon the Rotel on top. Sprinkle remaining chips over everything, followed by the cheese. Bake for 25 or 30 minutes. When done, garnish with diced tomato and chopped cilantro and serve immediately. Can be eaten as is or as a dip for chips or as a topping on lettuce to make a salad.

## No-Bake Chocolate Peanut Butter Pie

1 premade chocolate (Oreo) pie crust
4 Reese's Peanut Butter Cup Bars, regular size, crushed
1 cup peanut butter
¼ cup mini chocolate chips
1 8-oz cream cheese, softened
¼ cup peanut butter, melted, for drizzling
1 cup powdered sugar
8 oz Cool Whip

In a bowl, combine cream cheese, peanut butter, and powdered sugar. Beat until smooth. Fold in Cool Whip. Spread into pie crust. Top with crushed Reese's bars and mini chips. Drizzle melted peanut butter. Refrigerate for at least 2 hours before serving. May freeze if wrapped tightly.

# Cinnamon Quick Bread

2 cups all-purpose flour
⅔ cup whole milk at room temperature
½ tsp baking soda
1½ tsps pure vanilla extract
½ tsp salt
1 large egg at room temperature

The Swirl:
¾ cup white sugar
½ cup white sugar
⅓ cup vegetable oil
1 Tbsp ground cinnamon
⅓ cup sour cream

Preheat oven to 350° F. Grease a standard loaf pan (approx. 9" x 5"). Mix the Swirl ingredients in a small bowl, then set it aside. In a large bowl, whisk the flour, baking soda, and salt, then set it aside. In a medium bowl, whisk the egg and white sugar, followed by the oil, sour cream, milk, and vanilla, in order listed. Next, pour the wet ingredients into the dry ingredients and whisk until completely combined. Don't overmix.

Pour half of the batter into the loaf pan. Top it with the Swirl mixture, withholding 2 Tbsps Next, spread the remaining bread batter over the Swirl. Use a spoon to help spread, if necessary. Sprinkle the rest of the cinnamon mixture on top. Cut swirls through the cinnamon-covered batter with a knife. Bake for 50 to 65 minutes, until the toothpick comes out clean. Cover the pan with tin foil for the second half of the baking time. Frost if desired.

## Cowboy Stew

2 lbs ground beef
2 cans Rotel
2 pkg. kielbasa cut into ½" slices
1 10-oz pkg. frozen mixed vegetables
1 onion, chopped
4 cups of water
1 can diced tomatoes, drained
2 tsps cumin
4 medium potatoes, peeled and diced
2 tsps chili powder
2 cans pinto beans with liquid
Salt and pepper to taste
1 can whole kernel corn, drained

Brown the ground beef and onions in a Dutch oven. Drain grease and add all other ingredients, pouring in the water slowly because you may not want to use it all if you prefer a thicker stew. Mix well. Bring to a boil. Then, simmer for 1 hour. Serve.

## Taco Salad

1 lb ground beef
¾ cup cheddar cheese, shredded
2 Tbsps taco seasoning, store bought or homemade
1 medium avocado, cubed
8 oz Romaine lettuce
½ cup green onions, chopped
1⅓ cups grape tomatoes, halved
⅓ cup salsa
⅓ cup sour cream

Brown the ground beef. Mix in the seasoning. May add ¼ cup water to keep the meat from burning. In a large bowl, mix the lettuce and all other ingredients. Then, add the taco mixture. Can keep in the fridge for 2 days if the bowl is sealed well.

## Mounds Brownie

2 cups graham cracker crumbs
1 14-oz can sweetened condensed milk
¼ cup white sugar
2 cups flaked coconut
½ cup melted butter
1 12-oz bag semi-sweet chocolate chips, melted

Preheat 350° F. Mix cracker crumbs, sugar, and melted butter and press into the bottom of a 9x13" baking pan and bake for 15 minutes. In a bowl, mix the milk and coconut and spread over the crust and bake another 15 minutes. Spread the melted chips over the top. Let cool. And cut.

## Chocolate Peanut Butter Dream Bar

**Base:**
1 pouch (17 oz.) Betty Crocker
  Double Chocolate Chunk
  Cookie Mix
¼ cup vegetable oil
2 Tbsp water
1 egg

**Filling:**
1 8-oz pkg. cream cheese,
  softened
¼ cup white sugar
1 8-oz container of Cool Whip
1 9-oz bag of miniature Reeses
  Peanut Butter Cups, chopped

**Topping:**
¼ cup creamy peanut butter
¼ cup whole milk
2 Tbsps sugar
3 oz bittersweet baking chocolate, melted
1 cup unsalted dry-roasted peanuts
      (slightly salted peanuts may be used)

Preheat oven to 350° F. In a large bowl, mix the Base ingredients until they form a soft dough. Then, press the dough into the bottom of an ungreased 9"x13" pan. Bake 12 to 15 minutes until set. Cool completely.

In a large bowl, beat the cream cheese and sugar until smooth. Fold in the Cool Whip and the candy. Spread over cooled base.

In a small bowl, beat the peanut butter, milk, and sugar with a whisk until smooth. Then, microwave the mixture from 30 to 60 seconds, stirring after 30 seconds. Drizzle over the filling. Finally, drizzle the melted chocolate on top. Sprinkle with the peanuts. Refrigerate for 2 hours before cutting and serving. Store covered in the refrigerator.

## Crescent Roll Taco Bake

2 cans Pillsbury Crescent Rolls
1 ½ cup shredded cheddar cheese
1 lb ground beef
shredded lettuce
1 pkg. taco seasoning
1 cup chopped tomatoes
Sour cream and green onions for garnish

Preheat oven to 350° F. Meanwhile, brown the beef, drain the fat, and stir in the taco seasoning. You may need to add a little water to keep the mixture from burning. Then, in a 9" pie pan, spread the dough pieces until the pan is completely covered like a pie crust. (You may not need all the dough.) Next, add your beef mixture and sprinkle the cheese on top. Bake for 20 to 25 minutes or until the cheese is melted, and the dough is golden brown around the edge. Let cool for 10 minutes. Then, top with the shredded lettuce and chopped tomatoes. Add your garnish of sour cream and green onions before you serve it.

## Egg Roll Hot Dish

1 lb ground pork
2 tsps sriracha
1 tsp minced garlic
1 14-oz bag of shredded
   coleslaw mix

1 egg
1 Tbsp sesame oil
¼ cup soy sauce
2 Tbsps sliced green onions
1 tsp ground ginger

Brown the pork in a large skillet. Add the garlic and sautee for 30 seconds. Add the coleslaw mix, soy sauce, and ginger and sautee until coleslaw mix is tender. (You may need to add a little water.) Make a well in the middle of the mixture for the egg and scramble it until done. Then, stir the scrambled egg into the mixture. Follow by stirring in the sriracha, the oil, and the onions.

## Orange Jell-O Salad

1 8-oz can crushed pineapple, drained
1 16-oz small-curd cottage cheese
1 15-oz can mandarin oranges, drained
8 oz Cool Whip

1 3-oz box orange Jell-O
1 cup sweetened
   coconut flakes
2 cups mini marshmallows

In a large bowl, combine the pineapple, oranges, and Jell-O powder. Next, mix in the cottage cheese, Cool Whip, coconut flakes, and marshmallows. Then, cover and chill until ready to serve. Lasts up to 3 days in fridge if covered.

# Lemon Cupcake

1¼ all purpose flour
¾ cup sugar
¾ tsp baking powder
¼ tsp vanilla
¼ tsp baking soda
2 extra large eggs
¼ tsp salt

6 Tbsps milk
¼ cup unsalted butter at
   room temperature
¼ cup fresh lemon juice
¼ cup vegetable oil
1 Tbsp fresh lemon zest

Preheat oven to 350° F. Add liners to cupcake tins—12 to 14 tins. Combine flour, baking powder, soda, and salt, then set aside. Mix butter, oil, sugar, and vanilla in a large bowl for 2 minutes. Add the eggs one at a time. Add half of the dry ingredients and mix. Combine the milk and lemon juice in a small bowl, then slowly add it to the batter, along with the lemon zest, and mix everything until well combined. Add the remaining dry ingredients and mix until everything is combined. But do not over mix. Fill cupcake liners ¾ full and bake for 15 to 18 minutes. (Use the toothpick test.) Cool.

# Lemon Buttercream Frosting

1 cup butter at room temperature
5 Tbsps lemon juice
4 cups powdered sugar

1 tsp lemon zest
½ tsp vanilla
Salt to taste

Mix butter in a large bowl until smooth. Add half of the powdered sugar and mix until well combined. Add vanilla and 4 Tbsps lemon juice and the lemon zest. Mix in the remaining powdered sugar and salt. Frost cupcakes.

# Earthquake Cake

1 Box dark chocolate fudgy cake mix, including the
ingredients to make the cake per the box.
8 oz cream cheese, softened
4 cups powdered sugar
½ cup butter, softened
½ cup chocolate chips
½ cup creamy peanut butter
1 cup miniature Reese's peanut butter cups,
unwrapped and cut in half
1 tsp. vanilla

Preheat oven to 350° F and grease a 9 x 13" cake pan. In a large bowl, prepare the cake mix as directed on the box. Pour into greased pan and set aside.

In a separate bowl, mix together the cream cheese, butter, peanut butter, and vanilla. Add the powdered sugar, 1 cup at a time, stirring well.

Add the peanut butter mixture to the cake batter 1 spoonful at a time, spreading lightly. Sprinkle chocolate chips and peanut butter cup halves on top. Bake for 45-50 minutes, using a tooth pick to test. Best served warmed with a scoop of vanilla ice cream.

## Crock Pot Cube Steak

6 cube steaks
1 medium onion peeled and sliced into rings
1 can cream of chicken soup
1 can cream of celery soup
1 packet Lipton Onion Soup Mix
½ soup-can of water

Cut the cube steaks into small chunks and place in the bottom of a crock pot. Layer the onion rings on top. Then, spread the chicken soup and the celery soup on top of the onions. Next, sprinkle the onion soup mix on top. Pour the water on top. Cook for 6 hours on low.

## Spaghetti Hot Dish

1 lb ground beef
1 cup cottage cheese
1 regular-size jar of spaghetti sauce
1 stick butter
8 oz container of cream cheese
1 16-oz box spaghetti
¼ cup sour cream
2 cups grated cheddar cheese

Preheat oven to 350° F. Boil spaghetti noodles until al dente (firm). Drain and set aside. Combine the cream cheese, sour cream, and cottage cheese until well blended, then set aside. Brown hamburger, drain the grease, add the sauce, then set aside. Dot a 9"x13" pan with thin pads of butter, using 3/4 of the stick. Scatter half the noodles over the butter in the pan. Spread the cream cheese mixture over the spaghetti in the pan. Top with the remaining noodles. Dot with remaining pads of butter. Pour the meat sauce over the top. Bake for 30 minutes. Then, top with grated cheese and return to the oven for 15 minutes.

## Mexican Tater-Tot Hot Dish

(Winning recipe from Kittson County Central Food Class Students: Tyler Hennen, Annika Johnson, and Carter Pankratz)

1 lb ground beef
1 10-oz can of red enchilada sauce
1 onion, diced (about ¼ cup)
3 cups shredded cheese, divided
1 packet taco seasoning mix
4 cups frozen tater-tots
1 4-oz. can green chiles
Cilantro, optional garnish
1 16-oz. can of black beans, drained and rinsed
Sour cream, optional
1 15-oz bag frozen corn

Preheat oven to 375° F. Spray a 9x13" baking dish with non-stick cooking spray. Brown ground beef and onion. Drain. Add seasoning mix, chiles, black beans, corn, and enchilada sauce and simmer for 8 to 10 minutes. Stir in 2 cups of the listed cheese. Pour mixture into baking dish, spread evenly, and top with an even layer of tater-tots. Bake for 35 to 40 minutes. Sprinkle the remaining cheese over the top and return to the oven for 5 more minutes. Garnish with cilantro and sour cream.

# Raspberry Jell-O Salad

6-oz pkg raspberry powdered Jell-O
3 sheets of graham crackers
2 bags frozen raspberries (10oz each)
2 Tbsps unsalted butter
2 Tbsps fresh lemon juice

3 Tbsps sugar
¾ tsp salt
1 4 oz cream cheese,
  room temperature
chilled heavy cream

Bring 2 cups water to a boil in large saucepan. Remove from heat and add Jell-O powder and stir until dissolved. Add both bags of frozen raspberries, lemon juice, and half of the listed salt. Stir and pour into 2-qt. casserole dish and refrigerate until set—at least 2 hours.

Meanwhile, using an electric mixer on high speed, beat cream cheese and remaining salt in a medium-size bowl until smooth—about 5 minutes. Add heavy cream and 2 T. of the listed sugar and beat at medium-low speed until firm peaks form—about 5 minutes. Spread over Jell-O mixture and chill for about 5 minutes.

Crush the graham crackers into coarse crumbs in a small bowl. Melt the butter in a saucepan. Add the cracker crumbs, the remaining sugar, and the remaining salt, stirring often, for about 5 minutes. Sprinkle the crumbs over the whipped topping just before serving.